BOTTOMLAND

Also by Michelle Hoover
The Quickening

BOTTOMLAND

MICHELLE HOOVER

Black Cat
New York

Published simultaneously in Canada
Printed in the United States of America

FIRST EDITION

ISBN 978-0-8021-2471-5
eISBN 978-0-8021-9024-6

Black Cat
an imprint of Grove Atlantic
154 West 14th Street
New York, NY 10011

Distributed by Publishers Group West

groveatlantic.com

16 17 18 19   10 9 8 7 6 5 4 3 2 1

To my late father, Lee, my Aunt Irene,
and their mother, Bess,
the first to speak in these pages,
and whom I never had the chance to meet

Don't forget me, don't forget that hill
the horses cantered you down
to the bottom land.
From this stone, ageless heart,
remember your mother,
a mother who loved her children.

—Margo Taft Stever, "Bottom Land"

BOTTOMLAND

Part I: Never Make Too Much

NAN

I

It was little more than a month before winter shut us in when I last saw the youngest of my sisters. Our little Myrle. I woke to find her shivering just inside the front door when she should have long gone to bed. It was dark as a cellar in that hall and outside it would be darker—miles of field and grassland lay beyond the front porch. Our house sat alone on the prairie, far from its neighbors. The road to our place was a run of stubble and dirt. Myrle's hair shone white on her shoulders and she wore nothing but a nightgown, her arms and feet bare in the cold—not enough sense to cover herself though she was almost grown.

I raised my lantern to her face. "Why, Myrle," I said, "you'll catch your death."

The look she gave, as if startled out of sleep. Her eyes teared and she ducked her head. The door was locked at her back. After the war, Father would have made sure of it. A draft rushed our ankles from the doorstep. The rest of the house was still, nothing but a wind outside knocking the stable gate. I touched Myrle's forehead and felt it damp. She brushed away my hand. Her other hand she hid behind her hip, and when I asked her to show it, she glanced up the staircase and called our sister's name, as if Esther might rush down to save her. I turned my head and Myrle was off—the white of her nightgown a whirl up the stair. In their bedroom above, the two girls whispered together. When at last Esther stepped out, she looked down at me with her dark face, her hands very still where they gripped the rail. Without a word, she slipped back inside and drew the door shut behind her.

Later that night, I would wake again and remember Myrle as she stood in the hall. What noise had woken me a second time, I could not say. The hall had been cold when I'd found her, though her fingertips were colder. Her nightgown carried the smell of the riverbed. As she rushed away, I saw how her hair clung to her neck, her nightgown damp against her back, and the mat where she'd stood was dark with wet. When Myrle was born, I too was just a teenager, but when first I held her, I believed nothing was so fearsome and astonishing as a child. All the many times we had watched her and chased her and held her fast—brushing her hair, tickling her feet, clutching her hands. As I lay in my room, I imagined again the heat of the flame as I'd held up my lantern. I saw how it had burned close to Myrle's cheeks until she flushed. I took the blanket from my bed, wrapped it around my shoulders, and stepped out into the hall. When I tried the front door, it was locked as it had been, but the hall was empty now. Not a sound came from the room above.

I should have been wary of the stillness the next morning, but quiet in a house is a thing a woman likes to keep. The sun hadn't yet risen. A sliver showed against the eastern windows, and I sat on the kitchen steps, waiting for the others to wake. Through the fog, my brothers walked in the dark with their buckets of milk. Lee, the younger, was large as an oak and pale, while my older brother Ray was thin, bent. A tin cup banged from his hip, one he hooked to his belt to keep only for himself. They dropped the buckets by the steps and Ray grimaced, wrenching the door open with his good hand. "You're late," I told them. Lee shrugged, following his brother inside. "There's eggs," I called. The buckets smelled of hay, the milk adrift with dirt and hair until I strained it, though I couldn't convince myself to even start. I thought of frost, of the snow coming. We had the last of the harvest to bring in and the cellar to fill with canning, a new washhouse to frame if my brothers could get the lumber for a good price. Were Mother alive, she would have liked to see such a thing done. The door banged open at my back and Ray hurried off without another word between us. Lee stopped to nudge me with the toe of his boot. "Ray's in a mood."

"Ray's always in a mood."

"Right, right," Lee said with a wink. He put a knuckle to his ear. "Esther didn't come out this morning."

"She must be in the pastures."

"She said she'd come to the smithy, said she had something for me. Don't forget, she said. And I almost did. She forgot more, I guess."

Lee headed off and I opened the door to the kitchen. Esther, she didn't forget anything. Inside, my sister Agnes stood over the stove, picking through the pan of eggs. I might have scolded her, but the kitchen table was empty, the chairs pushed close. I had left a stack of plates by the sink for our breakfasts. Half of them were stacked just the same, clean enough they shone. The sun was starting now at the horizon, and Agnes still wore her nightgown.

"Why aren't you dressed?"

Agnes' curls were matted from her sleep on the back porch, her refuge from her sisters in the warmer months. She looked like a child standing there, balancing on her toes. "I couldn't. Our room is locked."

"It must be stuck again. Are you sure?"

She pinched her gown to show me what I had already seen.

"Where are your sisters?"

"I don't know," she complained. "They're sleeping."

I hurried to the foot of the stair, but the door at the top was closed. "Esther, Myrle," I called.

Agnes joined me in the hall with her plate.

"At the table, Agnes."

She made a face.

"Go on up, then," I said. "Wake them."

"But the door."

"Push *harder*."

I went myself into the chill morning. Without the two girls at their chores, a half dozen of our youngest steers would be out to pasture, their feed low, and both my brothers were off without knowing. Already the animals in the barn were restless, begging for attention. The potatoes in the garden were close to a freeze, three dozen or more tomato plants set to move to the cellar. In the distance, the Clarks' chimney smoked, the glint of a lantern in the Elliots' barn. I drove the cows from the pasture, my arms heavy with buckets by the time I returned from the well. In their pen, the hogs clamored for feed, and I carried a pail of swill to them and turned the horses out into the growing warmth.

Back in the house, the door at the top of the stairs was closed. When I put my ear to the wood, I heard nothing. When I tried the knob, it wouldn't turn. My baby sisters were huddled together in their beds, or so I imagined, and I felt old and dry and ever less a woman as my years went and I remained unchanged, except for the fraying of my hems. With Mother gone, I had tried my best, but our youngest were growing wild. They freed the animals from their pens, filled their pockets at the market without paying. For a month, Myrle had gone to bed without supper and in a teary state, and Esther had taken to spying at us from around corners, that mushroom cap of her hair short above her ears, like a boy's. *Aren't you too old for games?* I asked her. *Aren't you too old?* she returned. Too quick for her own good, that one, and with a terrible imagination. Why, she could convince a person the devil himself knelt in front of the parlor fire, warming his hands.

"Can't you open it?"

I startled. Agnes waited behind me on the stairs. "What's wrong?" she said.

"Go on, I'll take care of it."

"But . . ."

"Borrow something of mine. We're late for the chickens."

Agnes groaned and hurried off. I pushed at the door with my shoulder and it gave an inch. Finally I ran at it with my full weight. The frame popped, the wood cracking. Inside the room was dark.

What had Father taught us? Never make too much of something. Lest that something make a fool of you instead.

The smell of the girls hit me at once, earthy and sweet. Myrle's bed was empty, unmade, but Esther's was straight as a piece of wood. Against the far wall, Agnes' bed stood alone. Behind the door, a small wooden chair lay on its side, one of its legs broken—the very thing that must have held the door closed. In a draft from the stairs, the drawings Agnes had hung of our family stirred, Mother watching me as if I'd somehow forgotten her. The room otherwise appeared untouched, the dresser tops clean save for the girls' combs, the bone brown and marbled for Esther and dove-colored for Myrle. A picture of a woman's hand stuck to the mirror, the hand bodiless and pale with a bracelet cutting into its wrist, an advertisement Myrle had torn out herself. Under Myrle's bed was a shadow, and I crouched to my knees to know what it was. A hammer. The end of it was ruined and fresh with chips of wood.

"What's wrong?"

"Agnes, I told you . . . ." I took to my feet, but it was only Patricia, dull little Patricia. A lump of a woman and kind as cotton, Ray's wife was lovely in the way of ghosts, her hands forever gripped in front of her as if to stave off violence.

"They're gone," I said.

"What do you mean?"

"They're not here," I snapped.

Patricia stepped into the room with a puzzled look and touched Myrle's pillow. The woman was so slow and vacant, older than me though seeming not. She took up the pillow and started to plump it, only to sit on the bed as if tired. "But where could they be?"

I sat next to her, the hammer heavy in my lap. Surely the girls were hiding in the barn or had taken the bicycle. Gone to our neighbors the Clarks for breakfast, to the Elliots to see the new pups—though they avoided both houses as much as we ever did. Patricia stared about the room, her hands closed between her thighs. A tide was rising in my throat. On a busy morning such as this. On any morning at all, and the girls had gone running about. But there, out of the corner of my eye, the chair lay on its side with its broken leg, a damaged child.

"Oh dear," Patricia sighed. Before she could say another word, Agnes appeared in the door, my brothers behind her holding their hats.

"Agnes," I complained.

Ray shouldered his way in. "What have they done now?"

"Did you see them outside?"

He shook his head.

"Maybe they went to town," Patricia mumbled.

"But it's miles," I said. "And they couldn't have made it on foot. Not in the dark."

"It's Esther," Ray said. "She'd run off at any chance."

"No," Lee let out. He stepped in with chaff on his skin and the smell of the barn. "I just don't think they'd do that, run off. They've never tried anything the like."

"And what about the chair?" I asked.

Ray caught the chair in his fists and the leg dangled until he broke it off.

"It doesn't make sense," Patricia said. She tried to take Ray's hand, but both were locked around the chair, even the two stubby fingers on his bad side. Lee stood at the door and juggled the broken knob, stooping to eye the bolt. Without a word, Agnes waited alone in the hall. She wore one of my own dresses, and it draped the boards at her feet. I followed her gaze. The only window in the room hung low between the girls' beds, the frame so small a grown woman couldn't get her shoulders through if she tried.

"Let's not tell Father," Ray said. "Not yet."

"How can we not tell him?" I asked. But Father, he'd gotten into the habit of sleeping late. Ever since Mother went, the work had fallen more and more to us, while Father walked the property from one end to the next as if counting pennies.

"Yes," I said, thinking we might find the girls, we might settle everything, before Father knew we'd lost track of them for even a few hours. The others looked at me, waiting. Downstairs in the kitchen, the stovepipes shuddered. At the far end of the hall, the snap of Father's cane. We turned our heads. Soon he would appear in the doorway with his face red and sweating above his beard, his jacket gaping. Already at the bottom of the stairs, he called out, "What are you all making there?"

With a glance over her shoulder, Agnes drew up her skirt, took a step in. "The window's open," she whispered.

"So?"

She nodded at the hammer in my hand. "Father had it nailed shut last year."

We set off on our search. At first we circled our own acres, only to come up short when we reached the fences. Lee scoured the smokehouse and barn, as if the girls could have fallen asleep with the cows, and Father worked his way along the river, stabbing at the water with his cane. Soon we headed farther out, Agnes and Patricia to the Clarks' and myself to the Elliots', the men staying behind to finish stocking the pens. *Dutchy*, our neighbors had said of us before the war, though with Father's accent and the misfortune of his birthplace, they now knew us for Germans and believed that far the worse. The horses stood with their chests against the wooden gates, watching us. The bells on the cows struck a hollow note as they ate. The land rose up in front of me, a gray place.

The Elliot house was quiet. As I stepped onto their porch, I knew the girls would never visit by choice. The farm was ragged, what with only the old man to care for it, his son and the son's wife, flighty newlyweds as they were. The porch cracked underfoot. Rot had set into the sills. And there was old Mr. Elliot, opening the screen with a squint before I could dare knock. He worried at me as if trying to remember which of the Hess girls I was.

"It's Nan, Mr. Elliot."

"Haven't seen you in a long while."

"Have you seen any of us?"

"Nope, no." He scratched at his ear. Mr. Elliot was well over seventy. His eyes drifted and his forearm shook as he leaned against his cane. The poor man, waiting for me to explain myself. But what could I say? That the girls hadn't done their chores? That we had somehow misplaced them?

"Our girls," I started again. "The two youngest. They seem to have wandered off."

Old Elliot looked blank. An American flag hung curled around the porch post, stripped and bleeding its colors. "Wandered off, you say?"

"Have you seen them?"

"I haven't seen any of you. Those girls, they must be joking. That's what girls do. The kind I used to know."

"Would you mind if I looked around?"

The old man winced. Behind him, the door swung open again. His son Tom slouched against the frame, licking his lower lip. "What's this here?"

"She's asking about the girls," Mr. Elliot said.

"What for?"

"Have you seen them? Esther and Myrle."

Tom shook his head and shook it again. "Why would I?" His eyes were pale and dim, and a twitch made him blink every few minutes, lifting the corners of his smile into something different. The boy had been a wreck since the war, though he'd gotten a girl to marry him, and a surprise marriage that.

"Another time, maybe." I peered past them into the dark house, a light over the table and a greater darkness in the hall. "And say hello to your wife for me, Tom. In school, Dora and I used to be very good friends."

"That right?" Tom said.

"Well," said Mr. Elliot.

I headed home, my hand to my forehead against the sun. Only with a wary glance did I search their smokehouse and barn, the far corner of their stables. It was full daylight now and the fields were barren after harvest. Far off, a scabby break of trees showed at the horizon. The river that marked the border between our two families seemed no more than a run of weeds. The Elliots' house perched in its yard like an old crow, the wood blackened, while our own sat dust-colored and brown, a stretch of boxes with the girls' room a cap on top. For a good quarter mile I imagined the Elliots watching me as I went, waiting for me to cross the river again. Old Elliot had hung that flag on his porch when Tom came home from the service, and he'd posted a sign at the market in town, next to the door. "Shouldn't we be concerned," the sign had read, "about the enemy living among us?" Then in a larger hand:

TUESDAY MEETING
COUNCIL OF NATIONAL DEFENSE
SEVEN IN THE EVENING
THE ELLIOTS

At the riverbank, I turned at last to see Tom standing alone on the porch. I waved, but he ducked inside. A strange boy, but strange didn't mean badness. He could hardly rope a calf, least of all harm a girl, and surely Dora kept him in line. But if there were men like Tom Elliot after the war, how many worse had come home?

When Patricia saw me across the fields, she gave a sad shake of her head. The Clarks might have made for an easier visit, the group of them being the more talkative, but as a family of women—three rabbity sisters and their mother, their father an invalid in his bed—talk was often all they did. Agnes ran ahead of Patricia to the chicken pen, a coat across her shoulders and my dress dragging behind her. Off to the east, Ray worked the horses, bent to press the blades of the harrow to level the fields. I thought of the broken chair, the way Ray had so easily snapped the leg in two, despite his ruined hand. The girls must have propped the chair up to block the door, or someone had, making it difficult to leave the room or enter it. But who did they want to keep out—or in? At night, Father always locked the main doors both inside and out. He kept the keys on the hook by his bed, and I carried the same in the pocket of my apron. Through the fabric, I felt for their dull weight. Across the pasture, Patricia called my name, the sound like a swarm of insects. A grunt from the fields, and there was my brother bent over his work, his shoe coming down on the harrow's spine as if he had hit a stone. He had no time to search for the girls, not when they'd only run off on a stunt—or so he believed. Now Ray moved like a dark shape in those fields, driving the horses as hard as he could.

*　*　*

"Someone must have taken them," Patricia said. "That's what I think."

She scurried about the kitchen, gathering plates. I kept my tongue. Already the house had fallen into disarray, the beds from the morning unmade, the wash only just drying, and still the door open at the top of the stairs. The boys would come in soon from the fields though dinner would be late. Ray had insisted we finish the day's work and have our evening meal as if nothing had changed. "They'll be home before nightfall," he said. Now the sun had dropped low behind the washhouse. Another hour, and the light would be gone altogether. Patricia stared out the window, worrying the rings on her fingers. "It's terrible. Terrible."

"Oh, come," I said.

"There was that twelve-year old girl in Le Mars," she went on. "Alta Brown, Braun, something or other. They found her near those railroad tracks for the Illinois Central. Neighbor thought she was a store dummy lying there 'til she found out it wasn't. One day the girl was in her bed. The next, gone."

"You can't believe every story you hear."

"But it wasn't a story," she said. "They printed it in the newspaper."

"Well."

"And what about Villisca? A whole family killed in their sleep. By a minister no less."

"This isn't Villisca," I said. "It isn't anywhere close."

"It most certainly isn't." Patricia dropped a clean set of plates on the table. "You can never be sure of a place. That's all I'm saying."

My knife slipped on a potato skin, a bloody gash. I wet my finger in my mouth.

"And that window in their room . . . ," Patricia started again. "That window isn't much larger than my hips."

Agnes rushed in, my dress pinned so it drooped like an apron. I didn't have the heart to tell her to go to her room to find something else. "Myrle could have gotten through."

"I doubt it," I said. "And Myrle is far too timid."

"Someone came through that window," Patricia groaned. "Some strange little man."

"No one would have seen him," Agnes added.

"Stop it, the both of you. I don't see the use in talking this way." My finger pulsed, the taste of blood in my mouth. I bit it until it bled again. "As far as we know, the girls lost track of time and are staying in town." But there was no place for the girls to stay overnight, even I knew that. They had never kept away from home for so long.

Agnes sat at the table, her eyes turned up in thinking. The girl was bookish and no taller than my waist, far too stunted for her eighteen years. When she spoke, her voice sounded clipped, as if counting off facts on her fingers. "There's a trunk missing too," she said. "The one we kept in the front hall. It's gone."

"Father got rid of that trunk last year. I'm sure of it."

"And the chair?" Agnes asked. "I read a story like that. A man blocks the door with a chair after he kills his wife. That way, he keeps anyone from finding out until he's miles off."

"For heaven's sakes," Patricia said.

"You shouldn't be reading such things . . ." But before I could finish, my brothers swept through the door, their shirts caked with muck.

"Good Lord in Mercy." Patricia laid a hand to her chest. "You near scared me to death."

"Wash yourselves," I said.

Ray grimaced. "Aren't they back?"

"We should have gone to town," Lee complained.

"Yes." I sighed. "But Ray wanted to wait."

Ray sat at the table, leaning hard on his elbows. "We can go tomorrow, first thing, if they aren't back. You, myself, and Lee."

Agnes pursed her lips. "Do we really need to tell everyone?"

"Why not?" I asked.

Father's footsteps sounded in the yard. He opened the kitchen screen and sank into a corner chair. In his overalls and old leather hat, the one that smelled of smoke and damp, he gazed at the floor, his face hidden except for his beard. The cuffs of his pants were muddy from the river, a leaf sticking to the foot of his cane.

"We'll go to town at first light," Ray said. "We'll find them there, or someone will have seen them."

"I will go with you," Father said.

"It would be better you didn't. With all the trouble . . ."

Father raised his chin and Ray hushed. I set a cold plate of chicken on the table, a bowl of potatoes, and a loaf of our farmer's bread. The boys eyed the chicken, hands in their laps. The sun was setting. Through the window, the light blazed on the horizon until it vanished. "It's the only dinner we've got," I said. "We didn't have the time. Not with the girls . . ."

Father snapped his cane. "I will go with you."

We held our breaths.

"All right," Ray let out.

"Right," Father said. His hand trembled and he clasped it with the other, as if praying.

"Well now." Patricia pushed at the meat with her fork, her voice strained. "Eat up, why don't you?" We stared at our plates. The room seemed too full with all of us at once, the chicken an ugly cut of meat. Only Ray dared pick up his knife. A speck of rain struck the windows, the drops cold and sharp, then a rush. "Oh," Patricia sighed. And soon she was sighing and more. "Oh, those girls."

That night we lay awake in our beds, listening for the sound of footsteps in the yard. Sleep, it seemed a hollow chore. I thought of how young Myrle had looked in her nightgown. Her feet left their wet prints, as if she'd just stepped from a bath, and she held something in her hand. Myrle never lied. She had never before hidden anything from us. Esther was different. The way she'd stood at the top of the stairs, as if a warning. Then the thudding sound that had woken me again: A door closed? A hammer fallen? The chair wedged beneath the knob? How easy it would have been to pull the nails from the window and pry it open. I could imagine doing so myself. What if I had stepped out of my room a minute sooner? What if I had never gone to sleep at all?

It was months ago that Myrle had taken to her bed. She'd come down with a *sickness*, or so Esther had called it—so sudden and without reason that we thought to fetch the doctor, but Ray insisted we couldn't spare the expense. "She's in one of her fits," he said. I can't say I didn't agree. Myrle, our little bird. Once she almost cut off her hand while grinding feed in the shed. Why, if I had never snapped a finger at her, who knows if she would have reached her fourteenth year.

17

She asked for the curtains closed, the door locked, a lantern lit in her room all hours of the night. With blankets to her chin, she stared as if death himself stood at the foot of her bed. That girl, so pale her veins seemed to ravage her skin, her white-blond hair unwashed and wet with sweat. She was little more than a gown and bones between the blankets. "You can't go on like this," I scolded her. But the loss of a mother can turn a girl inward, no matter the time since. Myrle twisted away.

Later I often found Esther in Myrle's bed, whispering in her sister's ear. Myrle's eyes were open for the first time in days. A rash had spread from her cheeks to her throat, so fevered I yanked the blankets from her. Esther snatched them up again, as if I'd done something shameful—and for a moment I did feel ashamed, gazing at my sister, her nightgown thin over her breasts and stomach, the skin of her neck hot to the touch. Myrle, our beauty, even in her sickly state. Why, when she was born, none of us could keep our eyes off her, carrying her from room to room as if she were a pet.

Mother would have done better. The moment she sensed the door at the top of the stairs was stuck, Mother would have come awake. Why, the house might be empty with every one of us in the fields, and several rooms off Mother could sense a window open just an inch. But I had gone back to bed as if sleep was what needed me most, and now my sisters were missing. Before she died, Mother had taken my hand and craned her neck from her pillow. "What a girl you are, Nan," she said. "So tall." Then her gaze settled and her consonants grew long, as if speaking two languages at once. With Father, German sounded a march, but Mother's throaty vowels were bread and milk and eggs. "You might not have your own, my girl," she whispered.

"But those sisters of yours, they'll be everything to you. And you'll be everything to them."

The town had not seen us together for many months, not after what Governor Harding had done. Why, if German wasn't to be spoken in public, if even God could not understand a prayer in the German tongue—as our governor had said in his speech— then Germans and their brood might not be welcome in public, not all at once. And when only one of our brothers could serve, we had caused plenty of suspicion. Though we were born in this land and a part of it, still Father and his accent made traitors of us. More than a year had passed since the war's end, but the town's sense of wrongdoing remained.

"Well now," Lee said. The wagon pulled to a stop. He stabbed a finger in his ear. Agnes tied the horses and held close to their collars. Ours was a small town—the main street was three blocks long, with a handful of crossings, all of them dirt. The market squatted under an awning bagged with rain. The town hall stood with its one-eyed clock, the door closed and locked with a bolt. Off the end of the row, the doctor's house stood quiet, unused most months, a shop of trinkets at the other end. There was a trading post as well, open only on Wednesdays—and only, some said, when the man needed dollars for a bottle. Now even his windows were dark. The town was windswept, the buildings peeling paint. Still, this being a Saturday and harvest, a dozen or more children raced underfoot, men bent to haul their baskets to the market. Their daughters walked the street in their handmade hats, but none of them were my sisters. Not even close.

Ray lifted his boots and landed in the street in a spit of mud. "Ready?"

"I am staying," Father said.

I turned my head. "You're staying?"

He crossed his arms over his stomach. "If they see the wagon, they will surely come, and you will be off and I will have found them." He seemed calmed by this idea. When he took off his hat, his forehead was smooth, only a tight red line from the brim.

Ray held my arm. "Leave him be. It'll be easier."

"Easier for who?"

I headed to the market alone. A half dozen customers crowded the aisles, more than I had ever seen at once, though the shelves themselves were spotty with stock. After the war, the newspapers had predicted more of everything—hay and seed, canned vegetables, even meat—but not here. Few in town could pay the price. I stood at the door and wiped my feet. The place smelled of sour milk, and my sisters were nowhere about. Still, a group of women rushed toward me from the counter. I couldn't back out the door in time.

"Nan," the first called. It was one of the Clarks, flanked by her younger twins. Their mother swept in and the girls followed, taking their plump little steps. "The hens," Esther called them, and once at the county fair, my sister had ducked under their bench and pinned their skirts. The next day Mother visited their house to handle the complaint.

"Aren't they back?" Mrs. Clark asked.

I shook my head.

"But they must be somewhere. I can't even imagine."

Her daughters reached for my wrists. "It'll be all right."

"They're probably home," another said. "You'll open the door and there they are."

"So much fuss," the youngest let out.

"What if they were taken?" The oldest said this under her breath. "The men, they're so desperate these days."

"I really must go," I said. At my shoulder was the flat square of wall where Old Elliot's sign had been, though different signs hung there now—one begging a price for feed, the other selling acres of land. I imagined the group of them, the Elliots and the Clarks, the Conners, Wilkersons, and others, huddling in Old Elliot's parlor during the war. *Something has got to be done*, Elliot had said, and the women glanced at each other, wondering what that something might be. But our neighbors had plenty else to blame us for. Of the farms to the west of town, we owned the better land, the largest house, and the cleanest barn. Why, if we hadn't given the Clarks half our seed three springs before last, they never would have survived the season. But there was always something to be done about kindness, especially a kindness that reminded a person what little they had.

"Nan," Mrs. Clark said. "You'll let us know? If someone did something to your girls, the same could happen to any of us." In the corner, a woman and her son had turned to listen. An elderly man set down his basket of apples, his head cocked. "Really, I must be going," I said again. It was no use. In only hours, everyone in town would know the girls were gone, and now this knowing seemed worse than before. What kind of help would it be, if it only kept our names on their tongues?

The door of the market banged closed at my back. At the window, the sisters pushed together to watch. I hurried my steps. Our girls could be caught up with the trinkets at the shop. They could have taken refuge in the church, the doctor's. I searched the streets, ducked into corners, peeked inside wagons, and opened doors. The streets were sodden, the walkways splintered under the morning rush. When I spied one of my siblings, we raised a hand to each other and shook our heads before running off.

"Well, look who it is."

I stumbled to a stop. Dora, my old school friend.

"Don't be so jumpy, Nan. I haven't seen you in town in such a long while."

"No?" I asked. Dora studied me down her nose. I had seen her in town often enough myself, and even more across our fields. She was an Elliot now, after all.

"My dear, you look terrible."

I touched the back of my hair. "Have you seen Esther and Myrle?"

"Those two. Are you still after them like a mother?"

"If you know where they are . . ."

"Why ever would I?" She drew close to me and took my arm. She'd grown fat, her stomach taut under her dress, and I thought I might reach out to touch her, three months along she must have been or more—though I knew she'd been married less. It was a game we had played as girls, pushing dolls underneath our skirts, but never did we imagine forcing the man to offer a ring. "They're terrible, aren't they? Especially Esther," she went on. "I didn't want to say, but Nan, you've gotten so thin. What do you have of your own?"

I drew in my chin. "If you haven't seen them . . ."

"No, I haven't. But they must be somewhere."

I pulled my arm from her and she almost fell. "I've got to get back."

"Oh, Nanny, don't be angry. I was just saying, isn't it time you let go?"

"Thank you, Dora," I said. "I hadn't realized I didn't have that, something of my own."

"Nan," she called again, but I was off. Still that swelling beneath her dress stayed with me, my feet on the stones seeming narrow and hard. We'd sat in the same grade together, Dora and I, the desks for the other children lined up at our backs. Only Carl McNulty sat in front with us, tapping my chair with his foot. In that single room, Carl needed the extra watching, or so the teacher had said. Dora and I had been the smart ones. The teacher had said that as well. Why, if not for the war, we might have become teachers ourselves. And Carl and I, we might have become more.

When I found our wagon again, Father sat alone on the bench, his chin to his chest. "Nan," he sighed, wiping his face.

I took his hand. In the quiet between us, he squeezed my fingertips. "They didn't come." The morning was turning dark. Clouds thickened. Father dropped my hand. One by one, my siblings appeared without a word and climbed in. Ray snatched the reins and the horses lurched into the road.

"The deputy was in," Ray said.

I started. "You talked to the deputy?"

"He'll stop by in the morning."

Agnes hugged her knees. "You think they won't come home."

"I didn't say that."

"But not by themselves," she went on. "You think we need someone to bring them back."

I brushed a strand of hair from her forehead. "Hush now. Hush."

The way home was silent and hard. The horses thrashed under the wagon's weight, the roads full of muck. We threw blankets over our heads and the clouds grew darker yet. On the way to town, we had stopped to knock on doors, but the townsfolk kept to their porches, hands on their chins. Now here and there, a house stood gaping at the end of a long lane of dirt, the fields rutted. The Michaelsons, the Roberts, the Coors. After the war, they had pulled up stake when prices dropped and the banks had called in loans. Soon even some of the banks closed. Farther off, Carl McNulty walked his rows with a plow horse. One of his sleeves hung loose, pinned at the shoulder. Agnes tapped my arm. I had not seen Carl since he'd buried his mother a month after shipping home. He lived alone on that farm. As we passed, he took off his hat, looking up at the coming storm. Agnes waved to him, but I kept my hands in my lap. In another mile, a wooden sign hung nailed to a fence post, the words carved with a knife:

EVACUATION SALE
FURNITURE
ALL MUST BE SOLD

A growing line of trees, and there was the riverbank. The water rushed with rain, the only sound on the road save for the horses. In the distance, our house stretched with its many rooms, all of them dark. The girls had not come back. They had not come. Somewhere out there our sisters were lost, and the house seemed an empty place, the one I had lived in my whole life.

*   *   *

The next morning, the deputy knocked on our door just as we were washing the breakfast plates. The blinds were drawn, the lamps dim. My brothers' guns stood on their stocks in the hall. As if expecting an empty house, the deputy retreated down the steps before the first of us could answer.

Ray led him to the parlor and lit a fire, though we had never spent such fuel in the daytime. The parlor smelled of Mother, or the musty smell of something long past Mother. The man took the largest chair, crossed one leg over the other, and Ray winced. The rest of us sat perched close enough to the fire to sweat. Agnes pulled at her collar, her chin quivering. I rushed her out of the room at once.

"What could that man possibly do for us?" she sobbed. I put my arm around her, but still she shuddered. "Nothing, nothing."

"Come now," I whispered. She tore away from me and ran up the stairs. I thought to call out to remind her, but she swept into the girls' room and rushed down again, out to her porch. I returned to the others, their eyes on the ceiling. The deputy's Adam's apple seemed sharp as a wooden heel.

"So," the man broke in. "You have a missing girl."

"Two," I said.

"Two." He straightened in his chair. "How old?"

"Esther's sixteen," I said, "but Myrle just turned fourteen. We haven't seen any sign of them since the night before last."

"They left nothing behind? No note?"

"There's a trunk missing," I said. "A small one, though we aren't sure whether it's newly gone or been missing a long time. Father might have taken it away."

"Did you, Mr. Hess?" the man asked. "Did you take the trunk away?"

Father didn't answer, his eyes on the man. Ray turned his face to the wall.

"There was a chair in their room as well," I went on. "It was wedged against the door. I had to break it to get in."

"You saw it blocking the door even though you were on the other side?"

"Well, no."

"But you said . . ."

"Nan found a hammer under their bed," Patricia hurried in. "Isn't that strange?"

"Is it?"

Patricia drew up her shoulders. "Nan saw Myrle late that night too. She was standing by the front door. Tell him, Nan."

"She could have been sleepwalking for all I know."

"And they left Myrle's bed unmade," Patricia said.

The man sighed. "You're telling me that their door was wedged closed, a hammer was found, and a trunk is missing, and you saw the girls up and running about after their bedtime."

"We're not really sure about the trunk," I told him.

Ray cleared his throat. "I don't understand what all these questions have to do with anything."

"It sounds to me as if the girls have run off," the man said. "A night or two and they'll be back."

"But it's already been two nights," Patricia said. "This will be the third."

"They wouldn't run away like that," I assured him. "Not our girls. They were terribly happy here."

"And you've searched for them yourselves?"

"All day yesterday and most of the day before," I answered. "Everywhere we could think."

"Everywhere is quite a lot."

"*Wer ist dieser Man?*" Father grunted.

The man went on. "I'm saying that two girls, two at once, that's a rare thing. Either they ran off because they wanted to get away or someone did something to them, but I don't think we should be guessing at any wrongdoing just yet."

"They couldn't have gone by themselves," I said. "The window in their room is much too small and the house is locked at night, both inside and out."

"Locked?"

"Father worries . . ."

Father straightened. What could we say? That we were afraid of our neighbors? That the war had never left us? Father had insisted the locks kept us safe.

"Locking your family in. Is that wise?"

"They are young, those girls," Father said. "Everywhere there are boys and other troubles. *Doof!* A man who locks his doors. His reasons should be evident."

The deputy blanched at Father's speech. *Kraut,* he must have thought, though surely he knew who Father was. Our family had lived in the same house for more than thirty years.

"If the question should be of anyone," Father went on, "it should be the Elliots. That boy on their farm."

"The one who married this summer?"

Father grunted again.

"You've had some difficulties with the Elliots, haven't you? Something about the waterway between your properties?"

"Elliot is a sad old man," Ray said.

"He was confused," I added. "He's been ill since he lost his wife. But that trouble with the river is finished. I talked to the Elliots myself the day before yesterday, the both of them."

The deputy watched Father's face. Father's cheeks reddened, about to burst. "The girls' mother?" the man went on. "She died a while back. Isn't that right?"

"In the last month of the war," I said.

Ray put a hand on Father's shoulder. "I don't see how this matters."

"I've heard of families like yourselves," the deputy said. "Very strict. And two girls who have lost their mother, who are isolated on a farm and locked inside a house for months on end, I should think it's more than *evident* that a neighbor boy, a married man, isn't your greatest concern."

Father lunged at him. Ray tried to hold him back, but Father only stumbled into the bucket near the fire, and the room filled with ash. Patricia waved a hand in front of her face, and the rest of us took to our feet, everyone save the deputy, who covered his mouth with his handkerchief. Father stood breathing as if readying for another try. I pulled at his arm. He gave way, keeping his eye on the man as we walked out.

I settled Father in his room and sat myself at Mother's desk while he lay in his bed, his anger fading. "Never would I have thought," he mumbled. He touched his forehead as if it pained him. "Where are they, Nan? That man and his boy are at fault. I am sure of it. Elliot never forgave us."

"That's nonsense."

"Your mother and I, we believed we had found it. What is this word? Bliss." The word sounded thick on his tongue. "We were supposed to have a place to live." He snapped his fingers. "And it went."

"It hasn't gone anywhere."

But already Father had closed his eyes. His chest rose and fell, sleeping now or pretending to. By strength of will, he could disappear from us in a blink whenever difficulties raised their head. I turned down the lamp. On the other side of the wall, the sound of Ray's voice and the deputy's questions. In the low light, the room seemed a sanctuary, Mother's rosewater in its vial on her dressing table and her slippers beside the bed. Father rolled away from me and I reached for a blanket to cover him. Next to the headboard hung the hook where he kept his keys to the house, a set of four of which mine was only a copy. I dropped the blanket and reached for the hook instead. The ring seemed light as I turned through the keys, counting. I counted again. One of the keys was no longer there.

I closed my fingers and hurried to the parlor. The deputy sat with his hands folded in his lap. As if waking, he raised his eyes to mine. "Your brother explained that the youngest had been spending quite a lot of time in bed in recent months. He seemed to think she was sick or acting like it. Did you have the doctor come?"

"Ray, there's something . . ."

My brother put up his hand. "This is a working farm. We can't always have a man out every time one of the girls gets uncomfortable."

"She was sad over losing her mother," Patricia said. "That's what I think."

"But you said the mother died more than a year ago. Just before the end of the war?"

"Myrle's always been weakhearted," Ray said. "Our mother treated her as if she might break. Nan, tell him."

I gripped the keys. "They'd been upset about Mother's death. Both of them, but Myrle especially. We thought she was getting over it. She was going to school again, sleeping through the night. But in the last few months . . ."

"Was she too sick to run away?"

"They didn't run away," Ray snapped. "Something happened to them."

"But you have no idea what that something was?"

"Ray . . . ," I started.

"You might not understand," my brother went on, "but this town holds certain suspicions about us since the war, and they've acted them out."

"The war is over."

"It hasn't been so long."

I opened my hand. With a clatter, the ring of keys swung from my finger. "One of Father's keys is gone."

The room went quiet. My brother stopped his pacing, and Patricia stiffened, no longer kneading the skirt of her dress. Lee turned his head. "It's gone," I repeated.

"How can it be gone?" Patricia asked.

"What is this?" the deputy said. "What key?"

I reminded him about the locks, the keys on the hook, the copy I had myself. "The ring was on the hook as always," I said, "but one of the keys was not."

The deputy set his hat on his head. "That settles it. Your girls are runaways. They took the key when you weren't looking. There's little we can do about that except wait."

"But you can send out a search," Patricia said. "Can't he, Ray? The girls could be hurt."

"What about the chair?" I asked. "They couldn't have barricaded themselves in their own room and gone out the door at the same time."

"I still have doubts about that chair. It could have been just sitting there for all you know, already broken, and the door stuck."

"But you haven't seen the room," I said.

"I'm done with my questions. You'll get a letter from them in a week, maybe two, or they'll simply show up, and then it'll be settled. They're nearly grown, those girls. Remember that." With his final word, the deputy stood and worked his way between the chairs. I followed him. "I can let myself out," he said.

In the parlor, the bucket Father had stepped in lay on its side, a circle of ash on the carpet. Patricia touched her lip as if to clear away a crumb, and Lee sat nodding. I thought to take the chair the deputy had left, but the cushion held the hollow of his frame.

"What did Father say about the key?" Ray asked.

"He was already asleep when I found it."

"But we can ask."

"You know how steady he is in his habits. He would never have removed it himself, not with the other keys still there."

"He must have noticed it missing."

"Not last night. With the girls gone, he wouldn't have thought to lock the house. I didn't."

Ray eyed the ceiling. "Where's Agnes?"

"On her porch, I suppose."

"Tell her to come in and stop her sniveling. She needs to help with supper."

Outside the window, the deputy made his way across the yard, looking over his shoulder once, then again. If I thought it would do any good, I'd have locked the door at his back for good. But how then could Esther and Myrle ever return?

I found Agnes on the screen porch, sitting on her mattress, a book on her knees. Every year when the cold weather came, we had to beg her to sleep in the upstairs room. From the rafters, she had hung her drawings. Most of them were of family, but a dozen showed the Elliot house, dark and small in its lot across the river. Her head lay against the wall, her eyes closed.

I sat with her in the bundle of sheets and pillows. "Agnes, what's wrong?"

"I heard what that man said. About their running away."

"He wasn't much use, was he?"

"But Nan . . ."

"What?"

"Remember those magazines Esther keeps under her bed?"

"You weren't supposed to know about those."

"I looked for them last night, and they were gone."

"What do you mean?"

"I think Esther took them."

"Took them where?"

She shrugged. "They had those pictures, the big cities. New York, Chicago, Boston. Esther liked the ones of Chicago best."

"That doesn't mean she'd go there. Chicago is nearly three hundred miles."

"But she was always talking about it. Like she knew the place."

"Why would you believe anything Esther said?"

She took hold of my wrist. "I'll show you."

Agnes led me to the back of the house. The yard sat in shadow, mostly mud and brambles, little reason for us to wander there. A stand of trees leaned together above the curve of the roof and the grasses never grew taller than an inch. Agnes stopped under the girls' window. "Don't you see?" she asked. I strained my neck. Underneath the window frame, hidden from anyone in that room looking out, a gash showed fresh with splinters, as if something heavy and sharp had rubbed against the wood. Below it, the wall of the house appeared scuffed, a line that reached to the ground from the gash itself.

"What did you girls do to that window?"

"I didn't do anything."

"This could be from rainwater for all we know. It could have stained the wall."

Agnes closed her eyes, dismissing me. *Chicago*, she'd said. The name sounded the same as choking. Now with the window looking so strange, the missing key, and the way the deputy had turned everything around—I couldn't bear to think it. The girls may have left because of something we'd done.

"Agnes, when the deputy was here, why didn't you say anything?"

"I didn't want to tell anyone. I didn't even want to go to town. They'll all be talking about us again."

The shadows deepened at the back of the house. Standing on her toes, Agnes strained to see the window. The scuff on the wall might disappear altogether in another rain or two, but the gash itself seemed a kind of violence.

"I suppose we'll have to tell the others," I said. "Before dinner we will."

*   *   *

Around the table that evening, we ate what we could in silence. My brothers chewed with their mouths closed, and Agnes held her knife between the tines of her fork, the fork switched from left to right, as Mother had taught us for a cut of meat. "Chicago," Ray sniffed. The idea of one or the other of my brothers heading to the city to search seemed impossible. A hired car to Clarksville, then the Cedar Rapids and Chicago lines. A week or more to even try, Ray complained, and with all the work needed before winter. The price of a ticket alone was more than a steer at auction. How could the girls have paid for it? Deep within the house, Father groaned in his sleep. One by one we turned an ear to the hall. *Never make too much.* Father had taught us that too. But now spoken or not, there was something that made fools of us—why the girls would ever want to travel, why they might do so without telling. "No, we won't go," Ray decided. "It's just some idea Agnes has got." He rested his knife across his plate as if that finished it. The others took their napkins from their laps as they stood and dropped them on their chairs. Long after Agnes had cleared the plates, I stayed alone in the dining room and scratched at the table with my thumbnail until I'd damaged the surface. I scratched again. Who would notice such a little thing? And who would ever think I was the one who had done it?

When at last I went into the kitchen, Agnes and Ray crouched over the table by the stove, the crowns of their heads nearly touching. Patricia crossed the room in squat steps, stacking dishes in the pantry as loudly as she could. The stove burned, the light flickering. Agnes had laid out a handful of pencils and paper on the table, her face hard as she worked with her cheek inches from the surface. The photograph at her elbow showed our family together, a proper sitting Father had insisted on after Mother went, though it cost a good day's work. The older of us stood in a row in back. In front sat Father and the girls. Esther peered straight ahead with that furious look of hers, her hair a mop and her nose sharp. Not much was pretty in that girl, but oh, she was fierce. Esther knew you, the photograph said, and believed she was the better by twice. Myrle sat on Father's other side in a cream dress, a band of pearl buttons from her stomach to her throat. Her hair was held with pins, her hands folded. She leaned into Father, as if she might just rest her head on his shoulder.

"We're drawing up posters," Ray explained. "We can hang them in all the towns, the railway stations. Someone will surely see them." He leaned back in his chair and stretched. Agnes blew a strand of hair from her forehead. The photograph seemed small and dim in the low light, the girls' faces no bigger than my thumb. Patricia stood against the door, her eyes on her husband. "My, but it's getting late," she said. She rested a hand on Ray's shoulder. The kitchen was near to freezing, but Agnes sweated as she worked, wiping the paper clean. When she finished, Ray pulled the drawing from her fingers. "No good. It doesn't look anything like them." He pushed the sheet away.

"But the photograph is over a year old," Agnes complained.

"Ray," I said.

Agnes only wiped her face and started again, her pencil trembling.

"Isn't it terribly late?" Patricia mumbled.

I steadied myself against Agnes' chair. Agnes no longer looked at the photograph as she gripped her pencil, and the drops that fell from her face weren't from sweating now but from something else, something I hated to see.

Long after everyone had gone to sleep, I took my blanket to the front porch. The moon sat close to the horizon. The fields stretched without a wind. The house was dark, the lamps put out. How easy it would be to step off that porch, to fall into blackness as if nothing expected you back. I listened for any sound from Father's room, but nothing came. As a child, I imagined his every footstep weighing down whatever ship carried him to this country. What did it mean to spend so many months adrift? While the boat pitched the other passengers against the rails, I imagined him on deck, his stance wide, keeping the thing upright by will alone. I never would have guessed Father undone by anyone, but that deputy managed it in a matter of minutes.

"Nan."

I startled. Behind me in the corner, Lee held up a hand. Since coming home from the war, Lee had grown thick about the middle, his cheeks soft, though he was little more than twenty. He sat in the shadows. I could only see his face.

"It's strange," he said.

"It's more than that."

He chewed his lip, mulling over the words—a slow man gone slow in his thinking. Lee was blond-haired, like Myrle, and now likewise as dreamy. People often left the room before he'd finished speaking. "You can see everything from this porch," he started again. "Old Man Oak and Elliot's horses. They must be a mile off."

"Even more."

"That's the puzzle. You'd think we could have seen them leaving, but we didn't. From here, you'd think we'd see them days off." Lee scratched at his knee. Days, I considered, but that was impossible. Yet looking out, it didn't seem so very much. I thought Lee was done with it, but his mouth still worked at whatever troubled him. "Do you think they could have tried it, Nan? Chicago, I mean."

"I can't imagine."

"I'm going," he said.

"But you can't. It's only a guess."

"Next week, after the wheat is in. I have a little saved from the service. I don't care what Ray thinks."

"It's not just Ray."

"It doesn't matter that I'm here. But you, if you left . . ."

I turned to the fields with a shiver. I didn't want to matter like that. The moon was going. The dark sunk into the earth, the horizon vanishing. That the girls could have walked into the night by their own choosing, that they had done so without a lantern to light the way and traveled by foot, when grown men have died of wandering in such blackness—it was impossible, but since the war, everything was.

"Nan, I know I can find them." In the dimness, I couldn't make out my brother's expression.

When he was younger, Lee had come running from the barn and laid a creature on the porch's wooden planks. "Ran smack into the tractor," he said, worrying at it. He stretched out its wings.

"Why, Lee Herman, you can't . . ."

"Little bat nearly knocked herself out." He ran his fingers down its stomach as if to feel the creature's bones. "Don't think she hurt herself. Doesn't even mind me, she's so scared. And look . . . ." He held his fingers for me to sniff.

"Lee!"

"Lost control of her insides."

We watched the bat together as it woke and bared its teeth. It dragged itself off and climbed the closest rail with the claws on it wings, coming to rest on the banister. It seemed a dark tangle of fur breathing there.

"Why don't you leave it alone," I told Lee, but he didn't. He fretted about the dogs getting it and the cold. He must have been sixteen, seventeen back then, and he sat on the porch through the night to make sure the creature didn't fall from its perch. The next morning I found him asleep in the same chair and blanket, but the bat was gone.

I squinted to see my brother now, his fingers scratching at his knee. When the deputy came, Lee hadn't said a word but sat near the door with his head turned, as if listening for something. Lee had always been sweet on Esther. "Straw head," she called him. That bat had been an ugly thing with enough bite to hurt him, but how he worried over it. Esther had been his favorite, and he worried over her too. With someone like Esther, a man had to think hard not to go with whatever she told him, and Lee wasn't used to thinking. He'd sat until that bat flew off and though he hadn't seen it go, still he helped it to a high place where it could drop into the wind when no one was looking, easy as could be.

II

It is a strange thing to be a family of the missing. Deaths are commonplace. But a disappearance—it has the scent of murder in it, and there was little we could do to absolve ourselves. After Lee went, we continued our chores, but the work seemed dull without the promise of something new arriving to us. We canned our meats for the cellar, patched our woolens. We readied enough wood for the cold. There were repairs to be made and weeding to finish, plants going to seed and in need of pulling, the fields mulched with hay and manure. We had frosts by the end of October, a hard freeze that left a cake of ice on the sheep's drinking water. Our brood cow gave birth to a starveling, and Ray believed she wouldn't last the month. The summer crops were gone after that, save what we had already stored. With so few hands, Ray worked fourteen hours a day. Agnes grimaced at the layers of manure on her boots, and Patricia's knuckles swelled. "I do hope that boy can find them," she whispered in the kitchen. "I most certainly do." Already a month the girls had been gone. NO SIGN, Lee wrote in a telegram. STILL LOOKING. He never sent an address. At night with my eyes closing, I went through the books with a pencil, tallying our earnings and costs—three fewer stomachs, six fewer hands. I marked the difference at the bottom of the page with a shaky line. Hope, it was a terrible expense. We couldn't let anything go to waste. And we couldn't risk the extra we might set aside only to spoil if Lee and the girls didn't return soon, if the girls didn't return at all—though I couldn't let myself think it. Mother had said the same near the end. *None for me*, she'd said when I brought a plate to her bed. *This war. You're all thin as bones.*

This is not a place where people easily vanish. It is good clean earth for miles, straight as a table, our acres bordered by the river on one end and a rat of fenceline on the others, the distance between a long walk of cropland that takes more than a day's plowing. There is a low feeling to living here, the horizon far and wide with hardly a soul to break it, yet if you kick in your heel and wrench up a clot of dirt, how many thousands of creatures burrow through the earth beneath. In every direction our neighbors' acres are the same—more than a mile of farmland between us and the Clarks to the west, the Elliots to the south. In winters we don't lay eye on either family for weeks. The river between our acres and the Elliots' swallows its banks, higher from one season to the next. Bottomland, they call it, but the water could very well drown us. Father said we should be thankful to have so much. "There's nothing more honest than this," he said. But I think honesty is different from emptiness.

NOTHING, Lee wrote in a second telegram. NOT YET.

One night in November, hours after I had gone to bed, I had a dream. Myrle walked across the yard in the dark with the door to the house open behind her, and I saw myself standing just inside, watching. She was drenched to the skin. Her nightgown was sheer and stuck to her, her hair running with water. With the distance between us, I could not see her face. Instead of calling to her, I closed the door and locked it fast with my key. Outside the window, I could see her. She was running back to the house, to me.

I woke. The sound of knocking. When I sat up, the sound was gone. I took my lantern out into the hall and checked the door, the window. Both were closed, locked. Outside, only darkness. I carried my lantern up the stairs. The door at the top was open, the room now empty. On the girls' dresser, Myrle's dove-colored comb was gone, but the cutout of the woman's hand remained. Esther's pillows stood against the headboard but the wrong way, her bedspread crushed, nearly pulled off. The broken chair had been taken, as if to banish any thought of it. Only Agnes' drawings were the same—Mother with her pale hair, her eyes gray. If the girl had the chance, in forty years Myrle would be our mother's twin.

I opened the window to catch my breath. The ground below was dark as pitch. The gash beneath the sill felt sharp with slivers, as if something had bitten it. I thought of the hammer I had kept for myself, bundled in the linens of my room. It had a blunt rounded nose, its ears worn from pulling nails. The wooden handle curved just under my thumb, as if it had been mine all along. That gash, as wide as three fingers. The width of the hammer was the same, as if the hammer had broken the sill, pinned to hold something. Still, the gash itself seemed deeper than any my sisters might have left. From where I stood, the fields were gray with ruts of soil. Farther out, the trees were bare and black. Then nothing. Somehow, for some reason, the girls had gone running into that nothingness for all their worth.

They would have needed a rope. It might have been the dark of the room at my back that told me, or the way my lantern lit the side of the house. If only one of my sisters had used the key and the other had blocked the door with the chair and gone

41

through the window, they'd have needed a rope for the second girl to climb out—and it would have been Myrle. Close to hysterical at the drop and the only one slight enough, but Agnes was right. Esther could convince anyone to do such a thing, and Myrle more than that. Myrle, so sick those many weeks then suddenly not, and Esther with all her prowling—enough to make a plan. But what had made them want to go?

I walked out. The ropes we kept in the shed, the shed closer to the barn than the house and facing the fields. Around the foot of the shed, the mud was trampled, and the lock on the door hung loose, broken, the door gaping. It was an iron lock Father had made, as large as my hand and heavy. When I let it go, it snapped against the door. This farm never left things to ruin, not like that. I opened the door, but both our ropes lay coiled together at the foot of the wheelbarrow, the wheelbarrow rusted from the weather and the ropes wet to the touch.

A shuffle in the dark. I stepped out. Someone stood at the riverbank in the distance. An old man, stumbling along with his cane. Since Mother's illness, Father had often wandered. A dried-up dugout on our land had long been his favorite hiding place. Now he made slow going of it, stepping into the water as if half awake. In the low light, it lapped his knees, the thighs of his trousers. The water must have been cold enough to fill his boots with pins, the hour so late no man or woman would have wandered out unless driven. I thought to bring him back into the house, but he whipped at the water with his cane and whipped it again. I remembered my dream. How many times had Myrle come swimming here? But never in such darkness or as cold as it must have been. And never alone. I couldn't make sense of it, her feet wet on the doormat. I wouldn't let myself imagine what it might mean. I snuffed out my lantern and hurried blindly inside.

"I don't know why he sends each of you here," the deputy said.

I sat across the desk from him and drew my head back. I hadn't seen the man since his business at our house, more than a month ago now, and I didn't know who he thought was sending any of us. His office was a poor scrub of a room, the side door open onto the creek that ran through town. It could have been an outhouse, that creek, for how dimly it smelled. On his desk, a placard with the name SHEFFLEY in gold. The deputy dropped his chin, turning a pencil between his thumbs. "I've told you we've found nothing," he went on. "We will come to the house when we do."

"I know, Mr. Sheffley, it's just . . ."

The man groaned. "No, you do not know."

He puffed out his cheeks and I thought about the gash beneath the window and the hammer in my bag.

"Look," I said.

But he shook his head. "Miss Hess, this is a difficult time for all of us. Every other month, another farm goes to the bank, and there's who knows what in those empty houses. And every morning my wife asks for milk for our newborn, though she knows very well we can't afford enough. How can a father not have milk? We've got men on the roads, holing up behind every open door, and my wife sits in our house and weighs the child on the hour. When I get home, she never fails to tell me he hasn't gained an ounce more."

My face burned. What did he know of children, with only an infant? His worse complaint was that the child was thinner than he should have been? What if the boy disappeared altogether?

"You don't understand," I said. "If we stop coming . . ." But I couldn't finish. I drew my shawl to my throat.

The deputy returned to his papers, twisting his neck as he worked. The bag was heavy on my thighs, my hand gripping the hammer inside. Didn't its presence in their room, so strange in itself, prove something was wrong? That these girls, runaways or not, were different from the men in those sorry houses? And different needed attention. It must have had some terrible cause. I imagined the deputy turning the hammer over, an object strange to him—for surely he had rarely held a nail. He had never milked a cow or raised the wall of a barn. I imagined him dropping it in his drawer to be used for a later time, and Ray missing it, or even Lee. What good would giving the hammer to such a man do any of us?

I sat up straight and closed my bag. "If we stop coming here," I went on. The deputy didn't raise his head. "If we stop coming," I repeated, louder. "It would be like the girls have stopped. Like everything has. It would feel as if we had only just imagined them." My voice broke. "Why, my own brother has gone off to look for them. And he's not well. Ever since the war, he gets so easily confused."

"He seemed a perfectly capable young man." The deputy opened a drawer and drew out a pile of posters. "Beautiful faces," he said without a glance. "Someone in your house must have spent a great deal of time, but I don't know what good they'll do me. Those girls ran off. I'm sorry to repeat myself, Miss Hess, but you must listen. Everyone in town knows. Your brother, however confused, obviously does too. Girls, these days, they are so much older than they used to be. It's not my job to post advertisements, necessary or not."

"But these aren't . . ." I snatched the posters from him, a dozen of them or more, surely brought here by my own sister. The girls weren't so old as that. Not so old they might have done the very thing I had been thinking of for years.

"All right," Sheffley whispered. His pencil rolled down the slope of his desk and came to a stop near the edge. His eyes took on a dazed look, as if something had gone missing. He bent his head to his papers again, but his hand was empty, and he searched nervously about.

"Babies," I mumbled. I stood from the chair and left him looking, though the pencil lay neatly on the edge of his desk, as close as my own wrist. Puzzled by an ounce of milk and not a wink of sleep. If the man could not find a pencil, how could he find anything else?

It was more than cold now. The wind rose, ice glazing the roads. We expected snow. With the hammer in my bag, I stopped at the market to buy a dozen nails—though it seemed a waste with so many at home—and found a tree that faced the grocers. *Everyone knows*, Sheffley had said, but surely not the strangers that passed through town. Biting a nail between my teeth, I rolled out a poster and held it straight. MISSING, it read, the girls' faces copied by my sister's hand. "Nan, you want to know a secret?" I'd heard Esther say once. The hair on my neck had risen, as if her voice might know something worth whispering about. But with a laugh she was gone, and her whisper gone with it.

"Do you think that will help?"

I opened my mouth and the nail skittered away. A woman stood at my shoulder, the very likeness of Mrs. Clark. I remembered then that Mrs. Clark had a sister, though I couldn't remember her name.

"The younger was such a pretty girl, wasn't she?" she said.

"Both of them are."

"Young girls are often pretty simply by being young. Your girl was more than that. But the other one, she seemed a bit funny."

I turned my back on the woman and took another nail from my pocket, trying to hold the poster in place. When I swung the hammer, I swung too hard for posters, but not for other things.

"Funny," the woman said again. "She would come into town and stand at the market door to watch people going in and out. And when Nick Wallis complained, she folded her arms and asked him what he thought she should do about it."

"Esther is strong-headed, certainly."

"She wasn't like any other girl I've known." The woman stepped to my side, squinting as if to match the drawings to some likeness in her head. How similar she was to her sister—that hair a frizz around her ears and her cheeks fat, her eyes only slits, though this sister had blue instead of brown. "Don't you think those pictures are strange?" she started. "Aren't the girls a good year older now, at the very least?"

I drove another nail. "My sister Agnes did her best from a photograph. It was the most recent we had."

"When my girls were that age, they changed every month. My daughter's hair turned black and she was thin as a reed in less than a year. But that's the way with daughters."

"They aren't my daughters."

"That's right, your mother, poor thing . . ."

I headed off, determined to hang all the posters I could. "It was nice seeing you, Mrs. Clark."

She came after me in little bird steps. "No, no. Mrs. Meyers. You've gotten me and my sister confused. Of course, she is your neighbor." The woman looked at me blankly. That's what I remembered of the sister, then—she was a bit off in the head. Mrs. Clark, she was right as rain. "All I was trying to say," she went on, "is, what good will it do? With that picture so old?"

"It's only a year."

"You don't understand. Why, my own brother went off like that. He was a grown man. Thirty-two years old. I can't imagine seeing him now."

"I'm sorry to hear it."

She waved the words away. "All I'm saying is, sometimes it's best to let things lie. I don't know what I would do if I discovered Eddie on my porch today. Scare me to death."

I stopped and Mrs. Meyers came up short beside me. "You wouldn't be happy to see him?"

"Oh no, certainly not. It'd feel like a ghost knocking on my door. Like the dead. Nothing good could come of it. I think once people have gone strange, they aren't relations anymore, and you don't want any of those fists to come hammering. I wouldn't invite my own twin in after that."

If the brother was anything like the sisters, I pictured Mrs. Meyers opening the door to her very own image and shutting it at once. Behind me, she made her farewells and walked off. In the wind, the poster I'd hung had ripped at the corner, a tear that crossed Esther's forehead. I tacked it together. Myrle peered out from the other side, her chin longer than I thought right. Agnes with her pencil, sketching one face after another—but over the weeks, her drawings had grown careless and my sisters seemed little but strangers. If we ever had a chance to open that door, how much would they have changed?

"You shouldn't listen to her."

"Excuse me?" I turned. Carl McNulty stood watching me, and I stepped back. He raised a hand in surrender and only then did I realize the hammer was still in my grip, cocked as if I might strike.

"I said you shouldn't listen to her." He reached for my arm, pressing his thumb against the underside of my wrist. With a slow sweep of his hand, he lowered it. How well I knew the smell of him, sour like milking—and underneath, that warm cedar. *Something of your own*, Dora had said. I closed my eyes and saw instead a fence with four sides and an easy spot of land in between, the fence painted blue. I had dreamed of such a place ever since Mother went. When I looked up again, Carl had released my wrist. My skin felt terribly cold and I drew down my sleeve.

"Hello, Nan," he said.

"Carl," I said at last.

"I was wondering where you'd gone."

"I haven't gone anywhere."

"Neither have I," he said. "At least not for a while."

"Carl, look at you. I'm afraid we couldn't stop the other day. We were . . ."

"Not much, am I?"

"I was sorry to hear about your mother."

"And yours." He paused, seeing the poster above my head. When his eyes fell to me again, his grin had its old mischievous twist, though now he seemed as slow and even-tempered as his name.

"You must be alone in that house," I said. "You must be all by yourself."

"I've grown used to it."

"You have?"

He drew his hand through his hair, looking at the poster again and off down the street. The whole of Main appeared abandoned. How often I'd imagined that farm all his own, the quiet of this man and the house to ourselves, blue fence or no.

"I guess not." He caught my eye. "I should make you a visit."

"That would be all right."

He took the hammer from me. Wrenching the lowest nail from the poster, he fixed Esther's face, the way she must have looked those many months ago, when he might have seen her himself. He smiled at me then, slid the rest of the posters from under my arm, and carried them down the street until he'd hung them. At last, he turned back to me and slipped the hammer in my bag.

"It's cold as a brass button, don't you think?" He took my hand and I let him, leading me down a narrow alley, one I had never dared walk through by myself. Behind the low row of buildings, he knocked on a door. When it opened, an old man in an undershirt stood on the other side, the white crown of his hair twisted from sleep. The man's face colored, and he reached for a jacket. "Give me some warning with company, mind you," he said. "Come in, come in, before you freeze yourselves."

In a circle of lamplight, he sat us at a small wooden table and brought cups of hot milk with cinnamon. Canvas sacks lined the walls, the stink of meat. It was the back room of the traders, I guessed, and the man himself, he seemed to live there—a simple cot pushed up against the wall, a small stove, and a shelf of dry and canned foods. I hadn't recognized him when he opened the door, not in that state of dress.

"Nan, is it?" he said.

"I didn't know you at first."

"The eldest Hess girl. Yes, I remember you. But never so tall. How's the family? Your father?" He caught himself and dropped both elbows on the table.

"It's all right, Dennis," Carl said.

But Dennis squeezed his knuckles. "Such an awful thing. I'm sorry, I am. I heard about the girls. But for a minute I didn't. Do you have minutes like that? Sometimes I wish they'd last."

I felt the cup warm between my fingers and thought back to both my sisters' faces, posted high on wooden planks. "Why do you wish that?"

"Sometimes it's not so bad to forget a thing."

I let myself smile. "I'd never have known you were here. In town, I mean. Your windows are dark."

"Dennis likes to keep to himself," Carl said.

"Until this man here interrupts. But I suppose I can take interruptions from someone like him." Dennis eyed Carl's limp sleeve. "His mother was a good woman. Awfully good. And Carl, he's a hero to us. Any more of that, miss?"

My cup was empty. I wondered how long we had sat together in this room, and why I didn't mind, with so much to do at home. I licked the cinnamon from my lips.

"I better get her home, Dennis. Don't want to stay past staying time."

"I suppose it is after staying time, isn't it? Whatever time that is. Not that it's a bother. The two of you can come in for a warm-up whenever you like."

I stood, my head heavy, the taste of milk on my tongue. Carl carried the cups to the sink, the fit of his coat tight across his shoulders, and the pale hair at the back of his neck clean and soft—like it had always been.

"Remember your bag here, miss," Dennis said. Carl picked it up himself.

In the cold, I pulled my scarf to my chin. Carl carried my bag over his shoulder. With a smile, he tugged at the sleeve of my coat. "A good friend," he said. "Since the war, at least."

"I never knew him. Not really."

"You've grown up here same as me."

"But I'm different."

"What's so different?" He opened his hand between us, as if together we might find an answer in his empty palm. I felt the warmth of that room still, and the words of a stranger easy in my presence. Not for years had I heard so many words at once from a person outside my own family, none that were kind. Now because of Carl, I had. There had always been a lightness to this man, no matter that pinned sleeve, as if nothing in the past mattered and never truly would. He stared down at his feet, the wind pulling at the hems of his coat. "You'll be needing a ride then, won't you?"

I kicked the toe of his boot.

The way home was slow and clear. We rode together in his wagon, not a word more. It felt fine sitting there on the steerage, the wagon rocking, and the wool of Carl's trousers against my hip. The turn of our road appeared up ahead. Carl led the horses easily and I leaned into him around the bend. Soon the road straightened. Little changed, I thought, leaning away again. The lane stretched through the fields. The trees and hillocks were the same, every hill of grass so clearly set in my mind, every fence—and the sound of the river against the rocks, though we were some distance from the house. How could I ever imagine anything different?

"You can leave me here," I said.

"Here?"

"Please."

He stopped the horses short and I stepped out. The slope of our roof rose dully ahead, a run of smoke from the chimney. "I had been hoping to see you, Nan," Carl called after me.

I turned.

"I'd been hoping for a while," he said.

"So why didn't you?"

"I wasn't sure if you'd changed your mind. About what I'd asked."

"Mother died."

"I know it."

"I had to stay home for the girls."

He sighed. "And do you have to stay home now?"

"Now?" My eyes teared. "I haven't been much good, have I? My sisters must have hated me to do what they did."

"You don't know what they did, do you?"

I couldn't answer that. Carl looked over the fields. There wasn't anything to see on the horizon, not anything that might be called living, and the sound of the river was a maddening thing.

"If I made another visit to you," he asked, "would that be all right?"

"I don't think . . ."

He snapped the reins.

"Yes," I answered. "Yes, it would."

He smiled and tipped his hat. "All right." I waited until he was well out of sight, listening as the break of his wheels faded. At the bank, I watched the water and its muddy track. What trees there were had fallen, stripped of their bark. The ground underfoot was spongy and soft. The river cut the land in two, on one side our neighbors' acres and on the other our own, stretching so far at either end I had never found its source. A run of blackened leaves and twigs clung to the surface. They would drown soon enough. The keys were still in my pocket. When I fished them out, they glinted in my palm. With a shout, I threw them into the river, where I hoped the water would take them, as it did everything else.

III

It snowed. At first only a fine powder, but by the beginning of December, we had two feet or more. The animals stayed in their stalls. At the troughs, the cows kept their heads to their chests. We should have known from the coats on our horses that winter would be a trial, how the ears hung from the corn even before harvest. Now the air had turned to ice. Our layers offered little to protect us. Soon the snow grew high as the windowsills. Farther off in the fields, the fence posts jutted from the drifts, the only sign of our summer work. We tied a rope from the front porch to our outbuildings in case of storm.

We had known difficult winters in years past. During the war, we couldn't say they weren't a relief. The road to town became no more than a track, our sleigh old, kept only for sickness or accidents, and the wagon near to worthless. We planned our food stores well enough to carry us for months. Otherwise, we stayed to ourselves, eager to imagine that the town and our neighbors had forgotten us. With the few hours of daylight, there were only the animals to look after and the work in the barn.

But now with Esther and Myrle gone, I let myself sleep late in the mornings and did my mending by the fire in the dark afternoons, Agnes and Patricia at my side. The parlor smelled of wool, the walls seeming to thicken. When the wind was up, we felt ourselves drifting. Two girls, I imagined, their dresses no match for such weather, their judgment even the worse. If not for some terrible company, they surely couldn't make it through the winter alone.

"Nan, you're doing it again." Agnes sat in the corner with her book. "Stop picking." I looked down at my fingers—the small bloody tears—and took up my stitching again.

"Those poor girls," Patricia said. "What would their mother think?"

"You didn't know our mother," Agnes said.

"I heard about her plenty from Ray. Never seen a man so miss his mother."

Agnes gave me a look. I shook my head to keep her quiet.

"Except that Carl McNulty," Patricia went on. "The way his mother went, while he was over there fighting. Fancy seeing him again. So changed."

"Patricia, can you please hush?" Agnes asked.

"He brought me home," I said.

Patricia caught her breath. "When?"

"Just the other week."

Agnes stared. "Why didn't you tell us?"

"I didn't think it worth telling."

"My, my, isn't life strange." Patricia shifted in her chair, and the clock on the mantel skipped ahead. Agnes went back to her book, the skin of her throat flushed. Patricia hummed to herself. "That boy, out there all alone on his place. I sure do think he loved you, Nan. But I suppose a woman's feelings change."

My thread caught. "They didn't change. Carl left for the war and I stayed where I was needed."

"I suppose," Patricia said.

Agnes rifled through her pages. Now and again I caught her stare, but I dropped my head.

"When I met Ray," Patricia went on. "I thought I'd never seen a boy so handsome. Right out of the magazines. I'm sure I never told you."

"Yes, you did," Agnes said.

"A lonely boy. So much expected of him. He explained how your father counted on him and him alone. Of course, that's why he never could marry, he said. Until your poor mother . . ." She clicked her tongue. "Then it was a different story, wasn't it? She was always one of my favorites, your mother. A terrible time."

Agnes sighed. "How terrible was it, Patricia?"

"Oh, that war. If only she could have lasted until it was over." She shook her head. "I'm just saying when a boy loses his mother, he needs a woman by him. Boys like that, they're no good at doing for themselves. With Ray, I had to wait him out. Maybe if you gave your Carl another chance."

Agnes slammed the cover of her book. "Agnes," I said. Those fingers of mine pulsed as if my heart beat in them.

"Another chance," I repeated, as if such a thing were easy. "With the girls gone?"

The kitchen door banged, a rush of wind. Ray stomped his boots on the mat and found us in the parlor. He held up his hands to the fire. His cheeks glowed as if feverish, his bad hand gnarled in the light of the flame. Without a word, he dropped another piece of wood on the pile.

"Ray, did you see to the stockyard fence?" I asked. "I thought I saw a post down."

Ray grunted and swiped at a lock of hair on his forehead. He put on his cap.

"Aren't you staying?" Patricia asked.

"Can't," he said. He brushed by her hand and went out. Past the windows again, my brother stumbled through the drifts, a blur of darkness.

"He misses them too," Patricia said. "I know you don't believe me, but that man is just as sorry as the rest of us."

It was late the next morning when I spied Ray far off in the pasture, kicking at the snow. It was a blustery day, ice in my collar. In such weather as this, we feared for storm. Ray kneaded at the back of his neck. As I walked closer, the hindquarters of our brood cow showed by the barbed fence, her legs twisted and bloodied where she must have fallen. Ray took the animal's head in his hands and tried to move it, tried to place his fingers beneath her stomach, but she was frozen in the snowmelt. He stood, the wind hard against him.

I touched his shoulder.

"Nan." He wiped his eyes before he turned.

"Is she gone?"

He nodded.

"What was it?"

"Caught her foot on the barbs. I don't know why she would have wandered so far. Went off by instinct and got into trouble. Probably didn't see the wire until it was too late." He lifted her hoof with the wire wound tight, the skin bloody and bitten through to the bone. Her mouth was bloody too. "She tried to free herself."

I touched the cow's flank. "What should we do?"

"I can't carry her myself. She's well frozen."

"What about the horses?"

"We'd have to clear a path for them all the way from the corrals."

I sighed. "She couldn't have been out more than one night. Agnes told me she heard her calf crying only this morning."

Ray nodded.

"We'll have to leave her."

"I thought of that. But it could be May before we'd have her out. The dogs might get her. Wolves, too."

"Then the wolves will get her."

"This close to the barn, those wolves might think there's more." Ray went quiet, looking into the white of the fields. "Get the knives."

"It's too cold, Ray. You'll get nothing from her."

He studied the cow again, letting her chin rest on the lip of his boot as if he didn't want to drop her snout. "Just bring them, why don't you?"

I walked back to the barn. A butchering, so late in the season, when even the river was frozen to a standstill. My lantern we would need and torches. Something to keep a fire going. Inside, Agnes sat cross-legged in the hay, the calf quiet at her knees. It was loose-legged and weak, far too young to be feeding by hand.

"Will she eat?" I asked.

Agnes shook her head.

I opened a canvas sack and loaded our saw and knives. "We found the mother by the fence."

My sister looked up. "What are you doing?"

I threw the sack over my shoulder. Agnes had never done a butchering, had never seen more than a chicken on a block or used such a knife herself. None of my sisters had.

"We need your help."

Through the morning and into the early afternoon, we stayed by the fence with the cow. She was hard as bone, but Ray thought if we held the torches close, we could free just enough, and she wouldn't be such a waste. There might be something warm in her yet.

"Too good an animal to go," he said. Lee would have said the same.

His gloves turned bloody, his face grim. He didn't look at anything but the box saw in his hand. I held my knife, but it was Ray who cut at the animal with a vengeance, bent to get it done. The hide was thick with ice, but the saw was sharp, and when it finally broke through the belly, it cut straight and fine. Deeper in, the innards steamed. Ray stopped to shake his hand and started again. My own grip didn't have such strength, my cuts thin, and always the rush of bile in my throat. Agnes crouched near us with a torch, her head turned away. Ray had to remind her to hold the fire close, to look at what she was doing, but she never looked much. I tried to distract myself with numbers and meals—how this work might help us in the months to come, how good the meat would be to store in the smokehouse, saving another animal down the line. The cow's face had turned an icy gray, the ground around her melted to mud. Soon there was only the stillness of the fields and the snow stained under our boots. Agnes pressed her hand over her nose.

"Ray, isn't it enough?" I asked.

He stretched his fingers. "Agnes, if you're just going to stand there . . ."

"I'm holding the torch as close as I can."

"She's worried about the calf is all," I said.

Ray grimaced. His chin was trembling, but he bent to cut again.

"Agnes," I explained, "you have to try."

Her eyes shone. "Lee's the one who should be here."

"You know very well where Lee is," I answered.

"It's not fair, all of them leaving us to do everything. What if they never come back?"

"Stop sniveling," Ray said.

"But Lee is coming," I told her. "As soon as he can."

Ray wiped his nose. "She doesn't want to do the work."

"You never thought about going to Chicago." Agnes glared at him. "You never even tried."

Ray wrenched the torch in her grip closer to the open stomach. She nearly fell.

"Don't you care about anything?" Agnes cried. She dropped the torch. The skin on her fingers had blistered under the flame. I pulled her quickly to her knees, buried her fist in the snow, but she only cried out again. "You don't, do you?"

Ray raised his arm to strike her, but I caught his elbow.

"Ray!"

The shout came from far across the yard, a figure pressing through the snow. Father was bound in his coat and hat, walking with the wind. When he reached us, he tore the saw from my brother and bent to cutting, signaling to me with his chin to take up the torch. "Agnes, go home," he said, his eyes down. He cut with steady blows. "Nan, the torch." I lit it fresh. Soon Ray joined in with my knife, and Agnes stood in the snow, sniffling. She spun toward the house, her skirts wet and her hair sticking to her cheeks.

"I should go after her," I said. "She's burned."

Father lurched back and mopped his forehead. The cow was nearly quartered now, the meat greasy in the snow. He stared at me, his eyes cold, such a lost look on his face with the frost clinging to his beard. I bent my head and held the torch close.

Later in the washhouse, I leaned against the wall, if only to rest. We had finished with the cow well enough, and the house through the open door blazed with light, but I wasn't in any hurry to reach it, not in any hurry to sit at the dinner table and bring a fork to my mouth. I closed my eyes. It was rags I needed to dress Agnes' burn. We kept them in a bucket in the washhouse for scalding. They would want bleaching, yes, but already they would be torn in long slivers, a dozen or so for changing day and night. I dug into the bucket. These were our old long johns and underskirts, our coarser linens. Most were too threadbare to take a needle to again—though I had often tried—too outgrown to pass onto another child. Despite my every stitch, they ended up rags. Now from the bottom of the pile came something else. In my hand was one of Myrle's good dresses, a blue crepe I had made her for Easter the year before.

When had I seen her wear it last?

I laid the dress out in pieces and held up my lantern. My stitches stood along the hem. Stains spotted it front and back, as if the girl had rolled in something in her playing. The dress had been torn in half and half again, bundled up like a hated thing. Folding the pieces together, I crushed them in my hand, a sob rising in my throat. That girl. With no mind to the expense and the time I had spent. The time I didn't have.

* * *

At dinner that night, I watched the others at the table. Ray and Father hunched at either end, their faces chapped. Ray bit at a bloody tear of skin on his lip. Across the table, Agnes wouldn't look at him, her bandaged fingers heavy in her lap. Outside, the fire we had lit to finish what was left of the animal smoked low in the distance. It wouldn't last. I'd carried the dress back to the house, closed it away in my bureau until I could decide what it meant— if it meant anything. *Never make too much.* For so many years, I had lived and worked close enough to my siblings I could name their breathing in the dark, but now in every quiet face, I sensed something hidden. The way Patricia gnawed at her bread. The way Ray gripped his fork with those crooked fingers, his knuckles white. My youngest sister, tucking her good dress away with the rags. If she could do such a thing—so ordinary, one might think, but possibly not—what might my other siblings be planning?

"Such sour faces," Patricia let out. She helped herself to another bowl of soup. Unlike the rest of us, the woman had not lost weight the last few months but instead thickened in her grief. Ray caught her wrist to stop her spoon, but she shook him off. "Lee would have eaten two or more bowlfuls," she said. "Now, I'm not saying one way or another, but I never knew that boy to be gone for more than a day. Other than the war, that is. And not a word for weeks."

Father threw his napkin on the table. He walked down the hall, banging his door closed after he went. The dining room seemed to shrink, the lantern bright. Agnes tried to pull her sleeve over her bandage, but the sleeve was far too short—I hadn't once this season taken a needle to let out her hems.

"He must have run out of money," Patricia went on. "Even when he telegrammed, he never gave us an address that lasted more than a night."

"He will write when he writes," I said, but I wasn't so sure about that.

Patricia grated her spoon against the bottom of her bowl. "A little conversation at a meal. That's all I ask."

Ray raised his head, bleary-eyed.

"I don't see anything wrong with showing some warmth to each other," Patricia said. "Like normal people. Normal people talking about what's on their minds."

Agnes reddened, but I didn't have the heart to play peacemaker, not then.

"Nan agrees with me," Patricia said, "Don't you, Nan?"

"You want to talk about Lee," Ray asked. "Is that the kind of talk you want?"

Patricia slumped. "Well, yes . . ."

"The boy can't remember where he put his own hat when it's on his head."

"Nan," Agnes started. "Do you hear what he's saying?"

Ray swung his knife. "I wouldn't be surprised if he never finds his way back."

"You wouldn't?" Patricia gasped.

"You can't say that." Agnes looked at me. "He can't."

"And you." Ray pointed at Agnes. "If you want to run away too, then go on, why don't you? All of you. Just you try it."

Patricia dropped her spoon in her bowl. "Ray, I never . . ." He rested his arms on either side of his plate, too tired to lift a finger though his face seemed anything but. Patricia touched his cheek. He pressed a hand over his eyes. "No one's leaving,"

Patricia whispered to him. Down the hall, a door fell shut. We turned our heads. I pictured Father having listened to us in the dark, the door cracked open again, until he'd heard enough.

"It will be okay, won't it, Nan?" Agnes asked, her cheeks hot. "Like you said?"

I stood to gather the plates. A fork fell to the floor. When I dropped to my knees to fetch it, the dark under the table showed three pairs of legs and three laps. The empty chairs looked cold, the rest of us nothing more than cuts of wood. I imagined Myrle's dress again, strung up as if from a rope outside that window. In my mind it hung starched and ironed, a paper cutout for a paper doll. I made to stand, but something burned from my stomach to the bridge of my nose. I left the fork where it fell and headed for the kitchen, carrying away the rest of our meal, finished or not.

That night I shut myself away in my room and thought about Carl. A hero, the grocer had called him. He'd even won himself a Cross. Lee had served in the war, but he didn't have much but the limp to show for it. Both my brothers had worked the land for years, but it wasn't the thing of medals. And it didn't save our family from whatever the town cared to make of us. We were foreigners—no matter how long ago Father and Mother had staked their claim. And land grubbers at that. The parents who couldn't trouble themselves to learn their English proper, to change their name. The children who pretended they didn't know their native tongue. We were fooling no one. If anyone had seen Carl together with me, I knew just what they thought: What was the man doing spending time with the Hess girl again? A girl so tall and plain, the one the neighbors could only call handsome. The kind of girl too proud to keep a man's ring. Wasn't she rather old for such things? Before the war, even my family had been surprised.

A knock on my door. "Nan?"

"Go to bed, Agnes."

"Are you all right?"

I imagined her waiting, her hand raised to knock again, the one that had been burned.

"Nan?"

I opened the door and lay back in my bed. Agnes pinched at her skirts and eased herself onto the edge of my mattress. "You looked like you were going to be sick in there."

I didn't answer.

"How can you stand the way those two go on? It makes me want to scream." She fiddled with her bandage.

"Have you seen Myrle's comb?" I asked.

"Her comb?"

"The one she keeps on her dresser."

"I never saw it."

"Agnes."

She sighed and reached into her pocket. "I didn't think you'd want it." When she drew it out, the comb seemed nothing more than a piece of bone, no larger than her palm. She laid it on the mattress between us and I rubbed my thumb against the handle. "I've hardly used it," Agnes said. "Really. I only thought . . ."

Between my bitten fingers, the comb was soft with strands of Myrle's hair, the same ivory as the handle, and Agnes' darker strands threaded through. "Agnes, those posters you made . . ."

"You know how hard I worked on those."

"But sometimes when I try to think of the girls, all I see are those drawings. Their faces don't move anymore."

Agnes took my hand and held it in both her own, though it pained her to do so. "Nan, don't quit on me now. I couldn't stand it."

"I'm not quitting."

She turned my fingers over as a child would, studying them.

"Fine," I said. "Everything will be all right."

She smiled at that. The bandage on her fingers was trim and white. Earlier it had shown spots where her blisters had broken, but she must have changed it herself. When had she grown so old, this sister? She was nearly nineteen and far from a girl—though I had trouble thinking of her as anything but. "Can't we just say it's done?" I wanted to ask her, but I didn't. Not even to myself. Waiting was a grim thing. Just outside our door, years seemed to pass, when it'd only been months.

Come now, Agnes, Mother had said when it came to Esther and Myrle. *Be a big girl. Help out.* She was always one for helping, Agnes was. The forgotten one, stunted. The one in the middle of us. She sat across from me now full in the flesh. Without my having noticed, she'd dropped my hand.

"If I show you something, do you promise not to tell?" I asked.

"What is it?"

"In the bottom drawer of my bureau. Can you fetch it?"

She slipped off the bed. From the drawer, she drew out the pieces I had folded together. "This is Myrle's dress."

"I found it with the rags in the washhouse. Do you remember the last time she wore it?"

Agnes looked the pieces over, fingering the stains on the skirt and back.

"I can only think she went out playing in it and got muddy," I said. "She knew I'd be angry at that."

"Or Father would."

"Father, yes."

"But Nan, she loved this dress. It doesn't look like mud. It looks like something else." She held it to her nose.

I steadied my voice. "You said they ran away."

She went to the door and called Patricia's name. Our sister-in-law came running. "What is it?"

Agnes held out the dress. "What do you think this is?"

"It's a dress," Patricia said.

"But the stains."

Patricia sniffed them, and she drew back. "That's blood, that's what that is. I'd know it anywhere with all of Ray's wash after butchering."

"Then it's from one of the animals," I said.

"Maybe," Agnes said.

"This is Myrle's dress, isn't it?" Patricia pieced the fabric together. "I just knew something was wrong. Chicago. I knew it couldn't be that. Otherwise, Lee would have found them."

"It's only a dress," I said. "It could be mud for all we know."

"That's not mud," Patricia said.

"But you told us they ran away," I started again. "And we believed you, even if it didn't feel right."

"Something must have happened," Patricia said. "Something terrible."

"Maybe I was wrong," Agnes let out.

My eyes blurred. I raised a hand, wanting to slap away what she said. They both flinched.

"Nan?"

"Oh, Nanny," Agnes said.

"Get out. The both of you."

"We have to tell Ray . . ."

But I didn't give them the chance to finish. Taking both of their arms, I pushed them out into the hall and closed my door behind them. I bundled the dress tightly then and folded it away in the drawer.

The blame was mine. That's what I knew then. Why, I had forgotten my sisters so much as to raise my hand. I'd thought only of hems and bedtimes, chores that begged for doing, and all the many ways I could escape them. When Mother was ill, how often had I dreamt of it? That fence with its four sides and the small stretch of land. The fence painted blue. The square of earth in between, a place of my own where if I opened the gate I could invite someone in. *Hello, Nan,* Carl had said in town. *I was wondering where you'd gone.* I could only answer, *I haven't gone anywhere.* In the past weeks, Carl had not made his visit, and now I was convinced he never would. We were a practical family, he knew. We kept to ourselves. But underneath he must have sensed something new at fault. *I'm different,* I reminded him. The town had said as much in years past. And though we were innocent then, now with the girls missing, we seemed anything but.

Outside, a heavy crash. I sat up in bed, the wind fierce against the panes. Taking hold of my lantern, I rushed into the hall and opened the front door. A plank of wood lay on the porch. It must have blown from the barn or one of the outhouses, but the barn itself had disappeared in the storm. One of the Elliots' shepherds barked, and out in the southernmost field, a shadow quivered. For an instant, it showed itself against the snow, then it was gone. The calf. Looking for her mother. Somehow she had gotten out.

I pulled on my boots, looked back at the shuttered house, and stepped into the snow. My feet sank, the crest higher than my knees. The shadow loped and cried silently in the distance. Behind me the house seemed as if it might float, the snow blanketing the windows, and only the lantern I carried and a dim lamp in the parlor gave any brightness. The calf was running, stumbling as it went and caught near to stopping, and soon I was running too. The snow was thick under my boots. The cold burned my cheeks. The calf fell in the drifts, but surely when I caught it, I could take it up in my arms. I could deliver the creature from the storm, leave my coat by the fire to dry, and have done my part. I was close enough to believe I might reach out and feel the calf under my glove. Instead my boot kicked something hard. There wasn't a sound but the snow, nothing I could touch but cold and ice—and it wasn't the calf at all. A tree limb stood high in the drift, ripped from a far-off pine and blown. A tear of canvas stuck against it and swayed like a living thing. I touched the wood, felt its spine. The canvas tore away in my hand.

When I looked back, the house was gone.

I turned in circles, but the snow had thickened. My lantern grew faint, the wick low. How far I had walked, I could not say. In every direction, my light showed only a wall of white. My footprints were nearly covered, nothing that pointed one way or another. Crushing the bit of canvas in my pocket, I set out again, plunging to my thighs in the snow.

Surely I couldn't be far from the house. Only a few dozen yards at best, and the barn would show itself or one of the fences and I could follow any one of them back. In the dark, even my hands were invisible. Was this what it felt like when they went? For suddenly I was sure the girls had gone alone, dress or not. They had found the strength to do it themselves—what with Esther leading the way. I saw her clearly as I hadn't for months, pulling me along, her hand small and sharp and that fierce look she gave. *Hurry*, she said, as clear as the living, and when the wind tore up again there it was before us—an openness I had never known. The land was gone, the earth uncertain under my feet, and everything was possible at once. I could be forgotten, the oldest sister who would never be missed, and this was a release, the way sleep was a release, or that hour after the sun set, suppertime done, and I could sit with my darning and escape into myself while seeming every bit present. I could dream terrible dreams then, of my whole self vanishing while my knuckles cracked over one last trouser leg—and in that new place I could become boundless.

My toe struck the fence.

It was hours then or only minutes. I followed the fenceline with the barbs bloodying my fingers and soon wrenched the barn door open against the drifts. Under the rafters, my ears rushed with stillness, my lamp brighter now by half. The animals in their stalls shivered. In the far corner, the calf lay safe and near to sleep. She stared as I crouched next to her, her eyes shining—such a pretty thing, though Agnes worried she couldn't be saved. We should shoot her before she starved, Ray had said. But Agnes wouldn't allow for shooting, not with Lee gone. Lee, that soft heart. As I lay down, the calf shook her head, scared in the faint light and hardly ready for the living. I closed my eyes and let myself drift. A stream warmed my leg, as good as kettle water in the bath and a sudden softness in my hips. The calf nosed my shoulder, licking the snow off my chin. I took a scab of snow from my sleeve, held it to her lips to drink, and her tongue stung my skin.

I woke. The barn was still. The calf lay asleep in the far corner, its mouth wet. The rip of a hinge and the door flew open. I heard my name. It was then I was lifted up, a man's breath in my ear. He labored and fell and righted himself, another voice calling my name and asking to carry me, but the man wouldn't give in. Stumbling to the house, he grunted, nearly falling again as he held me fast. My cheek dropped against his shoulder, the smell of leather and tobacco. Soon I was awake enough to know it was Father who carried me, the way he hadn't since I was a little girl. When I was young, he let me sit on his knee and rested the flat of his palm on my head, as if in protection. He wore an old leather hat, a triangular sort the color of moss, and he gave it to me whenever I complained of the sun. His hands were large, pocked at the knuckles, the whole of him wide as a barrel. Often he had carried me to my room at night when I dropped off to sleep in the parlor, if only to stay with my parents and their talk. Now he lowered me to my bed. Someone pushed a pillow behind my back. When I opened my eyes, he stood watching me, wild and gripping his chest.

"*Mein Mädchen*," Father said, his face pinched. "You were found." He ran his thumb across my cheek and slapped me with a full hand. "Never have us find you again."

The room went quiet. My cheek stung. Around the bed my siblings watched like frightened children. Soon the room darkened and they hushed each other. I was falling asleep. I would sleep for several days more, hot as an oven and sweating through the sheets. The others came and went, tending to me. But it was Father who slumped always in the chair at my side, his head sagging. It was Father who said my name. I dreamt wonderful dreams then—of the girls returning home. Of Lee walking over the hill, not a limp in his step, and Mother taking hold of my hand. *What a girl you are*, she said. She opened the window and brought out her best skirt, fastening a belt around her waist. *Your father says we have new sugar*, she said. *How about a cake?* The girls ran to the kitchen to dip their fingers in the batter. *Not so fast*, Ray said. *Not before dinner*, I called out.

Then it was summer. It was late afternoon. Myrle was walking across the meadow in her bare feet, her fingers sweeping the grass. Her white-blond hair was dark and wet against her neck. On her back, the blue crepe. The fabric was soft and slim around her waist, the fit only just loose enough at her chest and hips. I couldn't help but think how fine the dress was, how my needle had done that—and the way she walked in it, a pale spirit. *Where's she going?* I asked my sisters. Agnes shrugged. *To see a friend*, Esther sung out. It was the last time I would see Myrle wear that dress. I would love if she could wear it again. I would bleach it clean, take my needle to the tears and hide them in new pleats—but Myrle was too far off now across the meadow to call back.

"Nan, Nan."

I woke. The room seemed clear to me again. A man sat close to the bed. I knew his voice before I knew him.

"Carl." I smiled at him and he drew his hand over my forehead.

"You're awake."

"I guess."

"They were worried about you. Agnes thought I might be a help."

Agnes sat on the other side of the bed. Her cheeks were raw, her hair twisted in a bun.

"Where are the others?" I asked.

"They're in town."

I tried to sit up, but Carl pressed a hand to my shoulder.

"Why ever for?" I asked.

Agnes stuttered and it was Carl who took my hand. He nodded to Agnes and she bit her lip.

"They found a girl," he said.

"The girls came home?"

Carl shook his head. "A girl in the river. They don't know who she is. The others have gone to find out."

Part II: The River

JON JULIUS

I

In the year 1892 I was a young man of little more than thirty, stealing passage from an old German woman who expired on the docks before she was boarded. She had blue cheeks in the time I discovered her. Her woolens were so thickly bound about her throat and chest I never could hope to save her, long past saving as she was. Her hand rested stiffly on her stomach. Her ticket wavered from the tips of her fingers as if offering it up. I touched her wrist and felt it cold, gazed back at the foreign village where I was friendless and sure to starve, and slipped that ticket from her grasp. God forgive the young their desperateness. Now nearly as old, I would pay for such unhappy luck. Yet little had I known of its opposite even then.

In the weeks as they passed, I stayed secreted on that ship, securing room for myself in the lower berths. I was a farm boy with a rent in his trousers. I reeked of pigs. If spied on the decks, I feared I would in an instant be pitched overboard, a trespasser no matter what ticket I held. In the evenings when the skies closed and the storms fell, I sweated in my bunk. The air was so very dense with smoke and stench my head itched. They offered us a mattress stowed with seaweed. A life preserver for a pillow. A tin pail for meals of herring and soup. My stomach turned. The lamps on such rocky waters were too dangerous to light. I tucked my knees to evade the rats. Still the ocean swells plagued my sleep. I stood in the mornings so sickened, I doubted I had opened my eyes.

In the daytimes, I dared walk the decks to escape the hordes below. When I grew tired, my legs unsure, I hid behind the vents and surveyed the horizon for land. One week more. One dreaded week. The engines of the ship bore on. On the upper level, a woman perched her child on the rail, gripping only his waist. The child was small, barely two years old. He was calm as he looked out. The woman cooed to him under her hat. She had a lovely pale face, little younger than myself. A ribbon bound a nest of hair off her neck. The hair was a fiery red, her cheek the whiter against it, and I felt a stirring when the wind lifted her skirt from her ankles. Now and again, she closed her eyes. Her fingers loosened from the waist of that jumper. The child was oblivious. He leaned forward in the arms of his mother, reaching for the sea.

When must we learn to fear? And if not from our parents, from whom?

I missed the land my father worked. I missed the house where my mother had me born. Sitting on deck on those dull waters, I missed my boots on the soil. In the dark of the evenings, I imagined that old woman as she snatched her ticket back. This voyage had taken from me something I never would have dreamed. My assurance there was a place for me. The steadiness of my limbs. Home. The idea alone is not solid enough to carry with us. Yet without it, on what can we stand? If I reached the far side, I prayed the new world proved steady. I might place my feet on the ground, build a life worth these many miles. Once I achieved that, I vowed I would leave the good earth never again.

*　*　*

I am an old man now. I sleep in my slippers because my feet grow cold. I know men who sleep far deeper than I. I know women who visit them in churchyards. Yet I cannot truly sleep in any sense of the word. The room is dark. I tug at my blanket. What a waste of time the evening is for the old. All those many hours between sunset and sunbreak. When I close my eyes, the swells of that sea always are with me. The never-ending tide of the river against its banks. How often I tried to keep the waters under my thumb. How much they have from us stolen. If the old woman and her ticket laid a curse, I have seen it play itself out, once and again. Why might a man lock the doors of his house? Why can he never forget the trespasses against him? He makes his confession. Yet confessing never erases the act. Try as I might, the language is wrong. The sentences slip. My ease with the old tongue is fading, and I am left only with this English. Its many contradictions. Its twenty ways of saying one thing.

Years ago when I stood on the deck of that ship, the sea reflected the sun. It lit my face from beneath. I believed I might go blind from the light. Even now I blink when I think of it. Me, only thirty-three and ignorant of everything save for what I could grow with my own hands. Born as I was a farmer. Raised in the northern German lands of wheat. The rest of my life, I learned little I would find important. About war, perhaps. About children and the duties of family. Yet these were not light. I could not make of them that.

When at last they released me from that prison Ellis Island, I wandered the streets of the city for a place to lay my head. With difficulty, I found boarding and determined to use it well. For two days I slept. Still I believed myself drifting on that ocean. On the third, a noise stirred me. A man stood next to my cot. His knees pressed into my mattress. I shared the room with a dozen others, and we had avoided so much as a glance. This man was short, powerfully built. He wore nothing save a stained undershirt, his naked arms and legs masked with hair. His breath more than stank. He watched me until certain I was alert, cleared his throat and puckered his lips. I turned my face. He let out a low guttural noise then, insulting me in some foreign language. In my innocence, I shook my head. Without another word he hurried to the toilet. From that room I heard worse from the man. His stomach seemed to drop out of him whole, leaving him gasping. When at last I sat up, I felt dizzy. Disjointed from my sleep. A spot of wet stained the blanket that lay across my chest. It was no larger than my thumb and just as harmless-seeming. Yet I remembered that man clearing his throat and understood such a spot never came from me.

Sleep on, Julius. Sleep on. The man had shared his pains as punishment. But for what crime? Come morning I would make my escape and discover the land they promised.

Early the next day, I packed my meager belongings and wandered the streets. I had often heard about the land in the west. New York seemed to promise little of such openness. How was it that its people settled on top of one another, never to fear trampling? In the afternoon, the streets shimmered with heat. I found only a bench in a park to give me rest. A church bell called once and again. I counted the bills that lined my wallet, wishing there were more.

Already I worried about my decision to leave home. To think I had wanted but a small bit of soil. Something not carved out by my father or his father before him. Yet almost every acre in my country had already been claimed. The thought of my father once he discovered my absence troubled me further still. The morning I went, I planned to leave hours of road behind me, long before my parents stood from their beds. I took a loaf of bread. A knife with which to cut it and keep for my protection. The cows I milked. The milk I poured in a jug for my mother. My bed I straightened, my church shoes placed at the door for one cousin to have or another. I had no heart to write a note. The cows would tell enough. The story, it would circle the village. How the son made well what was needed of him. How he had started in the darker hours to finish it. I imagined my father lifting his hat in the barn to find the cows asleep. Their stomachs would be full, their pails heavy with milk. I imagined my mother happening upon my bed and lifting the sheet. At its touch, warm or cold, she might guess the hour I had gone.

Week after week I trolled for work in that city, only to return to a different boardinghouse. I now had a room of my own with a lock. Still, my pockets had grown thin. My stomach suffered cramps. Outside in the hall, a washerwoman sang to herself as she scrubbed the floor. I opened my door to hear her better. "*Brauchen Sie irgendetwas?*" she asked, turning. Are you all right? Need you anything? "*Nichts,*" I answered. Her German held the thick lilting hum of the southern states, her *s*'s full between her teeth. Every word she spoke trailed from the roof of her mouth. At once I felt the home I had left restored to me. The woman wore hard wooden shoes. Her torso was narrow, her neck long. It rose to a faint line of hair, more white than blond and tied in a net. Without stopping her hands, she rinsed her rag in a bucket, wrung it, set it to the floor. Her singing never dropped a note. Despite the sorry house, she seemed to hold its very cleanliness on the tip of her thumb.

Mornings passed. I saw her many a time. Margrit was her name. An orphan. Her father gone to drink, her mother dead. At the age of twelve she had sold her family possessions to make the passage across. What little of Germany she knew remained in the language she spoke, her sense of work. She cared for that boardinghouse like her home.

"*Brauchen Sie irgendetwas?*" she asked.

"*Nichts,*" I answered again. Still I was growing more reluctant to close that door between us.

Inside the daylight hours, I continued my search for employment. Often I passed the same forlorn sheet of paper tacked to a post. An advertisement, in German no less. ACRES BY THE MILLIONS. LANDS FOR SALE. It showed a crude drawing of a railway cutting between miles of grass. I brought it to the man at the boardinghouse desk. Margrit held the sheet close, a translator for us. I was to purchase my train ticket. Labor in the place day and night to fill my pocket. Offer my bid within thirty days. "My own brother did it, and my dad. But not me," the man explained. "Nothing there but dust." "*Nur Staub,*" Margrit said. But dust, I thought, it needs soil to run beneath it. More land than could fit inside a fence. Margrit rolled the paper neatly, warmed it in her hands. When she offered it back, it seemed a gift. When next I saw her, I had a different answer to her question.

"*Brauchen Sie irgendetwas?*" she asked. "*Ja,*" I said.

Margrit and I were a week later married. With my last dollars, I purchased our tickets west.

They say one countryside is like another. There are horses and cattle. The smell of dung. At home, my father owned a small farm of forty acres where we raised wheat and maize. Yet as soon as our train crossed into the western plains, I knew this land would be different. The maps showed a state bordered on both sides by rivers. The Mississippi on one. The Missouri the other. A mouthful both of them, wide as any plain. Iowa. The word gives nothing for the tongue to hold. Still when we arrived, it seemed wholly settled, if only in the steadiness in its terrain. In Iowa, I held my hand level to the earth, my fingers splayed. If I squinted right, the very crevices in my skin disappeared into the dust. There was little difference between me and it.

Yes, this suits, I thought. It will a man and his family feed. It will bear a house on acres enough to build further still. With Margrit at my side, I believed this country held no trickery or grief. It was only as it seemed.

It was late in the summer when Margrit and I arrived on our stake of land. Our wagon was full. Our pockets drained. Bottomland, we had been promised. But I feared a rich soil swamped up to our britches. Only the spring before, we were told, the channels in the northeast had swallowed their banks. When the waters retreated, the soil was black as ink. Flat as an ironed sheet. Now the river stayed in its bed, a murky line that marked the border of our land. We had but a hundred and fifty acres, so far from the closest village we had earned twice our dollar. With the savings, we purchased a team of horses. A dairy cow and chickens. A plow and harrow for planting. At first only ten of our acres were broken in, the rest overrun with prairie grasses. An abandoned dugout stood in the southeast corner, so narrow it held no more than a cot. The door fell off at a touch, little better than a piece of canvas. The agent told us two brothers had run of the place. In the months before, the dugout had been found deserted. All that remained was a starveling dog tied to a post, a packet of tobacco hidden in the wall. Now both dog and tobacco were gone.

We ducked our heads. The roof was never so tall for a man to stand. Margrit reached for the ceiling. Her fingertips blackened. "*Wie ein Grab*," she said and wiped her hand on her skirts. No better than a grave. She left our bedding outside. "I am not sleeping in it. Might be fine for dead brothers, but I am far from that."

"If it rains?"

"We drown."

"And snakes?"

She considered. Out of her trunk, she uncoiled a woolen rope intended to hang sheets. She laid the rope around our blankets. "To confuse the snakes."

That afternoon we built a shanty from discarded tree limbs and covered it with bark. The sun would in a week curl the bark. Yet for our first evenings, the shanty suited us. A proper house, I promised Margrit, with a wooden frame. It would be finer than the log cabins we had seen, only earth and grass to fill the cracks. Margrit gazed about the prairie. No tree stood larger than an old man.

The animals we roped together behind the dugout where they ceased to whine. I scraped out a circle of dirt and lit twigs for a fire. What dried codfish we had was sweet, with meal to fill it. Our husks of corn buttered our chins. Around us, the fields stretched, the *zikaden* singing. Where we camped seemed the bottom of a bowl. So steady that wherever a man set his foot, it would remain. As would every wall he built. Every pole of a fence. When at last Margrit began to sing, it was a song I knew from my own mother. She had been born in the south of the country, where farming lands were little but gardens and German sons tried their hands at blacksmithing instead. Margrit stretched her legs to the fire and lifted her skirts. She rested my hand on the flesh of her knee. I felt every muscle of her thigh and the blood going there, alive as the good earth beneath us. She dropped her head against my shoulder.

"*Wo sich Fuchs und Hase gute Nacht sagen*," she said. Where the fox and hare say goodnight.

Later we slept. Margrit buried her hand in mine and rested a foot across my ankle as if I might drift. Clouds to the east grew heavy. What stars appeared seemed distant. Owls screeched in the trees far along the river. Farther yet, the moan of a wolf. We had arrived. Now we but needed to show how we deserved this place. How everything it held would with faith and sweat be earned. Our sons never would vanish and leave their good shoes by the door. The silence seemed to promise this very thing. I felt none of the loneliness I had often known. Still as I closed my eyes, I sensed myself floating. Waters ran far beneath the earth at my spine. In the quiet, I heard nothing save for the river as it gushed and I felt all of it spinning. We might in any moment be drowned.

II

It was more than twenty years before the letter arrived. Since the day I left, I had every month or two written my parents. I gained no reply. I imagined my mother and father sitting in their kitchen. They stared at my words under a dim kerosene lamp. Were she alone, my mother might push her plate aside and search for a piece of paper to write. But my father would surely hold her arm.

Selfishness, I had often heard him say. *I am not rewarding it.*

Those were the years I walked our land morning and night. Our crops transformed from seed to harvest. Seed again. Farther off, farmers brought their wagons to stake the land. At home my wife birthed four daughters and two sons. The years were months. The marks of a pencil on the wall. One girl replaced another in the same hand-me-down dress. With every child, I feared for Margrit's health. I swore I never would touch her again. It was the kind of thing that turned sleeping with a wife, as God saw fit, a terrible bloody business.

"We are from this place," Margrit told the children. "We are from nowhere else."

But then our youngest, Myrle. "We should not think to have another," Margrit said. I held the girl to my shoulder, her breath on my neck. The child was so slight, so strange. Her every cry moved me to distraction. How desperately I worked to spare her pain. Must a man reach his last before his children become more to him than their endless demands?

"Father, you have a letter," my eldest said.

It was a sweltering day in autumn. Nan stood at the stove, stirring a pot of soup. At the table Myrle clutched at her doll of buttons and rags. The other girls kicked their feet in their chairs, a pile of corn husks between them. The kitchen was in a state. The room was thick with steam, the sting of onions. The ceiling above the stove had gone black, the planks below caving beneath its stout iron weight. Our tabletops never were enough to feed so many at once. Still we were to host our neighbors for a picnic, as Margrit insisted. Their farms had quickly appeared on the horizon. Their children ran our fields as if ignorant of fences. I knew the men that owned these farms mostly by sight. An exchange of words about seeds or weather. That seemed enough. Now Margrit needed tablecloths, napkins.

"Why such a fuss?"

She squeezed my chin between finger and thumb. "I will wash them after for us to have curtains. Then you can close them all you want."

Nan stopped her spoon and drew the letter from her pocket. The blue envelope was mottled with stamps. "It's from Europe, I think. The postmark says Hamburg."

"Germany?" asked Margrit.

I turned the letter over. "My mother." Though I was not so certain. The writing on the envelope was strange, as if my mother had stooped beneath a candle with her pen.

Margrit sighed. "After so much time?"

I shook my head. The bread was rising in the oven, the soup simmering. A large sour roast and *spätzle* crowded the stove. The house seemed to breathe with every boiling pot. Our Esther gave up helping and raced screaming in a pair of trousers down the hall. "I asked her to wear her green dress," explained Nan. "You'd think I'd cut off her head." Myrle let out a wail, her doll fallen to the floor. Agnes gathered the husks close so they might not be swept away from her. Soon the kitchen spun with one girl after another. I stood unmoving in fear of collision, the letter pressed to my stomach as if it had somehow unmade us. Of that land I had left, I could not think. Could not so much as remember its smell. Calm now under the arm of her mother, Myrle whimpered. Her hair clung to her cheeks in pale strands. I slipped the letter in my pocket and rested a hand on her crown, soft as silk as her hair was.

"Go on now, Nan, take a rest," said Margrit. "But first convince Esther to wear something decent."

Nan swept her apron over her head and hurried out.

"And you, Julius," said Margrit. "Make yourself some use and see to the tables. I asked Ray to set them, but he wasn't too happy about it."

Outside, two tables waited in the shade of our yard, the new tablecloths fastened with pins. Ray had finished what his mother asked. Now he stood with Lee in the barn to see to the broken thresher. At the gate, Elliot and his wife hurried down the path with their son. Elliot dropped a platter on the table, and Mary scattered a handful of flowers. Their boy bounded off to the barn to join my own. In the distance, Mrs. Clark and her brood marched along the grassy lane. Like rabid animals, her trio of girls raced through the weeds. A house full of women. What it might make of a man. Mr. Clark could only but stumble along behind them, thin as a rake.

"Awfully nice," Mary let out. She fluffed her skirt, stretched a pale leg over the bench. Elliot watched her until she settled. She took a fair amount of time. "Awfully nice," she said again. She jarred her husband with an elbow. His sour expression remained.

"Look what those boys are doing," she said. Our sons had carried the topmost sieve into the yard. Now they sat together in the grass with the contraption between them. "Regular old fixer-uppers."

I nodded. "I have given the thresher over to them."

"Just the two of them and so many girls," said Mary.

"Thank God for those."

"You know what I heard at the market the other day? This will be the warmest year on record, that's what Mrs. Conners says."

"Has she?"

"The Conners, they seem to know everything. Terrible things. What with that fuss in Europe. I never would have given much thought to the Germans, but Linda says they're fighting for what rightfully isn't theirs. Everyone's for the Kaiser, she says. The Germans sure like their hops. That's all I could answer her. As far as I'm concerned, I hope Wilson holds to his senses and keeps us out of it."

I opened my hands on our table. *We are from nowhere else,* Margrit had said. Behind us in the kitchen, my wife called out instructions to the girls. Elliot eyed me under the brim of his hat.

"Our pastor says the Irish will never let us join the war," said Mary. She lifted the hat from her husband's head, clicked her tongue. "But Pastor Michaels is a pacifist. My grandmother was a Brit, Irish or not. That's our side of it anyway."

The hat lay on the table between us. Elliot coughed into his fist. "You don't . . ." Her eyes widened. "Do you still have family over there?"

"No." I winced. "Margrit and I left years ago."

"And you're no drunkards," said Mary. "You're not marching about. You keep up your fences."

"We try."

Mary reddened, her breathing fast. "Oh you're so much better than that!"

Elliot coughed again. "What do you hear of prices?"

"Well." Mary pressed a hand to her cheek. "That's my signal. I'd be a better help in the kitchen. Besides, Margrit'll want to hear about the Parsons." She bowed her head in a whisper. "That girl of theirs. With a child! Might well drive them out of town. That's what Mrs. Conners says." She stood and glanced back, fetched one of her flowers from the table to carry inside.

Elliot watched her go.

"Prices are two to one," I offered him.

"That all?"

"If a man could raise more stock, it would be something. That land of ours on the river, a plow or reaper can never run near it. But I have heard of some who are straightening their waterways."

Elliot squinted at me.

"To recover the land. A straighter channel, less flooding."

"Recover it," he said. "I don't have the hands to work what I have now."

"It could save us from falling behind the others."

He chewed at his cheek. "What you say we bring our wagons in together next trade. Keep them from underselling us."

I sighed at him. "Next time, then."

Elliot seemed relieved. He drummed his knuckles on the table and turned to watch the Clarks come. "House full of women."

"All that work with only the girls to help."

"Clark is sickly more than most," he said. "He was sick something awful last year. Heart."

I shook my head. In the churchyard two miles distant, the Clarks owned a stone and five empty lots. Elliot sat a while, his face fallen. He seemed to stew on something dark and close in coming.

"A good man," said Elliot again. "And no sons. We have ourselves sons for more than threshing, don't we? Should Wilson want them."

"Should Wilson not keep to his senses, you mean."

Elliot held up his glass as if to measure me through it.

"A man must support his president," I said.

"Right." His mouth softened, only just. "I suppose it's eating time."

"Always is."

"These women, they like to keep themselves busy."

"My Margrit works herself to the bone."

"I can't say I understand it, but it sure pleases Mary to have company. It pleases her a great deal."

The voices of Mrs. Clark and her brood carried over the fields. Our yard was soon filling with children. Mr. Clark could only but lift his hat and wave. A man such as him. He might well land in the grave from nothing more than a skip in his blood.

Our kitchen door banged.

"Ready!"

In a frenzy, Esther raced out. She wore an old canvas sack cinched with a rope at her waist. Nan chased after her. Esther stopped and spun. She curtsied to Nan before running again. The Clark girls screamed, and I reached for my belt.

But again the door to our kitchen opened. Margrit emerged with a tray of sausages. My wife had a flower in her hair. She smiled as she set the tray to the table. "*Würstchen,*" she said. "*Würstchen,*" Mary repeated after her. Her husband grunted. The children grew quiet. When at last my wife sat, her blue dress matched the flowers Mary had brought, their color a vision against her whiter skin. Once I had not known this woman. Now I knew her more than well. Across from her, our children crowded the single bench. How strange it was to see them lined up as they were, Myrle as always between them. They straightened the ribbons in her hair. Tucked a napkin to her collar. I felt the weight of that letter in my pocket. How loath I was to open it, with little reason I could explain. My children appeared so alike in every feature, their faces as sharp and fine as that of my parents. Once the meal came to its end, they surely would scatter. I could not so much as reach across the table to prevent it. But for now, my wife held them close, as if by a string.

It was late in the day when Margrit and I sat in the quiet of our parlor. Outside, the last of the sun lit the grassy trail the Clarks had left in their wake. Only Nan stayed with us in her corner, yawning as she sewed.

"Nan, dear," said Margrit. "You should take a rest."

"I'm fine, Mother."

Nan sat a while longer but soon gathered her things. Margrit touched her arm before she went. "You did so well with helping. Didn't she, Julius?"

"Very well."

Nan blushed and gave her mother a kiss.

I reached into a pocket for my handkerchief. I discovered the sharp corner of the envelope instead.

"I think our Nan has a beau," said Margrit. "Julius, are you listening? It's Carl McNulty."

"Carl," I said. "The boy who lives alone with his mother?" I drew the envelope out and studied the stamps. Hamburg, two weeks since.

"You're afraid of that letter."

"No, no." The envelope was thin as a leaf. The slightest tremor might turn it to dust. When I opened it, the German script came to me like an old scent.

Dear Julius,

Forgive me, but I only just found your address among your mother's papers, and I am writing to you with news of your parents. I'm afraid they've passed. Your father had a stroke in the fields a month back, and it must have pained your mother something to find him. Yesterday morning, Samuel discovered her with her head on the table, just after breakfast. She had taken her bread out of the oven, at least, so it didn't smoke the house. She was a good woman, your mother. Your father as well. He left the land and the house to us, what remains of it. I know your mother would have wanted otherwise. She often talked of you and your letters. Both are buried in Schubert's field, a small service as it was the best we could manage.

We will take care of the land and the house for as long as you wish, unless you can arrange a return. Travel here is ever the worse. Every boy has put on his boots for war, and the Kaiser would rather starve us than give way to France. We haven't the feed to keep our cattle. Our potatoes look blacker this year than the last. A quiet place like this might not survive all the trouble. I dare say your parents might have escaped the worst of it, if you can find peace in that. You are better off where you are.

Your cousin,
Martha Hess

"What is it, Julius?"

I closed the letter in my lap. The room seemed to dim. Margrit clicked her needles. Outside, the cicadas droned and the Elliot pups yowled from their barn. Oh, the food we had wasted. The expense of those tablecloths. I imagined them hanging in the parlor as curtains, sown in patches. Now with the letter from my cousin, the last string had been clipped. I had nothing in the old country left to me. Little way to return. How often had I wished the same? "*Schwierigkeit*," Martha had written. Trouble. The beginnings of a war. A thing so distant we could only but stand in the early dark and think of our milking. How could war be trouble any more than burying a mother and father? And only weeks from each other? I had been absent to witness both. I might never have stepped foot in the place. Never been born.

"Julius." Margrit rested her fingers on mine.

"Trouble in Germany," I said.

"What sort of trouble?"

Out the window, my daughters ran in their bare feet from the river. In her belted sack, Esther looked dry as a bone. Myrle plodded behind, her dress soaked. Her skin showed pink underneath, her hair wet on her cheeks. She shivered. I thought to call out to her, but could not find my voice. When the curtain fell back, the sight vanished.

"Julius." Margrit crouched at my side. She had turned the letter so she might read it.

I closed the page in my fist. "It's over now. It's gone."

Every day of that fall, I thought of little but Clark and his ailing heart, his five empty graves. I owned but a hundred and fifty acres, a decent lot of land for my sons. Yet others after us had bargained more. Every year at harvest, their wagons stood heavier with grain. Their horses strained. *He left the land to us*, wrote my cousin. I had never wanted the family acres. My own were far the closer and ever growing. Still, a good half dozen were wasted by their nearness to the river. A good half saved if I straightened the channel. Made that mud into something stronger to hold a seed, to drive the plow. The water lay like a boundary never to be trespassed. Yet I would trespass. Damn if Elliot helped or not.

My sons and I were thick in the worst of it. Two days of mud with only the aid of our horses, the tractor at the end. The water ran four hands deep at the driest times of year. Yet when it was full, those banks lost inches. Now with the river low, we had only strength enough to build a wall of timber and stone to shore up our banks, keep the river on its course. When at last our efforts held, a shadow broke over us.

"What's this here?" said Elliot.

I leaned against my shovel. On the far bank, Elliot was a gaunt figure. I washed the sweat from my face with the thick of my sleeve. "As I told you."

"You told me, eh?"

"Straightening the channel. It will give the both of us more usable land. If you want to bring your boy to help, we can make the going faster. Your side of it anyway. We are working on ours now. Just a portion to start before the freeze."

"You think we have time for helping?"

"Suit yourself," I said. "Come spring, we can begin your side."

Elliot marched off. I squared my hat. Lee and Ray had stopped their work, their blades in the bank. "Until spring," I said. "He will change his mind."

"What if he doesn't?" Ray asked.

I chewed my cheek. "You cannot help a man who will not help himself."

"With our banks holding, what if the water swamps his?" Lee stood next to his brother in waders. He was taller than Ray by a head, twice as broad. Still there was something small in the boy.

"It won't." I bent to my work. The water snaked round my boots. When I raised my face, the wind sent me to shivering. "Lee," I called. The boy gazed across the pastures on the far side. Elliot himself was gone. In front of their barn his son Tom stood, watching us.

The trees turned bare with winter. Margrit and I drove to town in our wagon for the last trade of the year. The snow had narrowed the road, the river only ice and stone. Beside me, my wife pressed her hands together in her lap. When we passed the Clarks' fences, she tapped her knuckles.

"Haven't seen the Clarks since weeks," she said. Their house was dark. In the barn, one of the daughters sang a tune. The barn was dark as well.

"I never see them much."

"Mrs. Clark missed sewing on Wednesday and the Wednesday before that."

"I suppose the county has run out of cloth for her."

Margrit smiled but quickly fell silent. Her eyes stayed with the house. "She has a fast hand. I'll give you that."

"We have no need of Mrs. Clark."

My wife stirred. "We have no need of her sewing. But she and Mary are the only ones who visit us."

I drove on. My wife often hid her worries, but she kept her eyes on me for now. When we reached town, the streets seemed deserted. The doors closed, shutters drawn. No wagons stood before the market other than a single four-wheeled cart. Only Mr. Wilkerson walked on the path. When I nodded to him, he offered a look back. A trio of boys played with their marbles. The tallest of them held his like a fist of stones. The horses grew restless, the boys leering at us. When I stepped out to secure the wagon, I rubbed at the horses' flanks and Margrit hurried to the market. It was then I heard a voice.

One of the boys lay on his backside in the snow. His cheeks were red as his hair, his lips bloody. The other two straddled him with their boots on his hands. They dropped one marble after another into his mouth. The boy squirmed. The marbles struck his teeth with a wet snap. If he dared close his lips, one of the boys pried them open again. I called out to them. The two dropped their marbles just the same. The mouth of the boy filled. He was close to choking. When I took to my feet, the two raised their heads, glanced at the other, and ran. The red-haired one rolled onto his stomach, spit the marbles out. The underside of his coat was soaked with mud and snow. He gripped his stomach, tried to lift himself. Before I could reach him, he had leapt from the ground and run off as well.

I stood in the street alone. At my feet, a frozen puddle of spit and blood and a handful of marbles, white as milk. The boys had vanished. The marbles lay sunken in the mud. I picked one up and rolled it between my fingers. At my back, the market door opened. "*Wo bist du?*" Margrit called. I slipped the marble into my pocket and raised my hand to her.

Margrit held the door with its bell ringing. From the wagon I hefted our jug of cream and carried it up the steps. The weight of the jug weakened me, as did the strangeness of what I had seen. Two boys. Intent on drowning another with playthings. Inside, the market was airless. An old woman sniffed, eyeing me as if I had somehow caused her sickness. I lugged the cream to the counter. The bell sounded again. Before I could turn, something sharp and wet struck my neck. Margrit pushed at my arm. "Ignore it," she begged. I looked to find an egg bleeding on the floor, and there was the red-headed boy, not lying now in the mud and snow but his face raw. His lips were bloody still. He stood in the door with his arm cocked from the throw of that egg, and slammed out of the place the way I supposed he would the rest of his life. An unthankful creature. A ruffian. A boy not much higher than dirt.

"Julius," Margrit scolded. "The cream."

At the counter, Mrs. Conners turned from her cash box. "That boy is my own daughter's."

My wife pinched my hand. "So grown. I never would have recognized him."

The woman looked us over. "No, you wouldn't."

Margrit blushed. "Always so many children about. Sometimes it's hard to recognize my own."

Mrs. Conners hummed and moved away from us. "Never known folks who keep so to themselves. The Schultes. The Meyers. They don't keep to themselves so much."

Margrit raised her voice. "We're ready with the cream, then, Mrs. Conners."

"I don't think we'll be taking your delivery today."

"Why? What's wrong?"

"With all the trouble."

"What sort of trouble?"

Mrs. Conners dropped a newspaper in front of us.

AMERICAN STEAMER *HOUSATONIC* SUNK

U.S. BREAKS WITH KAISER

"I suppose my boy has it right, doesn't he, Mr. Hess?" said the woman. "I suppose he knows what to do. There will be more of them, boys like that. They'll all know what to do when there's a need."

I drew back, looked out the door, where I expected the boy to hover still. I reached into my pocket and felt for the marble. When I pulled it out, I found it not a marble at all but a muddied tooth. I closed it in my fist.

"They'll be war," said Mrs. Conners. "Wilson is just waiting to set the Germans straight. Why, my own son, he's itching to go."

That evening, we sat about the dinner table. None of us stirred once we took our seats. Margrit set her hands to the bowls and circled to fill plates. "I never thought you would lose your appetites."

I counted empty chairs. "Where are Esther and Myrle?"

"In the kitchen," explained Margrit. "They say they have a surprise."

No one at the table seemed eager for surprises. Agnes and Lee were more than quiet. Ray never turned his head from the window. Nan sat in her corner, her face down yet her cheeks glowing. She twisted at one of her fingers.

"Mother . . . ," started Agnes.

"What is it?"

Ray held onto his knife and fork and cut fiercely at his meat.

"It's Harriet," said Agnes.

"Harriet Clark?"

Agnes nodded. "She said the whole town wants to know: 'Doesn't your father talk Kraut?'"

Margrit cleaned her spoon off the edge of a bowl. When she took up her chair again, she unfolded her napkin into her lap one square at a time. "That's not a proper word."

"It never matters how a person talks," I said. "Those Clark girls are not smart enough to rub two pennies together."

Agnes wiped her cheeks. "I don't care."

"Of course you care," said her mother. "A girl with a father so sickly. Who knows what comes into her mind?"

"Ray's the one in trouble." Agnes fidgeted. "Why don't you look at him?"

"What about your brother?" At the end of the table, Ray sat in shadow. When he raised his head, his eye appeared blackened. A bruise on his cheek. "Ray, what happened to you? What happened to him?"

"Answer your mother."

The children stayed silent. Nan kneaded her hands.

"Lee knows," said Agnes. "He was there."

Lee sat next to his brother. He pressed his fork into his potatoes. "We were in the old barn on Southwood."

"The Asters' place?"

"Used to be Asters'. It's empty now." Lee took another bite. "Some of us go there once in a while."

"Ray started it," said Agnes.

"She wasn't supposed to be there," said Ray.

"Even so," complained Margrit.

"Patricia was there too," said Agnes. "Ray was trying to get her attention."

"I don't need her attention."

"But you like it."

"Who's Patricia?" asked Margrit.

"She's sweet on Ray," said Agnes. "So he started a fight."

"It was Tom Elliot who did it. And Lee just stood there like a duck."

Lee chewed. "Didn't seem you needed any help." He took another serving of beans and filled his cheeks.

"He hasn't a spine on him."

"Ray Martin," said Margrit, "that's your brother."

"It's Tom I mean. He's already lost a cousin over there. Signed up early with the Brits. The Germans ought to be put behind bars, that's what he said. Said his father says the same."

"Nonsense," I said. "You can't outlaw a person."

Ray shook his head. "You should have seen them all agreeing. And Tom, he kept talking."

"So Ray hit him," said Agnes.

"He hit me back. But I got him worse."

"You don't hit a boy all the same," scolded Margrit.

"They'll take our land," said Ray. "That's what he said. They'll take the farm, and set it back the way it was, rivers or not. Any German-born loses the right to property."

"You see?" said Agnes. "It isn't just Harriet Clark."

Lee joined in. "At school, they made me and Hank Weber kiss the flag."

I struck my plate. "*Aber was, den!* You have gone to school with these children. You have known each other since you were born. And we have had this land years longer than the Elliots or the Clarks. There are laws."

My voice echoed. Lee slashed at his meat. Nan opened her mouth wishing to speak, but considered the better of it. I gnawed at the gristle between my teeth. Such a sour scrap I thought I might never be finished. The door from the kitchen gaped. Myrle and Esther rushed in. They held an enormous cake between them. Myrle stepped forward, her face bright, but Esther pulled up short, eyeing us. Myrle lost her grip. Catching it, Esther threw the cake onto the table. Scrawled in frosting by a fingertip: NAN'S GETTING HITCHED!

"Nan, is it true?" asked Margrit.

Nan tried to smile. "Yes, Mother, just this afternoon. I told them, but they wanted . . ." Her hand wavered at her mouth. "Then all this trouble. I said they shouldn't bother, but they went ahead." Nan reached out to take both the girls by the shoulders. The ring that hung on her finger was a narrow thread. The cake appeared caved in, a chocolate cream on the surface to mask the ruin.

"All this waste," I said. "Our good flour, our sugar and eggs. You thought of that, Esther, of not wasting?"

"Julius," scolded Margrit.

Esther bit her lip. "We didn't waste anything."

"You best be sure."

"But Myrle made it too. We both of us did."

Myrle nodded. Her hands were blanched with flour. Margrit held out her arms to her. "Julius, leave Esther alone."

Nan took up a knife, sinking it into the cake. The knife trembled.

"Why, Nan." Margrit stood to take the knife herself and cut where Nan left off. "Carl's a good man. We're happy for you, aren't we? Come on, everyone. This is a good thing. We have a cake."

Nan rested back in her chair. "That's just it, Mother. If there's a war, Carl will have to go."

"They'll be a draft soon," said Ray. "Wilson is just waiting."

I rubbed at my forehead. "Nothing will come of it. There are laws. Not even Wilson can take away a man's land on a whim."

"That cousin of the Elliots had the right idea," said Ray. "Join the Brits."

Lee had stopped his eating. Next to him, Ray brandished his fork.

"Wilson," said Margrit. "I don't want to hear about him. You eat now. We have a cake for Nan. We have something to celebrate."

The next morning, a sliver of cake waited before our bedroom door. After dinner, I had taken myself to bed. I could not bother to eat a shred more of meat or anything else. The cake lay on its side on a plate, a note beneath it. *For Father.* With my finger, I tasted the cream. It was salt.

"Oh," Margrit let out. "They saved you a slice." She rested her hands on my shoulders. "It was Esther's idea, baking that cake. She wanted something for Nan."

"It isn't much."

"Jon Julius, if you never give that child a chance." Margrit moved to straighten the sheets. She seemed to spend longer to dress, wrapping her belt about her waist and pulling it tight. "They'll never forgive us."

"It's thousands of miles away," I said.

"It's the Germans. I'm only glad the children know so little *Deutsch.*"

"Ray and Nan," I said. "They know what they should."

"I wish it were less. The Smiths, they changed their name when they first crossed over."

"Who are the Smiths?"

Margrit remained quiet. She eyed the plate in my hands. There was the shortening we had from Mrs. Conners, the salt and flour. No trade. We had purchased them with dollars no less.

"Lee and Ray won't go, Julius. They can't."

"Wilson has made nothing yet. Lee is too young by a year. If there is a war, it will be over then."

"What about Ray?"

"Ray." I sighed. "He has hornets in his stomach."

"Maybe that Patricia will settle him."

"First time I heard of Patricia."

Margrit sat heavily. "Poor Nan. What a day for an engagement. I so hope her Carl stays."

"I don't think Nan will have a say in it."

"And what was Elliot going on about?"

"The man keeps to himself, same as me."

"You keep to yourself too much." She looked at me then. "I don't like this business with the river. Could be the cause of it."

"Elliot will like it fine when he sees what land I save him."

"Have a visit with him. You can talk about the boys."

Outside the door, the children rose from their beds. The girls tumbled down the stairs in a rush and their chairs scraped the kitchen floor. Margrit touched her stomach and lifted her chin. "Breakfast."

My wife stood and wavered. I reached out my hand, but she set herself right. I watched her go. Her footsteps were quiet in the narrow hall. We had no need of others, surely. Yet had I kept her too much at my side? This house and the comfort in it, it was her own making. Her words to the children were always kind. For myself, I was helpless to extend more than shouts. "They'll take the land," Ray had said with his bruised face. "If there's a war," said Nan. Of the evening before, only the wreckage of the cake remained. War was coming. Though far overseas, I feared it was gaining on us. If it crossed that ocean, how easily it might bring us to ruin.

III

Wilson announced the draft at the beginnings of June. A million more men he wanted. A million he would gain. Mrs. Conners sewed a flag to raise in the center of town. Mothers scurried to fatten their sons before the arrival of notices. Ray spent his hours combing the winter crops for pests. The fences along our westernmost acres he insisted on mending, though they needed none. One noon dinner he wandered in late in his boots and cap. At the table, only Margrit and I remained.

"I don't see the point in waiting for my card."

I rested my cup beside my plate. "You will wait."

"Why?"

"We need you for the fall harvest. With the new acres I need two boys, not one, and soon those acres will double. Wilson can hang his war for all I care. We still have a third of the riverway to finish. Have you forgotten?"

"What if they draft me before then?"

Across from me, Margrit gripped her fork. Her face was flushed, her gaze fallen to Ray's throat.

"No," I said. "I have the new reaper. And the winter wheat is ready for a pass." I rose to my feet and gazed down at the table with its dishes and scraps. "Come now. If you don't plan to eat anything, we can start."

The boy raised his head to speak. He turned instead and rushed out. Margrit brought her napkin to her lips.

"He won't go if I can keep him." I touched her shoulder, but she flinched. Since months, the sure-bloodedness of my wife had grown thin. She stood to gather plates, though the plates seemed heavy for her.

At last she spoke. "We can't keep him."

Outside, both my sons were at work in the corral. They had the reaper brought out and two of the horses. They readied a third. "That old machine," I said, "it was little more than a scythe on wheels. But this . . ." I clapped the bullwheel. "This is mechanization. We need only two horses."

"Two?" asked Lee.

"Buck and Telly, they will make it just fine."

We led the horses to the northernmost field. The rest of our acres were corn and oats, yet the winter wheat was an earlier harvest by months. The following season, I planned not to plant a row of the crop, difficult as it was. Now I hoped it kept Ray from sitting at tables and making pronouncements. The boy trailed silently behind us. Yards from where we walked, the river ran with noise enough.

"Look at that," said Lee. The water kept to its channel on our side, yet on the far bank it stole clots. Elliot was losing more soil than gaining.

"You boys make a start. You'll be able to handle this alone. I'll be seeing Elliot about the river. We will set him right."

I had not since the fall seen Elliot. I had not gone outside our acres in the months following our trip to town the winter before. Our work in the spring and summer kept us home. Still I carried that tooth in my pocket, a reminder. In my heavy boots,

I crossed the fields. The beginnings of June, yet the month had rushed at us with the heat of August. Since a week, the soil had been hot to the touch. It steamed underfoot even after the sun had gone. Now the wind swung eastward. The sky hung above us with spits of rain, steaming the ground further still.

A clank of metal from inside the Elliot barn. I opened the door. The barn was dark save for a lantern lit too close to the floor. Another fire flared from the back wall. When it flared again, I made out the shadow of the man in his mask. He cut a wide sheet of tin with his torch, awkward for him to hold both torch and tin at once. The threat of rain, it must have driven him in. I took another step. A growl stopped me short. Two of the Elliot pups itched in the corner of the closest stall, large as wolves. With their chins on their paws, they bared their teeth. At last Elliot turned off his torch.

"Hess?"

I stood with my hat in my hands and eyed the dogs. "Margrit sends her best."

Elliot stepped from the dark. His eyes were red, the skin of his chest blotchy where the mask had failed to cover him. He sat on a bale of hay. "Hess."

"I thought I might call over myself."

Elliot worked his mouth. I found my own bale of hay. It was shorter than his and closer to the man than I might have wished.

"So you make yourself at home these days," he said.

"Home? Nothing of the sort."

Elliot checked the dogs with a glance. Outside, spots of rain stung the tin roof.

"I know what you want," said Elliot.

"Is that right?"

His eyes widened.

"Margrit was worried. It seems our boys had a spat a few months ago at the old Aster place. Ray earned himself a black eye, though it healed well enough. I am afraid this is the earliest I have had a chance . . ."

The man gazed at me. "Aster doesn't live there anymore."

"Yes, but the boys have taken it as some sort of den. Your Tom never told you?"

"Tom. What would he be telling me about?"

I cocked my head. "About the fight of course."

"Who's fighting?"

"It might have been Ray who started it. It might have been your own."

"Tom signed up for the merchant marines. He left a month ago for training. It'll be France next."

I leaned back from the stink of his breath.

"What do you plan to do, Hess? Scout out my barn? Run your water through that?" His torch had dropped to the hay-covered floor. He tore off his gloves. Underneath, his fingers were the dark leather of summer, as were mine.

"I have been meaning to talk to you. We could help shore up your side as I did my own."

"My southeast acres are mud."

"They would not have been if you worked with us."

His eyes flashed. I raised my palm.

"I know you are short on help, especially now with Tom gone."

"You've got two," he said.

I nodded.

"And not a one of them is going over there, is he?"

"Ray registered last week, just like the others. We are hoping he will hear nothing until after harvest. And Lee is too young."

"That means no."

"No. Not yet."

"What I thought." He lifted one leg after another from the bale, lowered the mask over his face. He fired the tank, his mask alight. His eyes behind it thought nothing of me and my two sons.

"Joseph!" A voice from outside. With his torch going, Elliot was deaf to it. I caught his arm. The voice called out a second time.

Elliot bounded after it and I followed. Mary stood on their front porch waving an envelope. On seeing me, she tightened her shawl and rushed over to meet us. "Julius!" she said. "We've got a letter from our Tom." She seized my hand. The woman in the last month must have aged tenfold. Her hair had fallen loose, her eyes shadowed. She offered only a flicker of a smile. "Are your boys gone as well?"

"Not yet," I said. "Lee is not of age."

"Of age?" The woman released my hand. She eyed her husband and touched her fingers to her cheek. "Why, I don't even know what that means."

Elliot led her back to their porch. The letter she crushed in her grip. The rain swelled. She fell into his side as they hurried, covering the envelope with her shawl. I blinked against the rush. The rain soaked the roof of their house, the timbers dark. Elliot never looked back and Mary, she had not invited me in, no matter the weather. Now they shut the door between us.

*   *   *

I stumbled home. Far off, the reaper stood motionless in the field. No sign of Ray or Lee with it. The horses stirred, strapped to the machine. I hurried to unleash them. The younger and smaller of the two appeared skittish, the river at her side gaining. As I led the horses to the barn, the young one strayed, brushing the flank of the male as often as she could. In their stables, I settled them both.

Outside, I gazed at the house. No one was in the yard, not even at the windows. The rain had stopped, the clouds broken. A glare of sun struck the glass. Smoke rose from the back, though it was far too early for supper. I quickened my steps. In the kitchen, a confusion of voices. I tore open the door. Inside, my children crowded the table. Margrit hurried to the stove where a large pot of water boiled, her apron thick with flour and more.

"Father!"

Margrit looked up. "Oh God, Julius."

"What is it?"

"It's Ray," cried Agnes. "Lee carried him in."

My wife stood at the end of the table and rent a rag in half. Ray lay with his arm stretched over his head and bleeding. The flour from his mother's baking clung to him. He kicked like a dog. The girls tried their best to hold his legs. Margrit grabbed hold of his arm and bound the rag tight, tearing off the end with her teeth. Lee hovered near the door. The front of his overalls were a bloody brown, his lips moving. "Thought Telly was all right. I thought she was." Nan rushed from the stove with another rag and set to cleaning Ray's arm. He swore at her. The rag turned dark.

"Julius," Margrit called. "Ready the wagon. We have to take him to the doctor."

"But what . . . ?"

"Julius, now!"

Ray was lucky, the doctor said. A crushed hand, lost to the ropes of the reaper's bullwheel, when he could have lost the arm. Yet how opposite of lucky such a hand was for a farmer or his son. Lee finished most of the work for the two of them. His older brother might milk a cow and carry wood. He could only just grip an ax. Yet the finer things were beyond him, the turning of a bolt or the tying of wire. The reaper stood in the barn under its heavy canvas. The ropes were twisted and stained, and Lee more than skittish with the horses. Ray rarely spoke to Lee now. I suppose this was a blessing. What spiteful things the boy might have said.

Throughout that fall and winter, I spent my evenings in the dugout. The door had long ago fallen into a heap at the threshold. The place smelled of earth and fur, some animal taken to sleeping in the corner. Still the roof held, the walls sturdy as stone. I braced myself on the wooden cot. It was nearly rotted through, only two planks to hold my weight. A discomfort, this. Yet I felt deserving of discomfort. My boys labored until dusk. Ray was more the stubborn in what work he could manage, and I was but an old man with little strength left to me and less the reason. Had the accident been a penance? For what crime? Nothing but a sliver of land. A muddy bank I wished to save from a relentless current. The whole of the harvest had been long, punishingly slow. Because of it, we had not the energy to channel the remains of the river. Nor the hands to have it finished. Even our Nan seemed less than willing to carry her share. Her mind was on letters, the war.

"They took her Carl," explained Margrit.

"But the girl shouldn't every minute be going on . . ."

Margrit hushed me with a finger. "Don't, Julius. Don't you say it."

The Elliot boy was sent home. We knew little what to make of it. Even in the coldest months, he stewed in the corral with their horses. I raised a hand to him across the fields. He stood with his face pressed against the fence.

Early into April, the snow lay frozen against the river-banks. We could not shake it. Our yard was polished with snow and ice, hard for walking. A new fall of snow drifted inside the dugout door. Only in sitting there as the sun set could I imagine that Margrit and I had just arrived. The land remained untouched, full of promise. Beyond the door, my wife arranged her ropes against the snakes.

A break in the gravel. "Who is it?"

"It's Lee, pap."

The boy crossed the threshold and sat on the far end of the cot. His breath showed white in the cold. He gripped his hands though he wore gloves. Together, we looked out over the fields. Soon enough, there would only be snow and whatever moonlight it threw back, if there was a moon at all. The howl of the dogs sounded near and far at once.

"Mrs. Elliot is sick," said Lee at last.

"Sick?"

"She has a bad fever. The doctor says he's seen fifteen cases like it."

"Mary is a good woman. I am sure she will pull out."

"I went to see Tom."

"He injured?"

"Not to look at him."

"No, I suppose not."

"I think it injured him some, one way or another. He's not telling."

"I never thought much of the boy."

Lee strained his eyes as the room darkened. "There's something else, see. Did Nan tell you?"

"Tell me what?"

He cocked his head. "They hung a man in Illinois. In Collinsville, near St. Louis. A whole mob of them did. For making speeches or the like."

"St. Louis."

"Near so."

"That's three hundred miles."

Lee shrugged. "Name of the man was Robert Prager. A coal miner. He was from a place called Dresden."

"Dresden? He's a German."

"They let Prager write a letter home before they did it."

"A letter to Dresden. I don't suppose he said much to explain himself."

"It was those speeches that got him in trouble. But it was just talk. That's what Nan says. Nothing worth hanging a man about. Still it's in all the papers. No one will leave it alone."

"Well." A hollowness turned in my stomach.

"So I've been thinking . . . ." The boy swallowed. "They say Wilson might lower the draft to eighteen. Maybe this fall, maybe before that."

"The fall is months off. The war might be over then."

Lee shifted. The wind swept through the door and fell to a hush. The yelps of the dogs grew in number. "That's just it," he said. "Suppose it's not."

"No use worrying ahead of a thing."

He shook his head. "I'm not worried."

"Well then."

"See, I got to thinking. With Ray hurt and all . . ."

"You can stop your thinking about that."

" . . . and Elliot the way he is."

"The man will be fine come spring. We'll fix the channel for him, finish our own."

"But what people are saying, the way me and Ray aren't over there. We've lost five boys from town. A sixth's gone missing. And it's only the start. Tom Elliot would never have been in Europe if it weren't for us. Now he's the worse, maybe his mother too."

"Because of the Germans, you mean. That boy was eager enough to sign himself up. And Mary, that's altogether different. I never heard of a homecoming bringing unhappiness to a mother."

Lee shifted again. "Suppose I drafted early. Then they'd know we're on the same side."

I turned to see him. Oil clung to his skin with whatever contraption he was in the shed fixing. He was always at fixing something. Now another of my boys wished to go back the way I had come. "Lee . . ."

"I've already decided, see. Every boy who's worth his weight is going. Even Carl McNulty. Even after he gave Nan a ring. And now they're all talking about who isn't. With Ray out, it's got to be me."

"So you're telling me, not asking."

He scratched his head. "If you don't want me to go, you can say. But if you want me to, you don't have to say a thing. I'll go to the office next week, sign my name."

"Your mother will never forgive us."

Lee was silent. The cold reached inside my collar, my sleeves. It seemed we could be anywhere. The solid earth lay both below and above our heads.

"Does that mean you want me to go?" asked Lee.

I could not speak. In the near dark, only the rising pitch of the wind and the wooden cot that creaked beneath our weight. All this time we had made what we considered right. We had worked the land. We had kept our troubles to ourselves. Yet keeping to ourselves no longer seemed an option to us. Even Margrit had said it: *You keep to yourself too much.*

"I am not saying go."

"But you're not saying don't."

I stood and peered out the door, my shoulder against the rotting sill. The two brothers who had the place built, I often wondered where they had taken themselves. To leave so much behind. To simply vanish. I turned and reached out my hand, my palm on my son's forehead. Lee leaned against it. His skin blazed with warmth. "I am not telling you one way or another," I said. Lee never moved. My hand trembled. "You may think it will fix everything, but people believe whatever is useful to them. If you are going, you go for your own reasons. I cannot keep you from that."

In the early dark the next morning, Margrit shook me from my sleep. Outside, a strange sun appeared on the horizon, our curtains colored with a furious light. My wife gathered her shawl to her throat and pressed her forehead to the window. She whispered my name.

It was a fire. One that rose from a mound of sticks in a circle of snowmelt, high enough the men seemed but children around it. Their clothes were dark. Their faces nearly hidden by scarves. In their hands, they held torches. When they saw us at the window, they turned and headed down the road on foot. Only four stayed behind. The fire spelled a crooked letter *K*, an *R*, and a cross at the end. When I spoke the letters aloud, the word came together: KRAUT.

In the light of the torches that remained, I could name them: Conners, Wilkerson, Elliot, and Tom.

I turned from the window. Outside our room, Nan and the boys stood in the parlor looking out. Their bedclothes glowed. The boys held their guns.

"If you'd only let us fight," said Ray.

I opened the front door and shut it behind me. From the porch, the fire looked higher yet.

"Pay up, Prager," they shouted.

Wilkerson stepped up, hat in hand. *Council of National Defense*, he might have called himself. "We've heard there are un-American activities taking place in this house. Snatching land. Keeping your boys from the draft. Five hundred in bonds should prove it otherwise. Eight hundred the better."

I kept my fists in my pockets. "I will not pay. Not with your torches. Not at this time of night. The one boy I have of age has his deferment. As far as the land . . ."

"We can't scare him," called a voice.

Wilkerson caught hold of my wrist. Conners joined him. They dragged me from the porch and bound my hands with rope. When I struggled, the rope jerked up sharp. I dropped to my knees in the snow. "I'm not afraid."

A gunshot cracked. The men ducked. Ray hurried between the torches, a rifle in the hook of his arm. He swung the gun and the men fell back. Lee joined in, unbinding the rope. He held me so I might lean against him.

Tom shouted, "You can't even aim that thing."

"I heard about you," said Ray. On the trigger, his good hand shook. "They say you went some kind of crazy."

Tom made a grab for the gun. Lee pulled him up short, and Ray pitched the barrel at Tom's throat.

"Stop it, the both of you," I yelled.

"You've gone too far, boys."

The group turned. Clark stumbled out of the fields. An ill man in his nightshirt and heavy boots, his cheeks slick, a coat loose on his shoulders. The others quieted. Ray lowered his gun. "My daughters saw the torches from our place," said Clark. "Scared them to death." He gave the men a sour look and took myself and Elliot aside. "Let's go into the house and talk."

"Eight hundred for those bonds, Hess," Conners spit. "And that's to start."

Clark waved him off. "Get buckets for that fire or I'll call the deputy on you."

The three of us climbed the porch steps, Tom and Lee following. Ray stood his ground. "I'll keep a watch." Margrit huddled at the door, waiting. The fire behind us had faded, buckets or not. She wiped a hand across her eyes. In the hall, Nan had gathered the girls, Myrle sheltered between them like the child she still barely was. As we passed, Tom gazed at her in her gown. Elliot jerked the boy by the arm. Nan rushed the girls up the stairs at once.

In the kitchen we sat about the table in the lamplight. The men seemed rabid, a fever in them. I ached from the rub of that rope, blood in my mouth. Lee stayed quiet.

"No more rough stuff, eh, Hess." Elliot tapped his fingers.

"Fires," said Clark with a sigh. "That's enough. Hess, the men just need to know you're on their side. Everyone else has paid their bonds and more."

I bristled. "Those bonds were not mandatory."

Lee rubbed his neck.

"Eight hundred," said Elliot.

Margrit stood at the stove. Already she had it filled with wood and started the kettle. Her smile was tight. "I don't know what men like you would be doing out on a night like this," she said. "Mary, now, she'll never believe it." Elliot cleared his throat. Margrit carried a tray of cups to the table. On the tray, a new lemon cake. Her knife shuddered as she sliced through it, scooped the pieces to our plates. "Ropes and torches," she said. "It's a hard thing when a wife is told something like that. A wife likes to believe better of her husband." Elliot flinched. With a flick of her wrist, the plates fell in front of us.

"Hess," started Elliot. "The bonds . . ."

"I will not pay a dime after being abused like this."

Elliot tried to gain Clark's attention, but the man was intent on his cake. Tom sat with his hands on either side of his plate, breathing it in. Behind him, Myrle appeared in her nightgown.

"Myrle," said Margrit. "You're to go to bed."

"But Mother . . ." The girl was shaking.

Margrit drew Myrle under her arm. "Why not some cake? Will that settle you?"

Myrle nodded and took a chair in the far corner. Margrit brought her a plate, but the girl would not eat. She sat with her eyes on her lap.

"I suppose we are finished," I said.

Clark swallowed. "All right."

Elliot's face was hot. "But he hasn't paid."

Clark whispered in his ear.

"All right." Elliot cursed. "Another time, Hess. You could save us the trouble and pay in town yourself. See to it that you do. And the river . . ."

The sound of laughter stopped him. At the far end of the table, Tom Elliot had picked up his fork with a piece of Myrle's cake. He fed it to her, stabbed at the slice on her plate, and fed her another. The girl chewed, her eyes closed. A blush ran from her forehead to throat. As the boy brought her another bite, she laughed again.

"Well," said Lee.

"What's that?" Elliot said.

We watched, not another word between us. Myrle was so very small sitting there, her face bright. She sat far too close to Tom in the near dark. The boy gave me a glance as he brought the fork again to her mouth. It scraped her tooth. Myrle leaned in.

Elliot's hand flew between them. Tom lurched to his feet, a hand to his jaw. Myrle cried out. Margrit took her in her arms and rushed her down the hall.

"What was that for?" asked Tom.

"You know what," said Elliot.

"Now, now," said Clark. "We're finished here."

They stood and I let out a breath. Margrit appeared in the door at the sound of our chairs. The cake on my daughter's plate was crumbs. On the boy's, it lay untouched. Clark picked up the piece between his fingers and slid it whole into his mouth. "A fine cake, Margrit. Very fine. Rhonda would say so herself. Apologies for keeping you. Those other men, the drink gets to them. They'll be asleep on their feet by now."

Clark swept his tongue against the inside of his cheek. The three turned and headed out, Elliot pushing at his son. By the door, Ray saw them off. We were alone in the kitchen with Lee then, my wife gathering the plates. I reached out to stop her, but her hands snapped away.

"Mother."

"*Alles wird schlimmer.*" She touched her fingers to my temple, my cheek. "More and more, Julius. When is it enough? You are all mad. All of you men."

She left the plates and went to our room. Behind her, the lock turned on its bolt.

Lee and I sat at the table across from each other. His bulk took nearly the entire bench. Above us, Myrle sobbed, and Nan ran up the stairs to settle her. The room fell to silence.

"It will be all right," I said.

Lee scuffed his boot on the floor.

"We can handle them. It's nothing we can't."

He leaned forward, his voice little more than a whisper. "I heard them. They called you Prager. Prager is dead."

IV

Lee enlisted the week after the next, and Governor Harding made his proclamation. Only English in our schools, in public conversations, on trains, telephones, in public or private meetings. Even in our churches. *The loss of one's native language,* William L. Harding said, *is a small sacrifice to make.* I closed up the house and fixed locks on our doors. I would not be opening them to anyone soon. Outside by the river, Ray roamed the fields with our horses, intent more than ever on finishing the channel. I never could muster the energy to join him. I could not ask him to pocket his own. What was the answer, to press on or to change direction? Instead I kept close to my wife. She stayed to our bedroom now after breakfast and was to bed again soon after supper. As the days passed, she never left bed at all. She complained of headaches and fatigue, a fever that spiked in early mornings. I sat with her in her wakeful hours, and Nan took up the housework her mother left unfinished. When at last he came, the doctor closed the door and whispered to me in the hall. "I've got dozens already in this county alone."

"What is it?"

"The flu. Mary Elliot has been sick more than two weeks. The whole house, but she's the worst of it."

"Is there nothing my wife might take?"

"Only rest."

"She is not as ill as that, surely."

The man chewed his lip. "They say it's the boys who brought it home. Tom Elliot and the others."

"Tom was in my house."

"He was in many houses. Mary Elliot will die by the end of the week, if not sooner. I'd keep your children away."

I opened the door to our room. Inside, Margrit sat propped on pillows, her eyes closed and her ankles crossed. Her chin rested on her shoulder, a blood-spotted towel in her hand. Agnes lay at her side with her drawing paper. Closer still, Myrle had curled herself up, a braid of her mother's hair wound about her finger. At the end of the bed, Esther raised her voice and waved her arms as she read: *"On whom,"* Stephen said, *"do you intend to seek revenge?"*

"Esther, please. You will tire your mother. You will tire your sisters."

"But they like it."

"That is hardly material for someone so ill."

"It's from our primer."

"Esther," I spat. The girl stiffened. Margrit tapped her finger on Esther's stockinged foot. When my wife looked at me, her eyes were stones. It was about Esther she worried. Esther she never wanted to restrain. *Let her go*, her look said. I could only repeat the thought for them all: *Let her go. Let her go.*

"Girls, you need not keep to your mother like squirrels." I dropped my voice. "She's not well."

Myrle tightened her finger on her mother's hair. Agnes never stopped her pencil. Only Esther watched me, waiting.

"Very well." I sighed and backed out.

* * *

Over the next days, Margrit slept late in the afternoons with few hours of waking. That bloody towel she held always in her hand. With the girls at school, I had her in the mornings to myself, only to leave her when her eyes closed and only as far as the other side of the wall. There I brooded at the dining room table. My eldest brought me a plate of scrappling and toast, a cup of coffee no larger than my thumb. I had little appetite. Still I liked to watch Nan lay a place and sit across from me in her housedress and apron, her hair pinned. Often she twisted the ring on her finger until her knuckle bled. Oh, what would this girl become? She had wanted to be her mother and now she so nearly was. I gazed out the window. The girls were leaving for school. Esther and Myrle walked arm in arm, Agnes trailing. When I turned, Nan had dropped her head. My daughter sat with me only out of duty, I knew, an empty hour when she might have gone to town or finished her sewing.

"Lee sent a letter." Nan took out an envelope. The envelope was stained, torn at the edges. As with the others, it was so heavily stamped the scrawl across the front barely was visible. Nan read:

Dear Family,

We don't get much time to think of home, but if there's a minute extra, we write. We have marched a great deal. The farms in France aren't a bit like ours. The land is divvied into patches no larger than an acre, every inch plowed. This makes for hard walking what with the hedgerows, and we move like turtles. Yesterday we hit open land. I took a bath and washed my clothes in a mountain stream and it was some cold. Had horse meat for dinner. Thought that was a strange meal, but I didn't tell. Corporal thinks I'm fine at chopping wood. We do so for as many as seven days when out of the trenches, and the others are slow. Corporal thinks I'm slow in other ways, but he doesn't say how. He calls me Hush. The boys do the same. I don't know what to make of that. This morning, an aeroplane battled in the air. Interesting to see, though the others say they've seen it by the dozens. The woods are so thick here the planes were soon out of sight. Had a sick spell a short time ago but it didn't stick. Well, Corporal is calling for us now so I must finish this. Tell Mother not to worry. I haven't seen a German yet.

Yours,
Lee

"Is that it?" I asked.

"It's Lee."

"Has your mother seen it?"

She shook her head.

"Best not, I suppose. Best not tell the boy about your mother either."

"Mother told me not to."

"What else has your mother said?"

Nan drew her shoulders together. "Do you want to write a note back?"

I sighed. "They will be sending him home, I would think. They cannot keep a boy forever."

Nan made a sound in her throat and folded the letter away. "They can keep him as long as they like."

The toast had run cold. The scrappling tasted of nothing more than skin and fat. My youngest son had long outgrown me. I hoped he would outgrow me further still. Too soft a heart never made a man any good. I prayed my son knew the same. Prayed it turned him sensible instead. Through the open window, the whine of a saw in the Elliot yard.

"Close it," I said.

A fog of sawdust broke from their barn. Soon the beating of hammers. Nan stood and shut the pane.

"Have you heard from Carl?"

She sat again. "Nothing." She swallowed and lowered her voice. "Mother said I should think of the girls if I think of anyone. I should think of them as my own."

I dropped my chin into my hands. "Family is everything."

She looked at me as if wanting more. The girls already had a mother. And Nan, she was engaged to be married. The man was miles across the ocean and not heard from in months, yet she had that.

"She thinks I might not have my own—children, I mean," said Nan. "Why would she say that?"

"Of course you will have children."

Nan covered her mouth. She took a breath before she spoke. "Mother said I mustn't leave the girls alone."

"No." The word came more as an echo than an answer. Outside, Elliot's saw had started up with greater force, and a thought burned in my throat. I knew at once I must speak to Margrit, no matter her sleep. I must ask her what she meant.

Nan closed her eyes. A sob escaped her. I looked to the window. When she spoke, her words were plain. "The note?"

I pressed my hand to my forehead. A note to my son, with his mother in bed. What could I write?

"Very well," she said. On the other side of the wall, Margrit coughed and coughed again. My daughter scraped her chair across the floor and picked up my plate. Her hands had roughened, the skin chafing. She worked too hard. But I could not have her work less. She stumbled against a catch in the floor, swung out an arm for balance, and quickened her steps. When I looked again, her ring lay small and thin on the tablecloth between us.

It was a week later when I lost Margrit for good. The flu, said the doctor. Yet I believed it far the worse. A fever that ran on ships. Ate slices of lemon cake at our kitchen table. I might as well have fed that fever to Margrit myself. With the Harding proclamation, we never could bury her in the churchyard with a German prayer. Never so much as inscribe HIER RUHT IN GOTT on a stone. I was left with not a child who dared speak my native tongue. Nor a neighbor who might welcome it. Beneath a slab of slate, we laid her in a field where she might see the house, the river behind it. The girls stood with bouquets of lilies. As the eldest, Nan was the first to throw hers in the dirt. She had the children dressed in black, their faces clean. By rights, a year they should wear the same, but in this place I imagined they would forget.

The winter became spring. Though the war had ended, Lee still had not returned. Our Agnes papered the house with drawings of her mother, all of them blurred. With the break in the weather, Nan stripped the linens from our beds. The stove was afire with boiling pots. The rooms puckered in the heat. Outside, just behind the smokehouse, my daughter starched and bleached the sheets. Shut the windows as I might, the children opened them again and leaned their faces out.

I lie now in this bed, the churchyard nearer to me, awaiting a doctor, a shovel, a hymn. The room about me is vacant. In the closet, Margrit's dresses draw moths. How often I hear the noise of that man from the boardinghouse. The sound of him losing himself in the toilet. The sound of his shame. My children are all that is left me, strangers every one. I am in the house I built on my own acres, more than thirty years in making. The blanket across my chest is white and laundered fresh by my eldest daughter, now grown. Have I escaped nothing? *You are not a father*, the man in the boardinghouse tells me. *You are no better a man.*

Do you know that the most beautiful word in my language, the word that forgives all actions and desires, becomes its opposite when mistaken for English? *Bitte.* The *t*'s are soft and the *e* at the end opens in an exhale. In German the word means *please*, as in *please forgive me*. I have heard no better word for pleading. Yet in English, the word sounds closer to *bitter*, a sour taste. The German word asks for absolution. The English only carries blame. How can a man trust a language that turns pleading into a kind of hate?

That spring, we suffered days of rain. It melted the last of the snow. The river overflowed its banks. It wrenched hold of fence posts and sent them drifting. The work on the channel was gone, our acres a brilliant sheet of ruin. Ray tried his best, but a boy alone can only save so much. Whenever I looked out, a heavy-set woman waited by our fences. Ray spoke to her with little kindness. Still week after week, she stood until he took off his hat, wiped his hands on a trouser leg. At the end of a month, he set out earlier to his work to wait for her at the fence. When later the boy brought Patricia home as his bride, I was not the only one to believe he had raised her out of the dirt.

Outside, the sheets hung on the line. On the porch, Myrle sat alone. The girl wore little but a cotton dress, one nearly sweated through, and not a shoe on her feet. Since the death of her mother, her hair draped her forehead, a sound like a cat rising from her. I remember my parents scolding me. Keep your face dry. Cold water on the cheeks. There is sorrow. *Tiefer Trauer.* And the sorrow that is silent. *Stille Trauer.* What better than silence could I teach?

I stepped out to join her. "I have a story about your mother."

Myrle wiped her face.

I lowered myself to the bench. I thought to rest my hand on the crown of her head, as always I had. The ashen hair of her youth never had darkened. But a man must not treat his grown daughter like a doll.

"I can tell you when first I met her. I was boarded in a house where she was the washerwoman, and your mother was always singing. The house was decrepit, but still she sang. She wore her hair in a bun, tied in a net high off her neck." I cupped my palms behind my head to show her. Myrle gazed at my knees. "When I asked her to marry me, she stayed on the floor. I reached for her shoulders to help her to her feet, took the rag to finish the floor for her. When she saw how clean I made it, she took my chin in her hands. *Ja*, she said."

Myrle scrubbed her feet against the wooden planks.

"Yes," I said. "She answered yes. You heard me?"

My daughter nodded.

"You are the only one with the color of her hair." I reached out to touch her, but dropped my head to my hands instead. This daughter, so alike in looks and manner to her mother.

Myrle took a strand of her hair and wrapped it about her finger. "What would have happened if Mother hadn't been a washerwoman? If you had met at home? Would you still have left?"

The question was strange to me. I shook my head.

"I don't know either," she said.

Together, we sat looking out as if from the deck of a great ship. The sun had in the late afternoon fallen low and flared against the fields. Our acres were drowned. The year next, I was certain we would suffer a fine crop out of this. What a terrible burden it is to keep a child safe, to hold to her in all your weariness, lest she jump. *Julius*, my wife had said. *A man can't keep his children in a fist.* But can you blame him for wielding hammer and nail for the few who remained? In the distance, the Elliot dogs had grown in number. The bitch must have borne a litter. They chased each other, barking the high keening of the young. Whenever the dogs started again, Myrle's face quickened. But when at last their shadows faded, her chin fell.

"Tom Elliot told me he almost died," she said.

"When have you and Tom been talking?"

"He told me Lee might die too."

I gripped her arm. A cry from her. "Stay away from that boy." When I released her, she rubbed at my fingerprints on her skin, her eyes filling. I tried to take her arm again, gently this time, but she held it close. I softened my voice. "You do not know what men want."

"Myrle!" Esther swooped through the door and gripped her sister's hands. I reached out to keep the girl with me, but both my daughters were off. They ran together down the steps and through the yard, their feet heavy with mud. I eyed the sky for a downpour, though the clouds appeared listless. The red of her skin stayed with me. My fingertips throbbed. My daughters could so easily be swept away by a torrent, something I never could save them from.

Part III: Motherland

LEE

I

I thought he was dead. My brother. Lying there by the reaper with his eyes closed and his arm strung up. A line of blood down his arm and it hardly looked an arm. Dead after the reaper jerked and I'd been leading it. Dead as I carted him back to the house. The field was longer than it once'd been, the furrows hard for walking with double the weight. But weight it was and would be, even when he opened his eyes.

We'd tied the reaper behind both horses. Old Buck in front and Miss Telly behind. Buck was straight and narrow an animal as he was old, Telly small for a draft, jumpy too. "Buck will lead her just fine," Ray said. Telly and the reaper both, he meant. Even if Buck didn't care to be led by me.

The reaper ran on a bullwheel Father had fixed. "That old one," he said, "it was no more than a scythe on wheels." *Mechanization*, Father said, though I thought the word wrong. Mechanization was for steam. That bullwheel ran smooth, so Father left us to drive it alone. Ray was twenty and one, age-wise. I had passed all of sixteen myself. I was bigger by a head, maybe more. But alone meant Ray would ride the machine. He'd straddle the wheel and clear the cutter, while for me, I sat the horses in front as I'd always done. Father had already given Ray a wooden pole with a sharp point for the job. "Just keep them straight," Ray told me. "I'll do the rest."

"He won't even have to do that much." Father grinned and set his hat on his head. "Boys." I had never seen Father with a face like that.

The north field was level plenty. Still it curved at the far edge to make way for the river. That would be the trouble. But I wasn't thinking of troubles then. The sun was low but rising. The soil caked our tongues. It would be hot as fry, but it wasn't so hot yet. In the house, Mother was baking her egg and butter crust. I counted up to twenty the times we passed the house, smelling that, while Ray was at the cutter. Ray, he never would give me a chance. "Elliot doesn't know fields from fish," he was saying. "Doing nothing, that's what Elliot wants." I cocked my head to listen for hoppers, a kind of singing. When I slept, they sounded just the same. Nan said night hoppers were different from the day. Why, at night they weren't even hoppers at all. But I knew some creatures sing different in the dark. It was a matter of being by yourself. Who you were then and who otherwise. In bed with the ceiling low and the lanterns put out, Ray slept next to me only an arm's reach between us. But he slept so quiet, I had plenty of time for believing I was alone.

"With Elliot, we could have gotten it done in months," Ray talked on. "Then I'd be free for cards, harvest or not." Ray's voice, it was a hard thing to listen to. To ease against it, I fingered a stone in my pocket. I'd found it the day before when one of the cows kicked it up. I don't normally take to stones. But this one showed bright against the dirt, even at dusk. It was smooth as the river, the shape of an egg and nearly the color. What so white a stone was doing in the pasture, I couldn't figure. While all the rest were muck-colored, broken in their rocklike shapes. I cleaned it nice at the pump, carried it back to the house. Must be others like it, though I hadn't found but the one. I watched Telly's hooves for kicking up more.

A musk of flowers and reeds, and I knew we were close to the river again. The water was high and rushing. The sun had fallen to clouds, those clouds spitting. Buck was slagging, while Telly was near to nipping his backside. With one hand on both reins, I managed the turn. My other hand was in my pocket, thinking of stones. How that egg-shaped one could be by itself mixed in with the others. How there must be more. Ray was going on. "I told him I didn't care if we finished it or not. I've got a right to go when I want." The rain made a low kind of steam on the ground and the horses stumbled. Could have been Buck, though with a jerk of her head I knew it was Telly. She was tired of backsides. I tightened the reins. Tried to get the other hand out of my pocket, but the hand stuck. The reaper jumped with Ray riding it. Ray's voice jumped too, the hoppers gone quiet, and behind me something cracked. I pulled the reins short. When I looked, Ray's pole had caught in the cutter and snapped. The ropes on the bullwheel puckered. Ray stood to fish his fingers under, trying to loosen the pole. Then the horses started again. As if told to, they did, and the ropes on that wheel pulled straight. Ray's fingers caught. I jerked the reins, but Ray was hauled up and flying over the wheel.

If I'd been quicker about it, I could have stopped them. The horses wouldn't have started. The rope would have stayed loose, and Ray's fingers wouldn't have caught. But Ray was already on the ground, his arm hung up in the ropes and strange behind him. His hand was tied good. Bloody as gutting a thing and not

even a hand anymore. He lay there white, his eyes dark. Looking at me and waiting for something. Then his head fell back.
I jumped to the wheel. Worked him loose. He was an empty
sack on my shoulder as I carted him home. It was long and
slow over that field, the house a far shot, and raining enough to
drown us. *If it wasn't for Elliot,* I thought, because now Ray was
quiet. *If it wasn't for rocks being in a place where they shouldn't.*
Father would paddle whip me good. *What were you doing?* he'd
ask. Only hours before he'd been grinning. *Boys,* he'd said. Not
for years would Father say that again, but my brother would say
plenty. About keeping your mind to how a thing worked. About
what a man without a hand could and couldn't do. The way he
looked at me before he was dead did. And the way he looked at
me after said it too.

If a person asked, I'd tell them war wasn't any different. Brothers by the dozen, accidents too. When I found myself laid up in
France, they said I was wounded. I didn't remember that. About
the hospital, I remembered plenty. One bed after the other, all of
us at arm's reach, some sleeping, some not. At night the nurses
kept the hall lit and there wasn't a quiet to be had. Not with so
many of us. Shudders and howls. Most of the boys worse the
better they got. In the daytime they made notes on my chart.
Did I see flashes? Hear ringing sounds? Doc said I was on the
mend. With my feet red and hot enough to burn, he said that was
what mending felt like. I said, time to go then, if I'm mended.
Not yet, he said to that.

I was in La Fauche, Base Hospital 117. The light outside
the windows was cold and clear. Must have been after harvest,

but I couldn't see more than fences in the yard. At home, I'd surely missed it. The doctors didn't bother about harvest. The stink of us, a high taint they called disinfectant, that's what they bothered about. Our bed frames were hollow as tubes, our pillows blocks. Those pillows carried the sweat of every worry in our heads. Morning and night, an old man mopped the floor, leaving behind his piney scent. I'd been in the woods, an infantryman in the 88th near Hagenbach, border of Germany and France. It was late October then. The mud in the woods nearly finished my feet. Boot rot, they called it, but it felt something worse. We had crossed the lines, the boys wild for a taste of something better than beets. Then the blast hit. I hadn't seen one man from our squad since.

"Private Hess, your dinner." The nurse spun a table to my chest. She had the accent of a Brit. Her hands were small, warm as a loaf. The food should've had a smell, but didn't. Some kind of chicken, a helping of pea-like shapes. The English tea, it was a brown stir of water, though I'd taken some liking to it. The nurse's hair was plain and brown too, her face milky. She wore it short and close to her face, the way Esther did. That smile of hers, it was hitched at the corner. Same as Esther's too.

"Be good," the nurse said. "Try to eat this time. Otherwise they'll never send you home."

I couldn't tell her. Since the blast, I didn't have the stomach to eat peas or anything else.

They kept us on a straight watch. 06:00 to wake, noon for dinner. At 14:00 there was exercise and 18:00 another tray in our laps. Lights out wasn't very dark. But I'd never thought sleep was good for much. The boy next to me favored talk. "Hush," he whispered. "You've got to hear this." Squire was his name, his bed nearest.

He had a mother who wrote him every day but Sunday, though he couldn't write back. His arms were as dead as drowned pups. Nurse said she'd do a letter for him. He couldn't even look her in the eyes. But to me, he told plenty. About a cousin he fancied. About a cellar back home, so dark he never went close. There was a Jerry he shot in the stomach. Couldn't finish him off. He talked about that. I thought to tell him about our farm and how I missed harvest. How with a man gone, Father and Ray might have it some hard. But I was the one who'd made Ray less than he'd been, and I stood for the draft to make things right. *Can't shoot with a busted hand*, the corporal had told my brother. *Can't even hold a pistol. But this one here.* The corporal had looked at me. *He's big as a horse. We'll take him, old enough or not.*

"Wake up, Hush. You listening?" Trouble was, I couldn't keep straight one story from the next, mine or his. Squire repeated a second time. Sometimes a third. He'd have snapped his fingers if he could. At night, I had dreams. I was sitting with the boys in a barn. Me, Critters, Stan, and Sam Bullet. That was us. Our stomachs were full. Our heads soft. That barn had a fair shake of hay, the nicest bed we'd had in weeks. Stan was watching me, and Critters too. They called my name. Then the hay blasted to fire beneath us. When I looked, there was nothing but straw burnt up where the boys had been. The ends of my legs, where my feet had gone to nothing, they were burnt too.

Someone pulled at my arm. "Private Hess." A doctor stood at my bedside, clipboard in hand. "Do you remember what day it is? Do you know where you are?" I said I knew the day just fine. It was November.

"Look out that window, Private Hess. Does it look like November to you?"

The nurse wheeled me out. The sun was hard on the grass. The garden beds, they were some full. I couldn't figure that. "I can lower these footrests now," the nurse said. I turned my head to see her, but felt dizzy fast. "You'll be right as rain," she went on. "Just a tingling in those feet of yours. Pretty soon you'll be pushing this chair yourself." But the doctors wouldn't sign my release, that's what I wanted to tell her. I thought of Squire too. How he might have made sense if I wasn't the one to hear him. How I might have something more than boot rot. The nurse shook her head. "Nerves is all. That blast, it knocked you clear out."

"What about the others?" I asked.

The nurse stayed quiet. "Tell you what," she said. "We can go off when you're feeling better. Have our own little adventure. The war's over. Why, even this place, it'll be closed in a month or two. Made into a boarding school. Wouldn't you like that?"

"That would be something." In truth I believed different. Those beds were no place for kids. Even with a man gone, he was still there. Even when they put another one in his place.

It must have been time for winter crops. That's what I thought that night. End of November, it must have been. No matter that garden or the doc. At home the rush of work before the snow. The first frost would have killed a fair lot, and they'd be trying to save the rest. By now, Mother would have picked her turkey from the pen. She'd be feeding it meal to get it fat, worrying about her cellar shelves. How many more jars they could hold. How much we'd need to make three months, maybe four. Nan would be a help to her, but not the others as much. If I was there, I'd be a help too.

"Here you are, Private Hess."

I woke, a ringing in my ears. No matter how I tried, I couldn't pry that ringing out. The doctor was back, the nurse too. Even

Squire was quiet in his bed, perched on his pillows, watching us. "Hey there, Hush," he said. "You all right?"

"You asked for a map," the nurse said. "Don't you remember?" She gave me a piece of paper wide as it was long. The doctor didn't seem happy about that. Still the nurse moved my tray to straighten the map out. "Look." She pointed. "That's France. We're in the east, near the Belgium border. And there's England across the Channel. In the south, near the Schonholz Woods. That's where they picked you up."

"That's where they picked me up," I said.

"That's right." The nurse smiled with her mouth closed.

"Right," the doctor said, sharp. He signed a piece of paper on his board, tore it off. When he left, that paper sat on my legs, but I couldn't reach it. I didn't even try.

The nurse pointed again at the map. I couldn't remember asking for maps. The shapes didn't add up to nothing much. And there wasn't one piece of land looked bigger than my thumb. "Private Hess," the nurse said. She was watching me now too. She'd pulled up a chair, her hand on the rail. I blinked, trying to read the map again. There was France and Belgium, their borders a hazy green. Then Germany to the east, England at the center. But to the west, only a wide drop. "We've received a telegram for you," the nurse said. "It's about your mother." Her eyes looked wet. "The doctor has signed your release. You can leave anytime you want." She dropped her hold on the rail and touched my wrist. Her hand was some cold. This nurse wasn't anywhere close to the same as Esther. *Private Hess*, she said again, but it was all a buzz. *Hush.* That's the name the boys liked. But better than that, the one Mother had picked from the start.

II

"Lee, ma'am," I told the woman next to me on the Chicago train. "Lee Hess." From the look on the woman's face, she didn't know what to do with a name like mine. Almost two years after the war and Dutchy by the sound of it. She squinted to fish me out. "I was with the 351st Infantry, in the 88th," I hurried on. At that, she smiled.

It was late afternoon. I'd been traveling since dark the day before. "Two girls who've lost their mother," the deputy had said. "Two girls like that." A strange thing, that empty room of theirs. Stranger yet, that chair against the door. Without Myrle and Esther, the beds seemed cast off in so much space. There wasn't any reason for the girls to leave, but Esther didn't need reasons. *I can find them*, I'd told Nan, though her face said not. With all the work before winter, the farm couldn't run more than two weeks with another hand gone. Her face said that too. *Two weeks is more than plenty*, I said. I didn't have a dollar more to last longer. Now on that bench, my legs were a twitch from sitting, my back a rail. Out the window, there was never so much as a tree or post in the fields to catch a person's eye.

"You're going to ruin that hat," the woman said.

I looked down. The hat in my lap I'd creased once and again. Like a fat piece of skin. Skinned and trying to be something. The woman said her name was Helen. She only gave her first.

143

"A man without a hat," Helen said. "That's not even polite. Not if you step off this train. Let me take it before you turn it to ribbons." She pulled the hat from my fingers and rested it on her knees, working to smooth it out. That smile of hers, it was still there. Her hands were soft and white. The cheeks of a mother, that's what she had.

"Sorry, ma'am."

"I've been watching you. You haven't eaten all this time."

"I'm fine, ma'am."

"No you're not. I know boys. They have to eat every minute. And pretty soon you're going to take a bite out of this hat." She opened her bag to show a napkin, blue and stitched at the edges with birds. Inside, five rolls the color of wheat. "Here you are." She dropped one on my knee. "I have too many for myself."

I bowed my head.

"Don't you worry. I had a boy your age, though he wasn't so quiet. Sometimes I wish he had been. Slow down, I was always telling him. Try to listen. You're a listener, I can tell. It will do you good, listening to people instead of always going on. Like me." She laughed. "But if you aren't going to say much, you should at least do me a favor and eat."

I took a bite and tasted butter. Raisin bursts and poppy seeds.

"My, you liked that one, didn't you? Here's another."

"No, ma'am. I couldn't."

"You can because you will. As I told you. I had a boy like you. If he was still with me, I'd fill him till he popped." Her cheeks fell. She hid a sigh behind her hand. "The 88th," she said, but I wasn't sure I was supposed to hear. "That sounds just fine." She folded her napkin as if bundling a living thing. After that, she fell asleep or seemed to. I thought of her boy and the age he must have been. The war had taken nearly all of us one draft after another. All except Ray, but he got hit with something almost as bad.

Mother would have fixed me plenty of rolls. She'd have tied an apron to her waist and filled the stove with wood. I could have done that for her, filling the stove, but she always shook her hand at me and did it herself. Mother's apron was white with blue stitches. It had flowers instead of birds. That apron of hers smelled of bread and something else. The smell of the river and the high cutting grass. I'd smelled it up close after the accident, when I sat at the table and she pressed my head to her chest. She wouldn't let me go for days after that.

If Helen had asked, I'd tell her that's why I was on the train. It was the accident that drove me to the war. It was the war Mother couldn't stand. Somehow, some way, something got broke. That's how I figured it. And when Esther and Myrle went off, it felt the same. It was me who broke it from the beginning. Me and the stone in my pocket. Now I was going to bring my sisters back.

The woman next to me woke with a kind of yip. "Ah, you're still here," she said. The train was moving again. Out the window, the fields whipped by like a wind. Helen looked as if she'd aged five years just by sleeping.

"Ma'am?"

"You don't need to call me 'ma'am.'"

"Sorry, ma'am. Do you know Chicago?"

"A nasty place, those factories. No place for a farm boy." She yawned. "But I suppose they need them. The factories. My sister lives farther out of the city. That's why I'm going.

Otherwise, I'd never step foot. A boy like you, you're not going there for work?"

I frowned. What kind of boy did she mean? Closer to Chicago, other trains cut past, near as spitting. Far off, towers smoked, buildings shouldering each other and too many people. Since the war, I'd forgotten there could be so many at once. The kind of boy who forgot, I guessed. The car was shaking. I thought it'd shake us straight off. But with the woman next to me and my stomach full, I grew some sure of myself.

"No work," I said. "My sisters live there too."

The train station in Chicago was brownstone and granite, close to a river and smelling the way rivers do. Grand Central they called it. But the words sounded wrong. Central wasn't so grand, not the way a sky was, or a summer storm. But words were better than numbers. It was numbers I forgot. How many months it took to get me home from the war. How many days this time I'd been gone. The station was high as barns. Higher than that. Glass and steel, the floor a shiny kind of stone. From the roof, a rush of voices dropped like a single thing. Outside the streets went off in every direction, the smell of burning. The clock tower was the tallest structure yet, pinning the station to the ground. I crouched against it. That wall was steady, at least, my head full of engines. All I knew about the place was that my sisters didn't belong.

"You're white as a ghost."

I blinked. The sun seemed brighter than it'd been. There was Helen, holding her bag. Others circled her feet. The sack I'd brought had only a poster of the girls. A blanket and a change of trousers. A square of soap. "I'm not used to the place is all."

"I supposed you'd be long gone," Helen said. She tapped the watch on her wrist. That blank space in my head, sometimes I lost minutes to it.

"Tell you what," Helen said. "You help me with these bags and I'll give you something for your pocket. My sister can't lift a spoon."

"I couldn't take money from you, ma'am. I'd do the bags for the rolls."

"That was a favor you did me, eating those. And look at you." She touched my forehead.

"I'll be all right."

"Hot as a gourd. I'll give you something for a good meal. Just a dollar for help with the bags. Any more and my sister will think I've gone loony." She studied me. "You don't know where your sisters are, do you?"

I wiped at my eyes.

"Are they together?"

"We think so."

"Do you have an address?"

I shook my head.

"Where do they work? Do you even know that?"

"Sorry, ma'am."

She stepped back and squinted at me. "Are they as young as you, these sisters?"

I nodded.

"They're even younger, aren't they?"

"Afraid so."

"My dear, dear boy. You're lost as a pup. You'll never find them here."

A trembling worked in my insides. That buzzing in my head, it was more than engines. I slumped against the wall and closed my eyes.

"Oh now, I didn't mean to scare you worse," Helen said. A car pulled up behind us and she gave it a glance. The car was running, but the sister didn't get out. Helen lifted my chin. "The factories, that's where you should start. Back of the Yards, in New City. Might take you hours to walk it, but the elevated is terrible for nerves, cost you some pennies too. You're young enough to go without it. Then I'd try the boardinghouses. If they're here at all, that's the only proper place for a girl to find sleeping quarters." Eyeing the car, she opened her purse and drew out a map. She pressed it flat against her thighs. "Look," she said and pointed. "There's the yard. That's the closest of the factories at least, though there's hundreds. And up here, whole streets of houses for workers. The Germans . . ." She stopped. I nodded it was all right. " . . . They're the ones who tend to the Near North Side. Or at least they did."

Helen eyed the car again. The sister had rolled her window down. "I've got to go." She put the map in my coat pocket and I helped with her bags. When I closed the car's boot, I was a run of sweat. But for those minutes of lifting, I knew the work even if I didn't know anything else. Helen opened her purse and dropped a dollar in my hand. Too much for bags.

"Lee, you're a good boy," she said. "I know you won't listen, but I think you should leave those girls be. Go home. They're surely here for their own reasons. You have to take care of yourself."

148

She got in the car and went off, waving to me before she was out of sight. I pulled the map from my pocket. It was worse than ten years old and thin as a leaf. In the corner the words CHICAGO TITLE AND TRUST CO. in red ink. Circles in the same ink grew around a center point. A mile marked by one circle. Two miles by one bigger than that. It was to that center point Helen thought I should be going. A place of some importance with so many street crossings, the names crowded and hard to read. Still, a good half of the map was nothing but white, and inside that, the words LAKE MICHIGAN.

I folded the map straight, careful not to rip the edges. I thought of what Helen had said about home. It was late morning on the farm. Nan would be in the garden, readying the winter vegetables for canning. She'd rake hay over the rest. After their chores, Patricia and Agnes would come in for noon dinner. Ray after that. But Father wouldn't. He'd stay in his room until dark. Maybe he'd go sit in his dugout. At the table, they'd have five empty places. One for Father. One for Mother. Two for the girls and one for me. If I could, I'd take four of those empty places back. *Lee*, Esther had asked. *You know how to trick that lock, don't you? If a girl asked for it?*

The doctors said I'd been in the hospital from fall to spring. Half a year, they'd said. I couldn't account for that. They said I'd have some trouble accounting for many things. I'd want to keep clear of noise, not work too hard when I got home. But home was work, I said back.

Now Chicago, that was work and noise both, and I'd been in the place only hours. I raised my collar to my ears. The city felt used. The men walked with their hats low, the women with purses tight to their elbows. Trains rattled overhead, fast with the smell of oil, the streets beneath shadows. Along every window and in the alleys, gray spots of snow. By midafternoon, my map was a sore piece of paper and I'd searched only a few blocks. The factories in the yards were wide and long as fields. High as three houses put together, sometimes more. The windows on the upper floors looked dark. The glass up there hardly bigger than a porthole, but what a noise. I imagined whole rows of engines behind those walls. Lines of wheels, pistons, and belts. And such a whir, the whole building breathing together. I breathed hard myself. *Back of the Yards* was a funny name, but it felt right. Nothing save brick and stone. Everyone was at work inside.

A whistle sounded above my head. I ducked into an alley to make it less. Minutes later, every door in the yard opened and out they rushed. Noon break. I stayed in the alley to let the men pass. Their hair was thick with a sticky kind of dust, their faces too. They walked and rubbed their eyes as if they didn't have time enough. Soon the yard emptied, all but a circle of men standing for a smoke. They gave me a look and I nodded. They didn't nod back. Not one of them seemed ready for talking. Least about two missing girls.

A hard place. Harder than I'd thought. The sun was high but the streets felt cold as knuckles. A whistle went off, my ears a drum, and the men filed in. Long through the afternoon I watched for another break, tracing one block after the next. At a store, I bought a spot of bread. Some cheese and a pickle. The man who sold it wore an apron over his front, and he dropped the change in my fingers like so much trash. "Here on business?"

he asked. I thought of pulling the posters out, but the man only frowned.

"Just seeing the place," I said.

"Best you keep to the Loop. Only workers here and only on breaks. We price for them. With the factories' help. The unions don't like a spare man wandering around, buying up someone else's bread."

I let myself out. When I looked back, the man stood at his window, arms crossed.

The afternoon was getting late. That whir from the factories, it never did let up. The light between the buildings grew heavy and still it was cold. It was colder when a person wasn't working, only walking about. The city was more than wind. Ugly with the sound. The pictures in the magazines, they'd looked washed clean. But here the streets were something different. They flattened every hill, constant as netting. And that dust, thick in the men's ears, thick in their hankies. Worse than any chaff in the barn. Finally, the whistle sounded again. A stream of men and women broke around me as if I was a stone. I couldn't get up my voice to ask questions, not with those faces. And not a one of them looked like my sisters, uniforms or not. In only minutes the workers were gone again. Then it was dark.

I hadn't thought about night. I didn't know where to take myself. Boarding, that's what Father had done. Helen had said the same. But a knock on one door after another and they didn't have room. "We're only for workers," a woman said. I walked farther, leaving the yards behind, and knocked again. "Too late," the last said. He was an old man, suspenders holding up his trousers. He hugged a hard role of salami in his fist and took a bite. "You'd do better tomorrow," he said. "If we lost a man or another, there'd be room. There's a George here, he might go. He might not." He eyed me close. The smell of that salami, it got my stomach going. "You look like a tidy one at least," he said, chewing. "Not like these others. Is that right?"

"Yes sir. I suppose." A doughboy face, Esther used to say. After the war, I wondered if it still was. "But I don't know the others, sir."

The man laughed. "You're a funny one. Remind me of my brother. Quiet like that. Look, if George leaves, there's a room to share. At seventy-five cents a night. Supper for seventy-five more if you want it. The missus does a fair spread. That's all I got."

I tipped my hat. "You're a sure help," I said. After blocks of walking, I found a street alley cleaner than most, near to dry, and I threw my blanket out. The alley was just wide enough to stretch my legs. A bit of dirt, something softer than bricks. I counted my bills, couldn't see numbers. Twenty-six, it felt. Twenty-six dollars. At seventy-five a night, seventy-five for supper, I could make it two and half weeks. More if the alley worked all right. I had my return ticket. And I had two extra for the girls. Already I'd imagined it, opening a door and there they'd be, Esther and Myrle. *Lee*, they'd sing out. I could be a George if the man wanted. I could be anyone. That's what I knew in France when I stepped off the boat. It was different than sleeping next to Ray and pretending at being alone. The boys had already made a name for me before we'd shipped out. *Hush.*

I turned on my side. A shadow scuttled along the wall. I didn't flinch. A barrel or two sat at the far end, a fair stink. I'd spent nights in worse. The cold was the same as the camps, the dark less. Here, I could see my hand if I held it to my face. In France when I stood watch, I imagined a German at every turn.

When a rat jumped, I had my Springfield on him. Some of the boys when they slept, they never kept their mouths shut. A man or two close to me as spitting, lined up in our bags like barnyard cats. Back then, you only hoped for a bit of space, but now the alley seemed a narrow block of nothing much. A hum far off, the rattle of the overhead cars, as if the city was running from itself. I missed Squire. I missed the others too, with all their talk. It kept a person from thinking too much. *Trust in God*, our K.P. said every morning with his slop. *Have Faith*. Our K.P., he wore a cross round his neck. His *Good morning* sure set a man right. Every hour over our heads, such a roar, the planes flying out to supply the lines.

I woke. It was nowhere near to light. There were no K.P.'s here, no planes either. I had more hours to sleep if I could. In the morning I would need to do better. If I could raise my voice, at least once or twice. Keep from being a stone. Why I hadn't shown those posters to Helen, I couldn't say. What my sisters looked like, seemed Helen already knew.

III

"Hey there, move on why don't you?"

I stood at the boarding docks in the morning, hands over my ears, and watched a man unload the trucks. Already he'd called me off twice. As dark a man as I had seen. Dark from his fingers to his nose, an even darker beard. I couldn't help but stare, thinking he knew what was important.

"Do they have girls working here?" I asked.

He spat and wiped his mouth. When he brought back another load, his face was fierce. "Listen," he said, "you've got it all wrong. We don't help with girls."

I reached into my pack, pulled the poster out. "These girls." The paper was creased hard down the middle, the edges broken with little tears. The girls' faces were sure different on either side of that crease. Esther with her stare, that turn in her smile. She was up to something. But not Myrle. With her coloring, the picture of her seemed too washed-out to be any picture at all.

The man frowned. "Never seen them. Why you looking anyway? Man comes around for girls and a man like me gets worried."

"They're my sisters."

"They don't look like sisters."

I studied the poster again. I couldn't tell if they did or not.

"So if they're your sisters, why do you have to find them? I'd think you'd already know where they are."

I turned my back. How much a brother knows. How much he forgets. Was knowing more than not what made a girl a sister to him in the first place?

"Hey," the man called after me. "You should go to the garments. South Market. This here's steel, blacksmiths. We don't hire skirts."

There was a rush of girls on Market, but they stuck together at breaks. What they were afraid of, I couldn't help but think. The men here, the ones who did or didn't work, some of them seemed ghosts. Hollow like that, starved for something. Smart as they were, the girls stayed close. In their navy skirts and aprons, they wore their hair tied in a bunch. Their lunch pails banged their thighs, their hands in gloves. When some took those gloves off, their hands seemed sure raw. I held my poster out, tried to look no worse than a brother.

"Have you seen these girls?"

"Who wants to know?"

"They're my sisters."

"Get lost."

One of the girls stopped. "What if he's telling the truth?" Her bangs were a black line, the tip of her nose red. The others tried to pull her with them, but she waved them off. "Don't worry about them," she said. "They think everything's fishy. But a person still has to be human, don't you think?" She stretched the poster between her hands. "What happened to them?"

"We think they ran away."

"Golly." She sniffled, pale drops. With her mitten, she wiped them off. "Place gets to me," she said with a laugh. "Just sitting at a machine, matching collars to shirts. Should be easy. But every time that needle goes in, it pulls something out. By the end of the day, all these bits are floating like bugs. It's like breathing with a sheet over your face."

A whistle sounded. I bit the inside of my lip, tasted blood.

"Hey, what's wrong?"

"Nothing." It was that high kind of whistle, tall and shivering. It was rain inside my head.

"You're all balled up, aren't you?"

I tried to take the poster from her, but she held it.

"Aw, it's all right," she said. "Most of the time, I'm balled up myself. What are their names?"

"Who?"

"Your sisters, silly."

"Esther and Myrle."

"Esther and Myrle," she repeated.

I cocked my head.

"Nothing. Just funny names."

"Not so funny."

"No. But it's those names, together like that. Seems I heard them before, but I can't tell when. Just a feeling you get, you know? On the tip of your nose. And that one." She pointed at the poster again.

"That's Esther."

She shook her head and squinted. "The tip of my nose. Then nothing." She shrugged. "I sure hope you find them. You should try the Y. They have all the lists. Boardinghouses. And the *Defender* too. They run the ads."

I looked at her, puzzling.

"The YWCA, silly. Don't you know anything?"

"Hey."

"Oh, you don't have to be like that. I know if my own brother came searching for me . . ." She sniffled again. "I know I'd go with him in a snap."

She opened her fingers and the poster curled into my hands. Finally that whistle was quiet. I touched my hat to her.

"Name's Bernadette," she called out, "but everybody calls me Nan."

I stopped.

"You don't like my name?"

"I like it fine." My face went warm. "If you see them, can you say I'm looking for them? Name's Lee. My big sister, I don't know what she'll do if I come home alone. She's like a mother to them."

"I'll tell them, sure."

I rolled up the poster. Nan watched me slip it into my sack. That black cut of her hair, it made her look some pretty.

"Lee, that's a good name," she said. "If I had a brother, I'd name him just that. And I'd never run off. If they know anything, they'll let you find them, easy."

A girl with my sister's name. A sign. And with Nan's voice in my head, that tip of her nose singing as if she knew something, that was good to keep me going. There were dozens of houses on that list at the Y, a dozen more in the paper, though those seemed the sorrier sort. I went knocking at the ones on the list first. The women who opened the doors were matrons. Behind them, the smell of coffee and sweets. Their arms cupped their heavy stomachs, their faces showing nothing much. When I took my poster out, the crease had grown so thick I worried it might well split in half.

"The nerve of you coming here," one of the women said. She had kettle-colored hair, her mouth a pinch. "We don't tell men what girls we have or not." With that, she stared me up and down. "If you're looking for your sisters, you best go home. You'll find a letter there. Then you'll know plenty about where they are." She moved to shut the door.

"Ma'am?"

"What now?"

"If they're here at all, will you tell them? Even if you don't tell me. That their brother has come looking. We miss them something terrible."

She swallowed, her voice quiet. "I miss my son too. But I don't go bothering people." She closed and bolted the door.

We miss them something terrible, I'd said. But for me, it was more than missing. My head felt hot, my stomach sore. All the way down to my bones, it felt. My face, maybe it didn't show what it should. That's why the women closed their doors.

I kept knocking. Sometimes the girls were in for breaks, eating dinner at the tables. Sometimes they weren't. Sometimes I could see them when they'd just taken off their coats. "You're no kind of gentleman," the matron said when she caught me looking. "Interrupting them at their dinner. Go on, why don't you?"

Those doors, they closed them fast. I couldn't help but think what might walk these alleys to make them do that. My sisters, maybe they already knew.

The other houses were the same. A *no*. Then another. *Not here. Never was.* A girl going up the stairs, a girl coming down. A glimpse of a scarf, the kind Esther wore. But I saw all sorts of scarves like that. When I tried to see more, the doors pulled shut. They were clean places, at least, the smell of bleach and flowers, while the streets they stood in were everything but. *You go on home*, the women said, shooing me. *Girls don't just disappear. They'll write if there's anything decent in them. They'd want to tell their mother where they are.*

"That's it, ma'am," I answered. "Mother's gone."

One woman touched her throat. "That doesn't change a thing, now does it? One person goes off, then another. You have to get used to it. We all have to get used to these things." She fiddled at the gold loops in her ears, as if they hurt her. "Daughters, they don't want to stay in one place anymore. Probably never did."

There was one thing I knew then: If Esther hadn't been the one to take Myrle off, Myrle never would have come to this place. But Esther was different. She was trouble to track. I walked from door to door, thinking about that. My breath was hard. The ball of my boots splitting, both sides. Hours of knocking and my feet did some ache, but never so much as France. That night in my alley when I slept, I felt myself knocking still.

The next few days, that's the way it went. I imagined Esther around every corner. Esther with her brown cap. Across the end of every street, before I could get a sure glimpse, she was there carrying a white bag, her flat-footed bounce. "Hey," I called out. Sometimes she was alone, sometimes a whole group at her side. I pushed through one girl after the other. A hand on her shoulder, swinging her around. The face was plain as the moon.

"Sorry. I thought . . ."

"You're crazy, that's what you are."

"Leave us alone."

At night my head knocked and Esther was there too. The way she'd slid into my smithy before she was gone, her hands polite in front of her skirts. She had never stood with her hands like that. Back then, she wore my old cap, but backwards. It pushed her hair close to her cheeks, hiding that she was a girl.

"Lee?" she asked. "What's that lock on the shed?"

I'd been fixing a horseshoe over the fire, the fire a smoke and my glasses thick. Esther reached a freckled finger to touch its sharp point. I pulled it back.

"No one locks their sheds around here," she said.

I shrugged. "Father does."

"Can you open it?"

"It's a hard one."

"That means you can? Ray couldn't do it, but you could."

I shrugged again, but already I was thinking: Ray couldn't. That was right. Esther straightened her skirt. She had never done much straightening before.

"You know what?" she said. "I bet Father's hiding something in there. You know how he's always keeping things to himself."

"Not so much."

"Aw, you know. Remember that time he didn't tell you about the new seeds he picked. He told Ray, but he didn't tell you."

"I don't worry about seeds."

"But that's the thing. He's always locking doors. Drives a person crazy."

I scratched my ear. "What about the barn? Nothing's locked in there. You can do anything you like."

"I'm not talking barns," she burst out. "Look, if you open that lock, I promise I'll tell you what I find."

I shook my head.

"I'll ask Ray then."

"Ray'll never do it."

"Maybe he will."

I sighed. The lock was more than Ray could fix. I knew that. The smithy fire was squaring low. I fed it, stirred the ash. The horseshoe, it'd be getting hard if I left it long. I might have to make it right over.

"Lee, you're not listening. Don't you care what Father's doing?"

My ears were abuzz. It was a buzzing like the nerves in my feet. "I care plenty."

Esther tried to smile, but her face didn't match. Those freckles on her cheeks, every inch, they had a way of looking dark. "So then you know how to trick that lock. You'd do it, if a girl asked?"

I sighed again.

"Thanks. You won't regret it." She was out the door, taking off the hat as she went. She threw it in the air, caught it easy. When she snapped it on her head, it was frontways. I never got that hat back.

IV

At the boardinghouse, George was away for four days. I had the sheets on a cot, a ceiling over my head. I didn't dream any dreams. The other two men in the room, they roared good as dogs when they slept. Those nights after the meal, my stomach was sure full. I might have roared some too. But then George came back. He was the wife's second cousin, the man with suspenders said. He turned up his eyes at that. Cousins had it good over strangers, even quiet ones, he meant. In the morning, I passed George as I left. He had his suitcase. I had my pack. He was small as a tailor, missing a circle of hair. A cold dome George's would have been. No good for alleys. No meat on his frame. He had a room. But in a week or less, I'd have a home again and acres. I'd have my sisters too. They were better than cousins. Already I had our tickets in my pocket.

Snow came. A fine cold shake, growing thicker with the wind. When I closed my eyes, I got myself to imagining Esther and Myrle. They were behind one door or another. And the way they'd hold up their hands, ready to come home. Ray would grip me by the arm. And Nan, even Father. *Didn't think you could,* they'd say. *But you did it. You did.*

I woke in the alley with wet cheeks, my boots soaked, jacket too. I bundled my blanket in the early light and walked. The snow fell for hours. The alley would be a cold floor by night, full of drifts. Not enough room to fit a man's legs across. The snow glowed like fireflies against the city lights. The girls from the factories kept their eyes down. With their hoods over their foreheads and scarves tight, I couldn't search for faces. At the factory doors, the heat let out in waves. I was cold in my throat, my ears, and walking tired. In France I'd learned to walk like that. On your feet and marching, letting your head slack. One man in front of you, one behind. You might march a mile or two and not even remember it. Now I wished I could walk to a place where the snow was gone, alleys too. My tickets turned soft as I fingered them. Still the print stayed clear. I put them quick in my pocket.

Before I left for the war, it was all of it snow. *I'll go to the office next week*, I said to Father in the dugout. *Sign my name.* He touched my forehead. That hand of his, it was some warm. *Your mother will never forgive us*, he said. It was almost a whisper, his saying that. But Mother, she was the one who'd thought accidents were accidents. No matter Ray's hand. There was no one to blame.

Father didn't tell me don't. He never really did. After he said his piece, he left me in the dugout alone. It was late. There was only a moon. Then the sound of footsteps by the door, but softer this time, and someone sniffling. I stepped out to get a glimpse. In the snow at my feet, the shape of my name, the words already filling. They looked carved by a mitten.

LEE DON'T GO

The moon pulled behind the clouds. The light was gone. Those words, I might never have seen them at all. Far off, the back of a black coat cut against the house. She must have run to get so far so fast. I imagined Esther's face wet, how she'd wipe it with her sleeve. Esther had never been much for feelings. But even if I didn't see it, I had that picture in my head. Even when I got to going the next week.

Already it was growing dark. Still the factory whistles for the night were hours off. The snow kept up and I was some cold. I was colder than that. I opened the door to a diner hoping for heat. The place wasn't bright, but it was clean. A lamp on every table, scattered spots of light. I found a corner where I could sit with my back against the wall, my shoulder at the window, and see out. My face was scruff. I rubbed at my cheeks. The place was not so busy, but it was busy enough. The smell of eggs and biscuits. The ovens hot. My feet burned even as they warmed.

"Be right with ya," the waitress let out.

I ordered coffee and toast, pretending at newspapers. The waitress chewed her lip. She didn't have a pad of paper when she took my order. I wondered at that. Her hair she'd tied in a bun under a net, her nails bitten to nubs. Working here, she would smell of eggs and biscuits every night. I wondered if she had a room for herself, if she could pay for it for even a month.

"Want another?" The waitress stood at my table with her coffee pot. With a heavy head, I lifted my cup. The owner eyed me from the counter. I dropped two quarters on the table. He went to the kitchen then, and a radio sparked. A couple sat at the next table over. The woman had taken off her shoes and wrapped her foot around the table leg. "Don't do that," the woman said, pointing her finger at the man. "What?" he asked. She pinched the scruff on his chin and laughed. "What?" he asked again. Outside, a gaslight blinked against the glass, keeping time with the beating in my chest. The sounds in my head, they blinked too. My coffee cup was empty. The toast had gone to crumbs. I'd read the paper twice, but couldn't make much of it. It would be quicker to find the girls if I didn't sleep. It would be quicker without the dark. But a person shouldn't wish for a thing like that. At home, the dark was a good place. Here it was something else. And during the war, it was worse.

Our squad, we made camp in the woods when a village wasn't safe. In our last week, we'd camped five days. Me, Stan, Critters, and Sam Bullet. With the flu in the regiment, that's all that was left of us. The paths in the woods were thick with mud, the sky wintry. In the daytime, it was a hard thing to find our way, and at night, a man couldn't move save to follow the telegraph wires. All the same, those wires were ankle blades and mussed with shelling so we stayed put. "Hold your position," staff sergeant had said. We hadn't had a message since.

"God damn if I have to spend another night," Critters whined.

We had a dugout in the woods, some two miles from the village. With the leaves gone, we'd lost our cover. Stan kept out of the trees, though he was lookout.

"We're holding," Sam Bullet said. He was squad leader, by the book he was, and as cold as his name.

The Huns still had it coming to them. That's what Stan said. "When we hit them again, they'll think it's worse than the flu." Stan was grinning with his big cheeks, his front tooth gone missing. But it wasn't so funny. Only the month before, our runner had a letter from home. His father, a man hardy to his fingertips, gone down to a thing a person couldn't even fight.

Our runner had been a sad boy, then he'd taken to the flu too. No runner for the squad, no orders in or out.

"You're all one for starting up again," Critters said. "But just get me to the village. A roof and walls. Fritz will sign for peace any minute."

"I'd keep my hat on if I were you," Stan said. "Fritz isn't signing anything."

Critters sank back against the fence. He was thin to his britches, thin even in his hands. He shook when he got nervous, and he was done with being nervous now. "We've been on the line ten days," he whined. Sam Bullet smacked him on the head.

It'd been a long run. Too cold and wet to take off our boots, the oil gone so we couldn't grease our feet. Too tight at night to sleep in the hole together. But the village was worse. Not a young man in sight. Only women and old hands. Plenty of houses emptied out. Plenty chance for surprises. When the guns were down, the village was fine enough for sleeping, but it was frightful dirty and the pantries dry. So much manure in the streets, the place was rich with the stuff. On the road, we'd walked through dozens of towns just the same. Fog heavy in the hills, columns of tanks and infantry lines. Many a dead German, too. To the east, the plains of the Rhine and no mountains. Artillery sparks shone far off in the flats, the echo of guns whenever we slept. This was borderland France, but most of the people spoke German, wore wooden shoes. They drank schnapps and wine in heavy cups, and they hated the Kaiser as much as any of us.

"I've got to have something to stick to my ribs," Critters said. "I'm dying here."

"You'll die faster if you go down to the village," Sam Bullet said.

Critters itched his feet.

"And don't you dare take off those boots," Bullet said. "You'll never get them back on."

"Stinks," Stan said.

"Hush's feet stink worse than mine," Critters said.

One stink was like any other. Numb, now that was something to worry about.

The next morning was quiet. By afternoon we walked to the village hoping for a meal and laid our bags in an empty farmhouse. They had a sofa in that place and a few metal pots, but not a picture on the walls. Nothing more than a lace dress hanging in the closet. We had a roof, but the cupboards were cleared and our men hungry starved, ropes cinching their trousers. Sometimes they didn't call me Hush anymore. "Hess," they said. "Hess, go fish something out for us from the Krauts." I didn't know the kind of German they used around here. I hardly knew German at all, but the boys looked at me like I did.

"I'd think you were one of them," Stan said through his missing tooth. "If I didn't know better. Walked right out of the fields without your lederhosen, that's what I'd think. We need a little grub is all. If our neighbors got the extra."

"What neighbors?" Bullet asked.

Critters sat up on his elbows. "You sending him for food?"

"That's up to him."

"He's not going anywhere," Bullet said. "We've got our orders."

Critters moaned and dropped back on the sofa. He took out his wallet and mooned at a picture of his girl. I looked over his shoulder. "That's Belle," he said. "She's something, ain't she?"

I nodded.

"You got a girl?"

I didn't answer.

"Guess that means no."

"Hush doesn't have a girl," Stan said.

"God damn if I have to spend another night."

"We're out of the woods at least."

"We're starving. Belle won't recognize me if Fritz signs. I'm walking bones."

I swung to my feet and put on my cap.

"Where you going, Hush?" Stan and Critters asked.

"Taking a walk."

I stumbled out. I had a rope around my trousers too, my boots too small by half. Critters said that was the better. His were three times over and he could fit plenty of socks. Still he fell on his nose with every root and pebble, and we had socks hardly at all. Days before when I took my boots off, my feet were some swollen. They felt full of pebbles. I didn't want to step too hard.

Bullet thought we wouldn't find a crumb, but I thought we could. Bullet looked like Ray, talked like him. He was sure solid in the woods and always at the ready. But maybe, if a boy tried a door or two and had the name of Hess. A face of a Hess too. Maybe there was something in that.

I passed row after row of houses set close to the road, most of them empty. A man could smell that. There were other houses a ways back, the barns in front, sheds all around. But there wasn't an animal left in those barns. A man could smell that too. Far off, a cabin sat high on the hill, a flash of light. I followed the road up, losing my breath. A garden of what must've been cabbage lined the yard, eaten to scrub. The fence had been set right, a dead German hanging over it. He was a handsome one with his yellow hair, his uniform old and crusted, his face frosted white. Not so handsome when I saw that. Strange they'd let him hang there, German or not.

The door of the house opened and I jumped. A man, tall as he was wide. He wore a hat and apron seemed made of straw, his thumbs hooked in his trouser pockets. Smoke drifted through the door behind him. Sure he would shut the door on me. Get his gun.

"*Essen?*" I asked. I lifted my arm to show him my uniform. "*Essen, bitte?*"

He eyed the German on the fence and eyed me some different. Then he pointed at his chest. "Schmidt."

"Hess," I said back.

He cocked his head and grinned, waving me inside.

The house was low and dark, but it seemed a good place. Simple enough. Brick for the floors, brick for walls. In the corner, a fireplace stood so large it took up the room by half, but it wasn't but a little warm. A girl huddled in a blanket, only her forehead showing. When Schmidt stepped out the back door, she spat a question I couldn't understand. Soon Schmidt stood at the threshold again, studying me and the girl. "*Alles in ordnung?*" he said. She didn't say a thing. "*Der tote Mann,*" he said, to me this time. He pointed at the man on the fence. "*Er hat sie angefasst. Verstehen?*" In his fist, three rabbits hung by their feet. They fidgeted and kicked, but that fist was as big as the three put together.

"The soldier?"

"*Ach, du verstehst,*" he said. "*Dieser Mann, ein Teufel.*" With a flip of his wrist, he broke the rabbits' necks.

In the backyard, the girl gathered wood and Schmidt laid the rabbits on a stump. He took out his knife by the blade, offered the handle. I had skinned rabbits plenty. Never had a taste for it. Still I wondered at how easy the coat pulled. How the innards rose when you split the stomach. *Save it for the foxes,* Father would have said, drawing them out. It'd been a while since I'd done such a thing. Weeks since I'd had a good bite. I tore back the skins, threw the innards to the ground. But even foxes seemed a waste of innards now. Everything I cut away, the head, the feet, it only made the meat less. Still Schmidt seemed mighty pleased. "*Gut, gut,*" he said.

We made a fire in a pit in front of the house. The smell of roasting meat brought the boys to the fence. The dead German, he was nowhere. I wondered if the boys'd had time to lay him out, cover his face. If I hadn't been eager for food, I might have done so myself. But maybe after what Schmidt said, the German wasn't worth even that.

"Hey, Hush," Critters yelled out. "You K.P. now?" The rabbits turned on sticks over the fire. I held another by its hind legs, threading it. When the boys showed, Schmidt seemed some worried. But with a nod from me, he waved them through the gate.

"This is fine," Bullet said.

"That's it, Hush." It was Stan this time. He squatted next to me as I fixed the rabbits. "That's how you do it."

We sat on logs around the fire to eat. The girl had joined us, edged close to her father and her face hidden. All but two eyes, she was, and Schmidt put an arm over her shoulder. She looked out from her blanket, studying us.

"What's up with the girl?" Stan asked.

I shrugged. It didn't feel right, telling something like that. Something about what a soldier might have done to a girl if he was hungry enough. A German soldier too.

"Haven't seen a girl in months," Stan said. He reached into his pocket, pulled out a tin of mints, offered them to her. With his grin, he moved himself closer. I jerked him back.

"What's with you?" Stan barked.

"Leave her be." I pushed at him.

Stan was on his feet. "Not so hush now, are you?"

"Hey," Critters called, palms out. Schmidt reared up. The rabbits spit and burned on the fire. Critters passed me a stick, passed Schmidt another, then Stan. "These are the old man's rabbits. He's sharing." Schmidt sat, pinching his knee. Stan bit the meat right off. "Hess," he whispered. "You've got some German in you yet."

Critters cleared his throat. "If the war's done, we have us some celebrating." He took a bar of chocolate from his bag and broke it into bites. "Peace!" he said, handing them out. "Thanks to the blondie on the fence."

That small piece of chocolate, it melted away in my hand. All day we'd heard our guns, but now Fritz stayed quiet. Still, done seemed different. Stan sat there, brooding. He wasn't even close to grinning now. The others licked their fingers. Schmidt brought out a jug of schnapps, tin mugs from the Huns. We raised our drinks. With a nudge from Bullet, Stan raised his too. We were soon enough blurry. Schmidt took the girl under his arm again and Critters, he started to sing.

There's a long, long trail a-winding
Into the land of my dreams

Where the nightingales are singing
And a white moon beams.

It grew darker than it'd been. The fire flared and dropped off easy. We were close to nowhere. We were closer to shadows. The sky above was black and clean, the fire cracking. Soon Critters' voice settled, the rest of us quiet. In the low light, we were noses and cheeks. Only the girl was different, being a girl. But as the fire settled and the rabbits were bones, she wasn't so very much. We sat loose and head-heavy on those logs.

When at last we turned to make bunks, Critters was the first to take to his feet. "Hey, Stan," he said. "Hush didn't mean it, right? It's just a girl."

I hit my fist to Stan's shoulder. He hooked an arm around my neck, like Ray had always done. "We're all right," Stan said. I smelled the schnapps on his breath. "War's near to over, Hush. We'll be the best now."

That night, we made our beds in Schmidt's barn and surely did sleep. I unlaced my boots. Didn't take them off. We'd beaten the Germans to a frazzle. Heard told, even the prisoners didn't care a fig for the war anymore. But it was days more for us to be brought in. My feet would have to keep until we got back.

As I drifted off, I could taste those rabbits. I could even dream them. Stan, he lay next to me and whistled as he snored. *We're all right*, he'd said. With the smell of meat on my fingers, I slept with my hands against my cheek to keep that smell close.

"Hush, you coming?" Out on the road that morning, I stumbled to keep up with the boys. Schmidt had left bread by the door for breakfast, but we couldn't find him in the house. Couldn't find the girl. Before the rest of us woke, Stan had gone looking himself. "Nowhere," he said, tucking in his shirt. "Not her old man, either." Guns boomed in the distance. From our side, they were going some loud. Bullet had gotten us a truck. We could ride with the men coming in from the lines. The driver, he was a sergeant, Bullet said. He could just as well order us. And he'd fit us in if we could hang onto our seats. Bullet waved me to hurry, but I walked on dead feet. We'd have to hold on some good. That truck couldn't take so many at once. I was closer then, I was closer than that. The guns went quiet. Critters let out a whoop. They all did, whooping, and I stopped and looked back. We knew what it meant. The sergeant whooped too as he started his engine. "We're leaving ya," Critters joked. "We're on vacation now." When he turned around, the truck jumped, the sergeant wheeling out of the mud. I was running as best I could. I could have been running on bread as much as feet. Another twist of the wheel and Stan waved his hat. "Hush!" he yelled. A sharp crack. A sound that snapped in my stomach. The truck broke skyward with a flash. I was thrown off my feet, the boys worse than that. The blast so loud it didn't have any sound at all.

"You can't stay here all night."

The waitress stood over me, holding her coffee pot. My head had fallen, spit running from the corner of my mouth. I raised my eyes and the room was a twirl. When the waitress snapped her fingers, the room came back. Outside, the streetlights had gone out. An hour or two, maybe more I'd lost. Without her hairnet, the waitress was red-haired and pretty. She poured another cup.

"That's it," she said. "I'm off my shift already. You drink that and get on with it, or Bill will show you another way to the street."

I stood, surprised to feel my feet under me, though they ached. The coffee tasted a razor, but it woke me up. I felt two places at once, the space in my head too big for comfort. I put on my hat and hurried out.

It was terrible cold. The snow was blue underfoot, the sky black. I walked. There wasn't a soul in the streets. That white space on my map with the name LAKE MICHIGAN, I could just as well have been walking on its surface if anyplace else. During the war, before rabbits, before those five days in the woods, I remembered standing on the German lines. We knew we were near the end. The Germans had pulled back. They weren't so much for shooting us. Looking across, I thought I'd see what marked them as different. But the land on the other side didn't show much. Grass and hills. A couple of shot-up houses, same as the villages where we camped. I don't know why I'd imagined it a separate place. Our maps showed that line, how it cut the land off straight. Over there, that was where Father was born. That's where he grew to a man. Must have been a drop of something in that water to turn Father so driven and a whole country to start a war like that. That drop, maybe I had it in me too.

I puzzled over that. It was a kind of white space splitting me in half. Out by that fire, I picked Schmidt and his girl over Stan. For only a minute I did. As if sides were required. Just a little thing, my pushing at him. But maybe little things were bigger than a person thought. It made a man believe in blood, good and bad.

I had stepped on a boat and stepped off someplace else. That's all I could figure. When I landed in France, the farm was so many weeks gone. I couldn't get the distance straight. Step off one spot of land and step onto another, as if a person could drift anywhere on that ocean. And not one of the boys knew what our farm looked like. When I woke in the hospital, that was something I couldn't get my head around. The boys were gone. I'd been missing for days myself, weeks even. Even if I couldn't figure how. Everything went missing, I thought.

V

Morning in Chicago. At the telegraph office, I wrote home. NO LUCK. COMING BACK. I was dizzy with walking, my feet pins. I had one more house to check. I didn't have much hope in that. As I headed out, the man in the office called my name. "You Lee Hess?"

"Yes, sir. Yes."

He looked at me under heavy lids. He was holding the order I'd just filled, my name at the top in caps. The man was gray as a squirrel skin, too old for his face to show much feeling. "This young woman here says we have a message for you. Been waiting here a week, she says."

The man ambled his way to the back. The woman took his place, picking at her fingers. Those nails of hers, they were painted a bloody kind of red. "He's getting it," she said with a squint. "I remembered your name."

I took off my hat.

"Lee Hess, I remembered it," she went on. "That's why I knew you had a message waiting."

"I should thank you."

"Don't thank me, a name like that."

The old man returned. "Don't worry about her," he whispered. "She lost a brother over there." He handed me a piece of paper. I was quick to fold it in half.

"Aren't you going to read it?" the man asked.

"I'll read it, sure." I made for the door. The cold outside was roaring bright, same as in my head.

"It's XU," he shouted after me. "That means they want an answer."

But I didn't have an answer for them. Not yet.

I knocked at the last boardinghouse. This one seemed different. Off on its own in the old town. The alley was a long block of bricks, not a window or door except one. A dog limped by the wooden steps, sniffing my leg. When I lowered my fingers to him, he bared his teeth. I knocked again. That telegram burned in my pocket. The girls might have come back, that's what it said. If so, I should be some happy. But *back* felt like I'd wasted it. My alley nights, they were good for nothing much. *Back* meant I still hadn't done anything right.

The door opened like a shot. The woman clapped a hand to her chest. "Young man, you startled me."

"Sorry, ma'am."

"What are you doing here?"

The woman was tall as a German and thick about the middle, a wisp of gray hair on her head. But that voice of hers, it was like Squire's. Irish.

"Are you crazy or something?" the woman asked. "You are, aren't you? A crazy man." She went to close the door. "I house girls here. Not men. And I don't have anything else you're looking for either."

I moved quick, took the poster from my pack. "I'm looking for my sisters." I unrolled the poster, trying to hold it straight. The woman studied their faces, pinching the poster between her fingers. Those hands of hers were small, square as a child's. "I don't want any trouble."

"I don't mean trouble."

She threw a look at the stairwell. "They're not here."

"Are you sure?"

"You think I don't know my own house?"

I checked the number on the door. "But this is the last one. I've tried all the others."

"Then you're out of luck."

She went to shut the door again, but I stuck in my foot. Those pins went deeper yet. "Ma'am."

"Young man, please remove your foot or I'll call the authorities."

"Their names are Esther and Myrle. Esther's younger than me by five years, Myrle's two under that. You can see them on the poster."

The woman sighed. "I don't need posters."

I leaned my shoulder against the door. My head was fevered. The snap of the dog and the smell of oil, a terrible roar at the alley's end. A whistle then, but far off, as if calling the dog to come.

"What's wrong with you? You look like you're about to faint."

"Sorry, ma'am." The poster slipped from my fingers, but I caught it fast.

"You can't even hold a piece of paper. You won't make it off this step."

"This is the last place."

She let out a sigh. "Come in, but stay to the parlor. I'll get you a glass of water. Then you'll have to move along."

She went off down the hall to the kitchen. Inside the parlor, I stood with my hat pressed to my chest, my heart going. There was whispering behind the kitchen door. When the woman came out, she left that door behind her swinging, but I couldn't see inside.

"You can rest your feet." Her hand made a show of the parlor sofa. "But be quick about it."

I perched on the edge of a cushion. The sofa was white with daisies. The arms had tassels at the end. I felt white and hot, though the glass of water was cool in my fingers.

"You're not drinking very fast." The woman lowered herself into the other chair.

"Sorry, ma'am, I just . . ."

"You've already said what you're doing. But why do you think your sisters are here?"

"They left our farm more than a month ago."

"And you haven't heard anything."

I thought of the telegram but shook my head.

She sighed. "Sit back, why don't you? I can't have a man big as you faint in here. I don't know the first thing I'd do then."

"That's all right, ma'am. I'll be good to go."

"Some girls just need to be left alone."

I held my water and took a long drink.

"Girls like the picture you showed me," she went on. "It's no use trying to get them to do anything. Not at that age. That's something I know."

I took another drink. The room was worn but bright. Books on a row of shelves, a coffee table spotted with fingerprints. The woman eyed those prints and wet her thumb to clean them. When the factories let out, the place must have filled to the brim. A long coatrack hung in the hall, the rungs empty, but still the smell of girls, a fresh wash. And with the white sofa under me, the place was some comfortable. Above the fireplace, a frilly line of text in a frame:

> *To be sympathetic without being sentimental.*
> *To care for the tired and sick.*
> *To be patient with the hysterical.*
> *To direct youthful gayety and extravagance.*
> *To help girls in danger of losing the heritage*
> *of womanhood.*
> *— Code of the Boardinghouse Keeper,*
> *Miss Edith M. Hadley, 1913*

The woman gripped her hands in her lap and stared at my glass, half full as it was. It took more breath than I had to drink it all at once.

"I'll tell you a story," she started. "Last winter we had a man here who yanked a girl out by the hair. His wife, he called her. But she couldn't have been a wife to anything, she was only a child. And you know what happened? She came straight back. All black and blue. I never have forgiven myself for letting her go. Then she packed up her things and went off. Without my knowing. Now when the man comes, she's gone but he keeps coming. Even if I knew where she was, I wouldn't let on. It was his coming after her that made her disappear in the first place. Now I'm not telling anyone anything, but chasing after someone never works out like you think."

I looked at my feet. *No use*, she'd said. A person could leave well enough alone. Or a person could do otherwise. One way or another, it was a guess what was right. If Nan had been here. If my brother had been. They could tell me which. Up and down the stairs, I imagined one girl after another. Other girls with other names.

"Why did they leave?" the woman asked.

"Why?"

"Of course, dear. It's the obvious question. Surely you've thought about it."

I shook my head. I could figure washers on broken door-knobs, but the *why* was a blank space. To leave a place, that took some doing. It took something else too. A town with their dark looks and torches, a German at the fence. Something that got a person to running. The woman gripped the arm of her chair, waiting. I pictured Mother in the kitchen, flour on her apron. *You should never have gone out to that field, working that machine,* she said. *I never should have let him send you.* Later when I couldn't let it go, when I turned it over in my head to try to change the way it went, she sat me on my bed. *Things come at you,* she said. *You can't always fix them. Your father will tell you different. But I say you have to sit and find some peace. Try to keep your mind on what is coming to you next.*

"What if they left for no reason," I said, because I couldn't think of anything else. I wouldn't. "But what if now they get themselves into some trouble. What then?"

The woman studied me. "A girl won't leave without a reason. If it's trouble you're worried about, then you'll know. All girls are the same when it comes to trouble. That's when they go home."

I let myself out. At the alley's end, the factories spilled their workers for the night. It was late again. It always was. The cold ran under my collar, the tips of my ears hard as nickels. I watched for the girls, but I didn't watch much. I would sleep the night in the alley. My legs just fit across. My blanket was a sorry piece of rough, but I had a dollar in my pocket. It was enough for a bite when the sun broke. I didn't want to remember the other tickets I'd bought. I didn't want to dream. When I thought of my sisters now, there wasn't a door to open. At home, not a hand on my shoulder. Out the window of the train, the fields under the snow would be straight as a sheet. As if such a thing as Chicago never was.

I stopped before the alley crossed into the street. Another set of tracks, when not one of those workers had taken to the alley yet. The tracks ran up next to my own, but turned around. They were small and scraping, flat-footed like. I followed them best I could, around the corner and up a dark path. Around another corner then, where those tracks mixed with dozens of others. Far off under a streetlight, a girl was walking fast. Her hair was a dark cap, a barn coat on her shoulders. Corduroy, that coat was, and hanging on her like a tent.

I ran. Around another corner. Across the bricked and muddy streets. The girl was running now too, but the snow kept her footprints. At every turn, she looked back. Sure enough, with her mouth open and that look on her face. Sure who it was. Through every alley, she ducked off. I spun on my heel. When she slipped around a line of trucks, the street twirled as if pulled by a string. My knees hit the ground, the snow soaking. The many times I'd missed her, I'd never been so close. I caught my breath and stumbled on.

But the next street was a blank. And the one after that. Now the Loop was awash with snowmelt and traffic. The trains clattered above. Every footstep, it was lost. My feet ached with a fire in them. I dropped my hands to my knees, my head spinning. There were alleys every hundred feet. Shop doors and overhangs. Plenty to hide a person. The streetlights over my head, they were some bright. A whole city of them. What was the use of so much light?

"Lee."

There she was, or the shadow of her. Where she stood across from me on the walk, Esther looked older. That coat big on her shoulders. Her hair was a helmet, her face bone-thin. But there were those freckles, even on her lips. So many, they made her darker than the rest of us. She wiped her cheek.

"I found you," I said.

She wiped her cheek again. "Don't be stupid. You didn't find me, Lee. And that's what you'll say when you go back."

"But I can't."

"You didn't find me. You didn't find Myrle. You'll go back because she can't be found."

She took a step into the street. She looked wild, shivering. "She can't," she said. "Not ever." And then the words that would undo me. Even she knew that. "I told you not to go, but you did. You owe me."

I coughed into my hand. My eyes burned, my whiskers were wet. When I looked up, the street was empty. The lights gleamed. I searched the sidewalks, only boxes and crates, piles high as rubbish and no Esther. But there in the snow melt, two footprints. If it hadn't been for that, I might have thought Esther was only in my head. My ears were ringing some hard. My feet like blazes. I sat in the snow so I wouldn't have to stand, reached my hand over those tracks. Sure enough, Esther had been there. And she had told me what she wanted. She always did.

But what she said about Myrle, I couldn't figure it. *She can't. Not ever.* Myrle, I hadn't seen her once.

I woke on a bench by the lake. My head was aching, my blanket wrapped around my chest. I stabbed at my ear. My bag was gone, but I still had my dollar and the tickets in my pocket. The city, it was a low run of traffic. In front of me, the moon showed on the lake. That light seemed a tunnel, promising something different. The sky above was fresh, the stars big as smarts. I could smell fish. A slow kind of wave that sounded thick with ice. At my back, the city was humming. A train in the morning. That way was home. But the water in front of me was wide open. That's what I liked. Wide was safer. It gave a person a choice. If you could leave parts of yourself behind, the parts you didn't like. If you could only do that. Since the blast, I'd known a thing or two that was close. At the hospital when I first woke, it was just me and a wool blanket on my chest. Me and the ringing in my head. The rest of the world seemed finished. It was strange to let go like that, even for a minute. Strange but easy, as if I'd never done anything wrong. At home, Father had said it too. *Look at this*, he'd said, his hand out over the wide open fields to show us.

I reached into my pocket, unfolded a piece of paper. The telegram was soaked. The type no bigger than a pebble. I read the words twice over. COME HOME. Underneath, in blurry ink, it said something that felt worse: SHE'S BEEN FOUND.

Part IV: Needles or Pins

ESTHER

I

We had to get away. Myrle took the key from Father's bedside, and I found the rope in the shed. Myrle would test that key herself, but it was me who unlocked the door that night and stepped off the porch. Me who'd tied the rope to the window and ran to the back of the house to help Myrle drop. She clung to the rope like a tired shirt. "Phsst," I whistled when I caught her legs. "Did you fix the door?" She nodded quick. The rope snapped against the house when we gave it a pull and fell at our feet. Myrle shuddered but I put a finger to her lips. Only the groan of Father sleeping and the trees against the gutters, the wind pitching the fields and the dark far over our heads. Not an inch of the house moved, what with everyone asleep, the doors closed and locked, and the cold enough for blankets. We had our boots and Lee's old trousers. We had the barn coats. I carried two loaves of bread under my arm and a bag tied to my back, Myrle with another as light as we could have it. I took her hand. We ran across the yard, over the grass until the grass became fields, and out to the pasture. Scrags of corn stuck up here and there, watching us. A dog wailed, one of the Elliots', and Myrle snapped her head to look. But the Elliot boy was done, I told her. She wasn't going to go there anymore.

The pasture led to the road along a path the cows had marked with grazing. Myrle walked in front and I followed, my fingers to her back. The moon was low to the ground, large as a house and barn put together. Then it was gone. I couldn't see Myrle but for the sound of her sniffling. I couldn't see my feet. But she was with me. Going better than I would've thought and not so much a word of worry, though I knew she did. When we came to the road, it was a white dust that showed itself between the dark of the fields like a bridge. We could go for hours before it turned light. We could make our way to Clarksville by next nightfall, some twenty miles, and the train after that. Father always said a person without a moon might wander off and be lost, fall into a ditch, a snake underfoot, or an ankle break, and no one would know to search him out. But that was just poor luck.

"Look," Myrle said and stopped short. An animal crouched in the dark of the road with its nose up. It jumped when I gave a whistle and vanished. "What was that?" she asked.

"A fox."

"I'm tired of foxes." She lifted the soles of her boots as if to show me how they ached.

"Remember?" I took her hand to pull her along, but she shook her head. The way she left her bed for mine when she was scared to sleep, I reminded her, and the picture in the magazine. *Do you dread the day?* the advertisement said. *Does washing tire you? Do you feel discouraged by the weary monotony of the old way?* The woman in the picture wore a pink dress, a black square of ribbon on her collar and sleeves. In a washhouse, she stood with her hand on a crank, the other palm up as if holding a cup of tea, and not so much as a blush of heat on her cheeks. Father would have my hide for looking, let alone taking the magazine from the market for free, but I had to think someplace there were women like this. *Hurley's Electric Washers*, the advertisement said, *of Greater Chicago*. I kept that magazine under the mattress ticking, folded it in a newspaper should Nan change the sheets.

"That's somebody, isn't it," I told Myrle.

She pressed her hand flat against the picture. "She looks a queen."

"A princess better."

I dropped my hand on hers and lined up our fingers. Mine were longer by an inch. "See," I said. "She's as pale as you." Myrle's eyes were puffy, a streak of wet on her cheeks. The Elliot boy, that's what that streak was. The magazine was the only thing that made her stop whimpering long enough to sleep. The light of the washroom in that advertisement, so bright it could kill shadows. Electric, always electric, when we might as well have lived in the bottom of a hole. Myrle curled her knees to her chest waiting for a story, and I would give her one if she wanted. Back then, I would have done anything for her.

The moon had come and gone again as we walked. The scrub in the ditches nicked us, our ankles bare enough for a bite. That fox, I wondered if it was trailing us on soft feet. But we would be fine as long as we stayed to the road and Myrle stopped her shivering. The way we made our plan, I was quick to remind her. The washing we wouldn't have to do, and the cows left in their stalls for someone else's buckets. Ray's voice out of our heads and Patricia's, Nan and her swollen fingers, pinching, poking, ordering us to break our backs. But Myrle whimpered again. "Esther," she said. "What about . . . ?" "Hush," I said. The pictures in the magazine, I reminded her. And Father's hand wide as my backside, me in my britches. It was one slap for talking back. One for tracking mud in the house. Two for freeing horses, and more slaps than I could count for stealing magazines. Did Myrle remember that? My ears rung to aching. My stomach sore against Father's knees. Father with his eyes closed, his wheezing. Nan called up the stairs, "She's learned her lesson." But Father was in such a state. Wild, he said of me, though he didn't know how much.

I ran to the cellar after every one of those lessons. The door was a heavy plank. Underneath, the wooden steps, cobwebs, and jars of what we saved from the garden, full to the brim. The ceiling was high as my head. The walls of dirt throbbed with beetles and worms. I breathed it in, that dark cool on my cheeks. Father was always quick with his slaps with me. No one else, especially Myrle, who he treated like a queen. If I closed the cellar door and pinched out the wick of my lantern, it was a cold, silent place where I could sit by myself with my knees to my chin. It was dark as dark then, the way it was those nights when I had to hold the rope from the barn to keep from losing my way to the house. If the air was warm, there wasn't any difference between me and it. My bones and skin, they were gone as easy as pinching wicks, gone as Father wanted me to be, and I was nothing but quiet and no one could find me. At home, that dark was all I was.

On the road, the sun was coming. The farms were spotty, the houses emptied, the barns boarded like thieves and not a noise. I laid our blanket flat under the cover of bushes. We dropped to eat. "Just a break," I told Myrle and took out the bread, a slice of

cheese I'd hidden in my bag. The bread tasted of nothing. The
cheese even less. She chewed at the food in small bites, half
asleep. The ground was cold but thawing. With the wind, the
bushes caught our hair. It was a fine place for stopping, out of
sight of the road and not a farmhouse. Only a wide trail of grass
in every direction. Far off, the smell of a wood fire, but not any
smoke we could see. Myrle used her bag for a pillow. An hour
or two before we needed to get going, just enough to rest our
feet. Already we'd walked six miles, maybe seven. We had hours
of sun to make the train. Myrle was breathing easy, huddled as
she was and her eyelids jumping. I knew what she dreamed. It
was always the same.

The Elliot boy. At home before we went to sleep, she'd told
me every little bit. The smell of him, musky and warm, different
from what she'd thought. His fingers on her back, teasing her
neck. His hands so large she imagined he could hold all of her
at once. The first time he helped her climb into the loft, made
sure she didn't slip. His mother was gone by then, ours too, and
Lee finally home, but not by much. After the war, none of them
came back, not all the way. The Elliot boy had holes in him you
couldn't really see. "Look," he said when he showed her the scar
on his belly. In the loft, he showed her the money he'd buried
too. He had a tin box, and inside it, a heavy roll of bills. "I can
take care of you, see?" he said. "With what they paid me at least."
That's when he asked if Myrle wouldn't mind lying down for
a rest, and she said she didn't. The Elliot barn wasn't the same
as ours. The loft pushed into the rafters and the boards gaped,
wide enough you could spit on the cows and the hogs below fast
asleep. He touched the collar of her dress, brushed her stomach
between the buttons of her blouse. Bursting, he seemed, as if

all he needed was at his fingertips. He touched her lower then. "Please," he said. "You're the prettiest little thing." The way he asked her, she'd never been wanted so much.

I couldn't help it. After she went to sleep, I imagined I was the one in the loft with him instead.

Months later, the gossip at the dinner table. "The Elliot boy's gotten himself engaged," Patricia said. Myrle hid her face. *The prettiest*, he'd told her. He must have changed his mind.

But it was after that, after what Patricia said. The boy asked Myrle to meet him behind their old smithy. Said he was sorry. His father, he told Myrle, that's all it was, because Old Elliot would never take a Kraut for a daughter-in-law. Still, maybe he could make it right. He stood there shivering, an arm too heavy on her shoulders. The smell of his breath was like milk from our cow. She'd worn her Easter dress for him, thinking something nice might change his mind. So he took her hand gentle like, got her up in that loft again. He got her to lie down for a rest too, but it was different this time. Only later did I see how different it was. "He never said a thing," Myrle said. Just did what he usually did, only hard as knives and twice as fast. His mouth smothered her. His shoulder bucked her chin. And after he finished, he threw himself off as if he'd never wanted to touch her. He didn't help her down that ladder, though her dress was ripped. Didn't wait for her to make it out the barn door. He ran, she said. Like he was scared of himself. All the times before, she'd thought this Tom might be someone. A Tom who whispered sweet things. But that Tom was gone, and she was skin-sore and shivering, making her way through the fields alone.

It was near dark. The grass was full of midges, hoppers too. They scared her with the way they flew up at her feet. She was lucky I saw her coming, looking after her the way I did. Her cheeks were scratched, her lips bitten. I drew her into the washhouse quick. She had more scratches on her legs, the straw splinters in her so deep I had to use pliers. But the worse of it was the bleeding, like he'd tried to split her in half. I scoured her drawers that were nearly black. Her dress I shredded for the rags. Her skin I scrubbed raw of fingertips and everything else. After Tom's wedding, Myrle hid herself in bed in a sweat, everything that boy put in her pouring out. Sick, I told Nan. Nothing else. We kept our door closed, the lamps bright, our food untouched on plates in the hall. I tried to imagine what it was like, being wanted so much it left scars.

After that, I knew I was going. And Myrle, she was going too.

In the daylight now, we walked in the ditches with the scrub. I held the tail of Myrle's coat, she had me by the wrist. We crouched in an overturned wagon to eat the last of our bread, drank from a farmer's buckets. The water tasted like feed. Our boots fit like boxes by then, our barn coats thin. With Myrle slow as she was, by the time we made Clarksville, the sun had risen on us twice. "Where are you two going?" the man at the ticket counter asked. The stitching on his jacket spelled SHELL ROCK RAILROAD, his ears red under his cap. He tapped his knuckles at us. But we had a pocketful of fives and tens from that tin in Elliot's barn. Myrle had taken it herself. She'd surprised me doing that, and the boy could never say he missed it. Not after what he'd done. "All right then," the man said. He scratched at the bald skin under his cap. "Two tickets to Chicago. You girls be careful out and about."

We slept on the benches in the station. We slept in the train. It clumped over the tracks, slow through the boxcar end of town before speeding up. The smell of smoke from the engine, the flicker of kerosene lamps. Outside it was dark and fast and we held onto our seats, the train as loud as a tractor three times over, tearing at the rails as it went. A boy gripped the headrests as he walked the car. A woman put her stitching down, her hand on her stomach. I closed my eyes. Next I knew, the sun was coming again. It had rained the night through. The fields and farmhouses shone. My breath on the window was white. "Myrle," I whispered, but she slumped asleep with her arms over her face. I wrote our initials on that window with my finger. *MH*, I wrote, and *EH* in larger letters. Across from us, the lady glared, and I wiped the letters off quick.

We changed at Waterloo for the Cedar Rapids, rode through McAuburne, Shellsburg, and Bridgeton. We took the Chicago Northwestern across the state line. The Mississippi was a long stretch of water, and we were in a place called Illinois then. Later, roads broke across the fields like splinters, lines of wagons and motorcars. At the railway stations, men in suits crowded the planks, raising their hands. Soon there were sidewalks full of people with long coats and shopping bags, buildings taller than a person could count, and the pitch of horns in the streets. When at last we pulled into Chicago, it was larger than looking up had ever been. The porter tipped his hat at Myrle and we knew we'd made it.

The night before we left, we stayed up near to morning in the kitchen to make sure of our plan. Myrle was set to get the key, and the rope was under my bed, that tin already empty and hidden back where she'd found it. When at last we climbed the stairs to our room, the sun was just rising. It was low and grand, and we watched from our window. The birds were quiet, though I felt they were restless. The fields looked black under that run of light, as if something new waited for us. There were all sorts of sights we didn't know beyond those fields, all sorts of wonders. Myrle rested her head on my shoulder, already dreaming, and I helped her to bed. We'd have only so many hours before break-fast, only so many before Nan knocked on our door to wake us with the day of chores, before we could make our escape after night fell. When I closed my eyes, I could see the road and the brightness up ahead, the long trail that whispered to us, and I felt I was nothing and everything at once.

Later when I came back and Myrle didn't, when I lost her for good, I would think about what it meant to leave and never return. At the window, maybe that was the last time she trusted me so much.

II

Our train pulled to a stop late morning. I had the address of Hurley's Electric in pencil on a card, asked at the station office for a map. "A nickel for that," the woman said without looking.

We sat in the station and ate buns, a cup of coffee Myrle spat out. "This is where we're going," I showed her. "The factories, they're all along the river and the tracks. There's work there." Myrle traced the lines on the map with her finger, mouthing the names of streets. Outside, the city through the windows was a gray lump of clouds. A sweep of strangers' coats hurried through the doors, a woman carrying her dog in a cage. The man at the shop who'd sold us the buns was reading his paper, a group of boys in the corner filling their cheeks from a tin can. The trains whined to a stop, took up passengers, and headed off. My eyes ached.

"You've got your bag now," I told Myrle. "I can't carry it for you."

She stopped her tracing.

"Ready?"

Myrle folded the map neat and put it in her bag.

We walked for hours after that. The streets were cramped and thick with dirt, the motorcars fast as axes. No one paid us any mind. At every corner we stopped and looked down the spill of streets, as if looking could tell us something. When finally we reached the address on my card, those streets emptied out, but the warehouses hummed, the walls as long as blocks. There didn't seem any numbers on those walls, not even a door for knocking. Only vents and docks, the windows starting two floors up. When we stopped at what looked an office, the door was locked. On the front, a square of old paint, where a sign for Hurley's Electric might have been.

"What is it?" Myrle asked.

"Nothing." I hid that card in my hand.

Myrle shifted her bag.

"It must be down a ways," I said. "Come on."

We scuffed our feet. Hurley's wasn't at Clinton and Monroe, and that map of ours didn't do us much better. I checked the same number on different streets. Checked ways those numbers might rearrange themselves into something different. By midafternoon, the lake was in front of us and we crouched on the stones. We couldn't see the other side, not even a speck of land larger than a finger. The waves were slow. Far off, tugboats and ships moved by inches. If anything, the water looked like rutted dirt, as close to home as home ever was, and I wondered if Father was missing us.

"Esther," Myrle said. She sat with her bag tugging at her neck, her mouth to her knees.

"We must have passed the street."

"We're nowhere."

"It's a whole city worth of places."

"It's not Hurley's."

"I must've got the address wrong, but that doesn't mean it isn't somewhere."

She closed her eyes, rubbing at the palm of her hand like it itched. I tapped at her foot. "Hungry?"

She nodded. Before I could take up my bag again, she'd thrown hers over her shoulder and headed back the way we'd come.

The bakery had four short tables and a mess of chairs. A bell rang on the door. We sat with our cups of tea, and out the window, a man stumbled down the street. "What now?" Myrle asked.

I took out the magazine. It was more than crumpled. The woman with her invisible cup of tea, she didn't seem so pretty. Myrle watched me with a dark look and eyed the customers, all of them men. Behind the counter, the baker reached into his oven, pulled out a pan. The men at the tables eyed my sister back. Foxes, I thought.

"Do you know . . . ," Myrle asked them, her voice cracking. ". . . Hurley's Electric?"

I shushed her.

The man closest sat up in his chair. "Hurley's?"

"Hey now." The baker came out, flour on his knuckles, his apron. "What you bothering them for, John?"

John held up his hands.

Myrle reached across the table for the magazine. She gave it to the baker, holding tight to the corner like he might not give it back.

"Oh, that Hurley's," he said. "They've moved most of the business to New York. Nothing but an office on Jefferson now."

"Phsst," I said.

The baker gave me a wink. "That's right. I can't tell you how many of the boys felt the same. A bunch of them companies went to New York. In this neighborhood you'll find textiles more like, garments. What's that you're looking for?"

But I didn't want to give an answer, not for them. Myrle had taken the magazine and rolled it as fine as she could. Bowing her head, she tucked the magazine into her bag.

"Aren't you girls a little young to be wandering?" John asked. "This side of town specially."

"Maybe not," I said.

"This one?" He pointed at my sister with his chin. "She can't be more than what, thirteen?"

"She's none of your business."

"Listen," the baker started. "You two don't want to be around here in an hour. Those whistles go and it's another place altogether. Some of those factory men, they don't care how young you are."

Myrle sat up, her eyes filling.

"You don't got a place, do you?" John asked. I shrugged. He turned to the baker. "Who's your aunt that runs the boardinghouse?"

The baker wiped his hands. "This time a year, I'm sure she's full up."

"Is she?"

"You can try her. Place is on Wells, the North Side. You have to cross the river again. The door is in the alley. You know the North Side?"

"They don't know nothing," John said.

"Geez. What can I do about that?" The baker went behind his counter again and came back with a stack of cards smeared with butter and flour. He looked through them, spitting on his finger when they stuck. "Listen, the North Side is thataway." He pointed out the window. "And Wells is almost straight up. But you got to take the alley behind Huron to find the door. The number's on the card. And it's Mrs. Keyes you want. She's my aunt."

"Is that Mary Keyes, Ed?" John asked.

The baker waved a hand at him. "They don't need to know. Just Keyes. She's got the boardinghouse. But I'd head there fast. She closes her door soon after those whistles go, sometimes even earlier if the girls are all in, and then you'll never get her."

John reached into his pocket, took his wallet out. "Here now, I'll pay for those cups you've got."

I left a quarter on the table instead.

The alley was full of stink and weeds, dark with shadows. At last, a door as clean as a whitewashed fence showed against the brick. At our knock, a woman opened the door an inch. She was wide and pasty-faced, dressed for bed. "Yes?"

"We're here for a room."

"It's awfully late." She yawned. "What are you two doing out this time of night?"

I pointed at her sign. ROOMS FOR LET BY THE MONTH. "We can pay." I handed her the baker's card.

She wrinkled her nose as she dusted it off. "Ed, that old dog. Well, hurry yourselves in. Either that or I'll catch my death." She opened the door. A set of chairs crowded the hall, a rack with a dozen coats or more, bundled with scarves, and a line of shoes, all of them small and worn. Still, the socks in most had lace tops. Girls, I thought.

The woman lit the lamp in the front room and sat with a sigh, her hips tight between the arms of the chair and her thighs fat as muttons. We sat on the sofa across from her, hands in our laps. The room had a mother in it, every inch. Plain and scrubbed. A needlepoint over the fire grate in blue and white stitching. *Code of the Boardinghouse Keeper.* In the corner, a stand of pipes banged for dear life. Myrle gripped my hand.

"You must be farm girls," the woman said. "Those pipes always scare them. But they're just for heat. What good they do. The name's Keyes. Keyes with an extra *e*—no jokes about it. The board is twenty a month, includes breakfast, dinner, and laundry every other week. More and you pay fifty cents a wash, but no proper girl I know needs more than that. We keep on time here for meals, no running in last minute. No leftovers either. We're a proper board, rules and all. You'll have to share a room of course, and the lavatory's down the hall. Bathing is on Sundays, behind the kitchen. I'll need your papers for starters."

"Papers?"

"I assume you have work in one of the factories."

A girl came running down the stairs. She wore her hair combed short above her ears, a blue dress that showed her calves, and shoes like slippers. "Isabelle," Mrs. Keyes snapped. "It's almost curfew." Isabelle let out a huff and was out the door. Keyes stretched her neck, looking after her. With a quick turn of her head, she remembered us.

"Work?" she asked.

Myrle opened her mouth. "We just started," I hurried in.

"Because I only let rooms for the workers. This isn't a flophouse. It doesn't do for just a night, not even a week. We expect long-term. There aren't so many of us boarding houses left . . . ."

Something caught in her throat. Her eyes teared and she slapped her chest. "Your papers?" she coughed.

I opened my bag, rustled through the blouses and skirts.

"What's wrong with this one?" Mrs. Keyes asked. "Doesn't she talk?"

I elbowed Myrle, but she was near to a fit. "Just shy."

"And exhausted by the look of it, pale too. That girl needs iron if I ever saw one."

"Yes, ma'am." I went back to my ruffling.

Mrs. Keyes yawned again. "If it's so much fuss . . ." Her eyes were closing. She blinked and opened them. "I suppose since it was Ed who sent you, you can show me your papers in the morning. It's much too late as it is. You're lucky. A girl left this morning. Otherwise, I wouldn't have opened the door. In bed with my tea, I would've been. And that would've been a lesson to you, wouldn't it?"

Mrs. Keyes put a finger to her lips, and we climbed the stairs, her bottom so wide I couldn't see a thing. On the second floor she stopped at a door like all the others and held out her hand. I counted a night's worth of rent, then a week's when she clicked her tongue. "Wake up is five a.m.," she whispered. "You'll hear a knock. If you need more than that, you've got bigger problems than you think."

When she left, I opened the door. Even in the dark, the room looked no bigger than a stall. A single bed and a desk, a sink in the corner, and a closet large enough for five hangers and a pair of shoes, but just. The pipes banged out little heat, the floor like stones. Myrle lit the lamp and threw herself still dressed under the sheets. I counted it out: Ten nights we could afford. Never thought that pile of fives and tens could go so quick. But we wouldn't tell Keyes we couldn't pay the month. Across the room, a mirror showed me in my boots and coat. They were slick with dust, as if Keyes couldn't guess what we did and didn't have. I stripped to the skin. In that mirror, I had never seen so much of myself. The pipes kicked up a storm. Myrle quiet under the sheets. But I was naked as I wanted to be and open in the open air, spinning one way and the next to feel that air on my skin. The mirror had me straight as a board, nothing in front to fill out those dresses in magazines. I pinched my chest. Still every day could be different. Even mirrors knew that.

"Esther . . ."

I spun around, my arms to my chest. Myrle sat with her hands over her ears.

"It's only the pipes," I said.

"Sounds like someone's under the floor trying to get in."

"It's nothing."

She sank against her pillow, scratching at her hand again. "We could send a letter home, tell them about Mrs. Keyes."

"We can't write letters."

"But won't they worry?"

"You want them to come get us? And Tom Elliot too, after his money."

Myrle went quiet. "I don't think he'd come."

I pulled my nightgown over my head so she couldn't see my face. "We don't have paper for letters." My nightgown fell. I could have been any girl I wanted, but there was Myrle watching my every step. "All right, all right," I said, but I didn't look at her. "We can get paper tomorrow."

Myrle turned to the wall. I searched through the desk drawers. No letters without paper. Under the top ledge, a thinner drawer, no deeper than a finger. It whined when I pulled it out, but Myrle didn't give a twitch. Inside, a single sheet with a girlish scrawl: *sister*. The rest was a blank space, the word *sister* crossed right through. I folded the paper up tight and looked to hide it, but the room was bare as a cup. Not a rug, a crack. At last, I dropped it in my mouth. It was a sour piece of chew, but it couldn't be used for letters, not anymore. At the back of the drawer, something rolled against the wood. I reached in. It was a small silver ring. The ring was lighter than a dime, a flat blue stone and a silver band, just sitting there wanting to be someone's. I tried it on, but it wouldn't budge over my knuckle. I tried it again. Crouching on the bed, I shook Myrle's shoulder and called her name.

"Look, isn't it something?" I slipped the ring over her finger.

"Whose is it?"

"It's no one's."

She held the ring close to her face. Already her eyes were closing again.

"It's yours," I said.

She smiled a little. "Isn't it time to go to sleep?"

"Sure." Though I was more than awake. Still I slipped under the sheets with her and turned out the light. It was only then I thought of that piece of paper in my stomach. *Sister*, it'd said, and nothing else. As if a girl knew I would read it, knew I was just beginning at that blank space at the top. A strange thing to keep a girl fed for the night.

The wake-up knock rattled down the hall, one door after another. Five a.m., Keyes had said. The windows were black. Black when we'd gone to sleep and black in the morning. I lay against my pillow and wondered if it would ever turn light. A slip of curtains hung over the windows, hardly enough to stop drafts. Papers, Keyes would want, just like Myrle, but we didn't have any papers. We didn't have anything yet. Myrle slept curled to the wall, her nose whistling. Our clothes were wadded rags and smoky from the train, a fine stink. A snatch of dirt in the bottom of our bags had left smudges. I wondered where that dirt came from. The train or earlier, when we'd slept by the road under the bushes, listening for anyone who might come looking. But no one did. No one seemed to have tried.

Voices rushed from below. Myrle sat up, rubbing her eyes. "What's that?"

"Come on. If we want breakfast, we've got to run."

Down the stairs, a dozen heads turned at the sound of our feet. The girls were a blur in blue uniforms, their hair pulled into ponytails with strings. On the table sat bowls of porridge and muffins, glasses of yellow juice with pulp on the rims. I stopped on the bottom step, Myrle at my back. At the far end, an older girl sat with her elbows on the table, the yellow tips of her fingers pressed together like a tent. She had red hair and curls, the rest of her bluish pale. She didn't look up with the others, but when she did, she stretched out her arms, offering us the empty chairs at her side.

The others went on eating. Some were skinny and big-eyed, some not. Some so dull-looking, I feared I'd be the same in under a month. But it was the redhead who Myrle watched. The redhead gave back such a grin, it could have spun milk.

"There you are." The kitchen door swung and in rushed Mrs. Keyes. "Most the girls come dressed. You won't have time before the whistle if you don't." She gave us plates, silverware. "Go on, why don't you? Serve yourselves. This isn't a restaurant."

Myrle kept her head down, her sleeves pulled tight to her wrists.

"You have those papers I asked for?"

I started to speak, but something crashed in the kitchen. Mrs. Keyes looked sharp. "Ellen!" she called and pounded back.

The redhead ducked her chin. "You don't have work, do you?"

I kicked Myrle to keep her quiet. "We have a place."

"You don't even have a uniform," Red said. "Listen, you can't let on or Keyes'll have a fit. I know Kupp's got a spot. That's garments. You can work a sewer, right?" The girl looked at my hands. "Right. A spot for one, but I don't know about your sister. She old enough?"

"Maybe. Maybe not."

Mrs. Keyes rushed in again, the flowers of her blouse loud under her apron. "Those papers?"

"I'll bring them tonight," I said.

She huffed. "Very well, but that door closes at nine. Not a second after. And you best be in or you two will be sleeping on the steps." Mrs. Keyes stopped herself. "What place did you say again?"

"Kupp's."

"Ah yes, Kuppenheimer's. Like nearly every girl here. Garments."

Another glass broke in the kitchen, then what sounded a whole tray. "My sakes." Mrs. Keyes ran off. My napkin flew from my lap as she went. The other girls pushed back their chairs. The kitchen door swung. On the other side, a girl in pigtails stood pale-faced with a mess at her feet. Mrs. Keyes loomed over her like a bear. "That's the last I tell you, Ellen."

The redhead laughed. "Ellen's dumb as a plate. But don't let those pigtails fool you. She's been here for years. Longer than me, at least. I'm Charlotte." She held her hand out. Like a man, she did.

"Esther," I said.

"And this one?" Charlotte turned her head. "You're some pretty, aren't you, and shy too."

"That's my sister."

"Myrle," my sister whispered. When she glanced up, her cheeks colored, seeing Charlotte all at once.

"Sisters," the redhead let out. "I never had one myself."

"Never?" Myrle asked. "I've got three." She covered her mouth.

"Never," Charlotte said again. "Not yet."

The table was empty now of everyone but us. Charlotte slapped her hand on her chair. "Come on now, we have to get you to Kupp's. We'll be late." She stood with a rush. Tall as a tree, so much I straightened to see her right. "Meet you in front, five minutes," she called back and raised her hand to show five long fingers. Without another word, she disappeared down the hall.

We sat alone, staring at our plates. The blush in Myrle's cheeks had stayed. I thought about Charlotte. I thought about our room, small as a stable. There wasn't a Nan at the door. Not a Father with his cane. No Agnes eyeing us, either, watching for what we'd do, as if we'd do anything. Tom Elliot, he was gone. No more lofts, no fires in the yard. That room, it was all our own. The walls pocked with nails and tape, a key for the door, a desk, and a bureau's empty drawers. All of it, ours, and only strangers in the rooms down the hall. Every morning when the house woke, we could be anything we wanted. Now Myrle stretched her fingers, liking her ring. Already she seemed different. In the café, speaking up the way she did. At the table with Charlotte. Even now, not a drop of worry and me almost out the door.

We had a room and a bowl of porridge. We had the city and a wide stretch of lake. We had Kupp's too, and not even a full day yet. Home, it seemed a long ways off. And trains, they seemed hard. Already I felt I'd eaten breakfast at this table for weeks. I'd learned the name of every girl in the house, easy, as if I'd always known them. As if I'd been born here, and I might as well have been. I couldn't imagine a better place.

"Are you going?" Myrle asked. For a flash, her eyes watered.

"Have to."

"Remember the paper," she said. "You promised."

"A heap of it. Envelopes too."

Myrle brightened, took our plates, the mess heavy in her arms. The kitchen door swung open. Mrs. Keyes steamed out only to pull up short. "My heavens," she said. "I about knocked you sideways. Don't you have any sense?"

Myrle offered up the plates. Mrs. Keyes rested her hands on her hips. "Cleared the plates already," she said. "You must have some sense after all. Come on in then. You can put them on the counter. Ellen!" she called. The door swung closed behind them. "Watch this new girl with the plates. That's how it's done."

Charlotte had us down the alley in minutes. The first whistle. That's why she was running, and I was running too, that red of her hair a flag. While the streets churned with people, that red was the only thing that kept her in sight. When at last we stopped enough to slow our chests, we stood at the foot of a large iron door. The building was stone and brick, as great as a ship, and it breathed the way I guessed a ship might, a wheeze from the upper windows that looked small and black and not really windows at all. "This way," Charlotte said. When she pulled the door open, the building roared. A line of workers with punch cards and lunches, women and men in dusty blue uniforms. Charlotte swept a sweaty hair off her cheek and took me by the hand. Around the corner, a hall longer than anything ever was, and a sign with the word OFFICE in gold.

"Now listen," Charlotte said. This close, even her eyelashes were orange. "When you go in there, you pretend you've been doing this for years. Longer even. And you tell them I brought you. Charlotte Byrne. Don't forget." She squeezed my hands. Then she was off.

I took a breath. Inside, a large man sat at a desk in a room big enough to store wagons. His lamp glowed through its green glass, the name MR. PRESTON on a block of wood. He bent his face to his papers, a sad circle of hair on his head. When at last he looked up, he grimaced. "Name?"

"Esther."

"Esther what?"

"Esther . . . Byrne."

"Another one," he said. "Well, Esther Byrne, come out and show yourself. You want a job?"

Come out yourself, mister. But I didn't say it. I didn't for once.

The workshop at Kuppenheimer's was long and narrow as a train car, five floors up, the ceiling almost on our heads. When Preston opened the elevator, I saw waves. A line of girls sat at their machines, fingers flying with scissors and thread. Those machines were close to on top of each another, a hundred or so at once, and the needles whirred. Unless a girl watched herself, any bit of hair or skin might catch. Clouds of cotton kept the air thick. Fuzz of every color stuck to their cheeks. The windows were so dirty the day didn't show itself, the girls closest to those windows sewing by lamplight like all the rest. Preston led me down the line, but not one of the workers turned her head. The girls were sweating through their collars, the muscles in their necks jumping with Preston at their backs, but their machines never quit.

For me he found a chair at the far end. A large black sewing machine waited on the desk. Preston threw me some scrap and crossed his arms. The man was bigger than me by twice, and those hands of his, they could sure fix fences. "Go on," he said. "You practice on these, just a hem at a quarter inch. Straight is good but quick is better. If you keep your head about you, we'll give you a uniform."

"What about . . . ?"

The girl next to me gasped, but she kept on spinning.

"What about what?" Preston asked.

"Nothing." I picked up my scraps, and he went off. The girl wiped her nose on her sleeve, her fingers a blur. Her eyelashes flicked at me.

"You don't know what you're doing, do you?" she whispered.

"Maybe," I said. "Maybe not."

"Do it then."

I turned to the machine. A dragon, it sure looked, twisted the way it was, and the heat of the wheel every time I hit the pedal. Electric. But this wasn't light and cups of tea. The place smelled like burning. A single lamp hung over our heads, my face close to the needle so I could see. When I pressed the pedal, that needle pulled fast. The scraps flew, and only my fingers were left. I pushed at the pedal softer then, but still that dragon caught me every other time, just when I was going grand. After an hour or more, my fingers were scraps too. I stuck them in my mouth. The taste of blood. Around me girls worked without even looking, like they'd always been sitting there, cool as dolls, and they were the ones who got the uniform and walked out with their paycheck every week. The room was spinning. I wouldn't get my papers. Wouldn't last Chicago more than a day, though I'd promised Myrle something different. Everyone watched me though they pretended they didn't, sitting as I was with my fingers in my mouth.

The girl next to me sneezed into her sleeve. She sneezed again, worse than a cat. But with every sneeze, her elbow slipped against my desk. It was then I saw it, a new scrap and then another under that elbow of hers, and not so much as a smile on her face. "Thanks," I whispered and started my pedal again. This time, I pulled against that needle, kept my fingers light. By the end of the shift, I had that wheel going inside my head, but I'd hemmed the rest of the lot he'd given me and some of the girl's too, straight as I could.

A whistle, loud as knives. The girls stood from their chairs, the place going quiet as the machines stopped. "Byrne!" Preston called out. He took up my scraps. "Pretty good, pretty good. What's this?" He eyed a bloody one. I hid my hands behind my back.

"Nothing," I said.

"These are expensive machines, young lady. They aren't for fingers."

Phsst, I thought, but I didn't say it. I knew I'd done better than he might have guessed.

"Practice," he said. "We'll give you to the end of the week and see if you're worth keeping. And here." He threw me a uniform. Old, with a stain, but it was something. Preston walked off with that heavy gait of his, and I stood from my chair and followed the rest. The girl next to me, she was all elbows and knees, but she grinned. *Worth keeping*. That's what the man had said. And there was Charlotte, waiting by the door at the far end with that red of her hair a sign.

"Guess we're sisters, now?" She winked.

I took her arm, strong and muscle-thin, a smell like smoke in her hair. But it was the whir of those machines I remembered. I never thought I would hear so much. I could feel it in my bones. Electric in my skin. With that uniform over my arm, my chance to become something else.

I started as a shirtwaist maker. Not a cent those first weeks, though at home I'd worked Mother's pump machine to turn out plenty. "Nothing more than a bicycle," Preston said to that, but soon he gave me six dollars a week. If I could make a year, he promised seven. But I would never take all of that seven home. If I laughed or spoke, I was fined ten cents. Five cents for a mistake. Five off our checks every week for needles and five for benzine, what they used to clean collars and waists, even if I never soiled a waist once. If I was one minute late, I was fined a cent. If five minutes, I lost half a day's pay. I got five cents an hour except breaks, thirty-three dimes a week, though those fines made it less. Seven to seven we worked, twelve hours a day. Saturdays the same. Still those dimes were mine. Mine and Myrle's. It was more than I ever thought we'd get.

Factory girls. That's what they called us. It wasn't women with pink dresses and washing machines, but it was something. In any case, the heat from those machines made me think electric could be anything I wanted. And Chicago, it was the only place I knew other than home. *Chicago.* Even if the name sounded like spitting. Charlotte told me better. "I've seen plenty of girls leave the factory for a ring, but I've never seen one leave this town. It sticks."

III

Every night after shift, I came home with my fingers curled, my feet pinched from the throb of that pedal. I was almost asleep when Keyes cleared the dinner plates. Upstairs, Myrle sat at our desk with a stack of paper. At the end of the month, she'd run through so many fits and starts, her balled-up letters filled the garbage pail. But that night when I came in, she stopped her pencil, closed it in the drawer. She was more pale than ever, a milky glow to her skin. She folded up a single sheet and dropped it in an envelope, licking that envelope twice.

"Can you mail a letter tomorrow?" she asked.

I lay on our bed with my eyes closed. "I'll try." *I told you,* I'd argued. *They'll find us. Tom Elliot will be wanting his money, sure.* She slipped her letter in the pocket of my coat. I heard her pat that pocket twice. Then she was out the door and down the hall to the washroom.

I waited until her footsteps faded and slipped out of bed. That pail was full to spilling. *Dear Father,* one scrap said. And the others: *I wasn't sure . . . I couldn't help . . . I'm sorry that we did.* The pencil blurred, a scratch where she'd tried to black out what she didn't want. I wondered how that letter in my coat was different. How she'd finally gotten it right.

The doorknob turned. I hurried to bed. Coming in, Myrle wiped her mouth.

"What's wrong?" I asked.

She dropped beside me, her hands to her face. I threw my arm over her stomach where I could feel her breathe.

"Esther?"

"What?"

She turned until our noses almost touched. "You'll send my letter, won't you?"

I swallowed. The house below us had fallen to a sure hush.

"I'll send it," I promised. "First thing tomorrow."

She lay on her back, gripping my wrist. Soon her breath was slow and even, but her grip on me never let up. At night my hands snapped and flinched the way they did on the line. Threads and needles, that's what I dreamed about. Pinpricks up and down my arm. Myrle had her dreams too. But after a month, I didn't have a clue what they were. As long as she stayed in this room, in the house, I didn't have to worry if she was safe or not.

The next day, I took her letter before shift like I'd promised. I opened it a crack and read what I could. But when I tried the postbox, the door wouldn't budge. The Elliot boy and his money, that's why we couldn't write. And the Elliot boy's new wife, the way we'd left without a word, and how they'd track us if they had an address. Myrle wouldn't listen, but I'd never have to tell her what I did with that letter. Right where I stood, a garbage bin loomed big as postboxes, and no doors to get stuck. I dropped the letter in, wiped my hands on my thighs. No matter what Chicago did, that old house we'd left didn't have anything new for us. Everything would be forgiven as long as we never went back.

*   *   *

The next night at dinner, one of the girls was missing. Her chair stood empty at the far end, and Mrs. Keyes hadn't set a place. Keyes stayed in the kitchen, and the girls were quiet. All I could think of was Myrle's letter. *Dear Nan,* she'd written with her pencil. *We're safe in Chicago and working hard.* She talked about her work in the house, how I came home in the dark every night and didn't have a breath to talk. And then: . . . *I should have explained before, and now we're so far away. Just let me try.* But why would Myrle write about Chicago if she didn't want them to find us? What did she have to explain?

"That was Isabelle's place," Charlotte whispered.

"Isabelle," I said, as if tasting it.

"Don't you remember her?"

"Jezebel, more like," I heard. In the chair next to me, Dolores stared at me like the nit she was.

"What did you say?"

"Jezebel." Dolores grinned. "It's not like a person couldn't guess what was going to happen to her."

From across the table, Abigail let out a chirp. "What do you mean?"

"What do you mean?" Dolores aped. "I *mean* that anyone in their right mind could tell she'd get herself in trouble, going out every night. I don't know why Mrs. Keyes didn't throw her out months ago."

"Heard they sent her to Loretto Hall," added a girl at the other end.

"The Catholics!" another said.

"She'll be a sister next," Dolores laughed. "Hey, Abigail, what kind of girl are you, pins or needles?"

"What?" Abigail looked around.

"She doesn't get it," the girl at the end said.

"I mean *pins* . . ." Dolores sat up straight and blinked, her hands clasped in front of her like praying. " . . . or needles?" Making a circle with forefinger and thumb, she stuck her finger through. The girls shrieked. Dolores crooned, "Here comes Abigail in her white . . ."

"Knock it off," Charlotte snapped. The table went quiet. Every eye shot to the kitchen, but Keyes was humming to her radio. "Just wait until your chair is empty too," Charlotte said. "Nobody's here for good."

The others went back to their food, not a word. *For good*, she'd said, but what if this place was everything I wanted? I'd thought Myrle had wanted it too, but when I looked, my sister was staring at the empty chair. Her plate was full. She hadn't even touched her spoon. "Myrle," I hissed. Abigail elbowed her. Myrle's head snapped back, her eyes wide. She pushed at her chair and was up the stairs in a rush, the others staring after her. In the kitchen, a bell rang. A creak as Keyes opened the oven door and dropped a pan of bread on the counter to cool. That bread smelled like earth. Our room upstairs, it smelled like that.

"She's sick," I said.

"Mr. Preston was sick something awful today," Abigail let out. "Every time he walked by, I was scared he'd sneeze on my head."

"You wish," Dolores said.

Abigail giggled.

"She's got a crush," Dolores went on. "And the man is old enough to need bifocals."

The kitchen door opened. Keyes bounded out. "You girls have been awfully quiet. Where's Myrle?"

"She's sick," Abigail said.

I would have kicked her if it had done any good. "She'll be fine by morning. She's never sick for long."

"See to it that she isn't," Keyes said. "I've had just about enough of sickness and who knows what else. You girls have got to learn to take care of yourselves. Terrible things can happen. The kinds of things you can't take back." She shook the thought out of her head. "Now hurry up, the rest of you. It's time for bed. Esther, you can help me with the dishes if your sister can't."

Keyes blew into the kitchen again, the radio louder by a good turn of the knob. The chairs at the table banged, everyone off in a rush. Everyone except Charlotte. She squeezed my knee, her face hard as Nan's. "Myrle's all right," I said. But that look on Charlotte's face, it didn't change. Not an inch. What business was it of hers? Charlotte squeezed my knee all the harder. "She's fine," I spat and tore my leg away. With her sitting there, I snapped up the plates and rushed into the kitchen to wash.

After an hour Keyes let me go. I climbed the stairs and opened our door. Myrle stood in front of the mirror in her nightgown, staring down at herself.

"I thought you'd be asleep."

She jumped to the bed, covered herself with the sheet.

"What's wrong with you?"

She didn't move. Her eyes were closed, the rest of her curled toward the wall.

"Myrle?"

"It's nothing," she said.

"If it's nothing, you do the dishes next time." I dropped onto the mattress and let out a groan. I couldn't bend enough to take off my shoes, my hands swollen. The chain clicked against the lamp as I turned it off, the heaters kicking for who knew what, and outside an icy rain scraped the windows. Lightning flared, flashing shapes on the wall: a tree, a bird, the face of a stranger.

"Esther?" Myrle said. Her voice was muffled. Her back to me still.

"What?"

"I'm sorry."

"Phsst," I said. My feet ached, a pulsing in my fingertips. Myrle sniffled, but I didn't have anything more to give her. The windows shook and the storm flashed. I had never seen so much coming from a light through our window, as if the world had turned or we ourselves had, the whole place moving every little inch, and no one knew why or when it would stop.

It was another month before Myrle wrote a second letter. She wrote one every week after that. In the morning, she left them on her desk or tucked them in the pocket of my coat. I carried the letters off, swearing to send them. *Father*, they'd been addressed, or *Nan, Lee*. Even *Agnes. We're sorry to have left*, or *Tell Father, we're sorry*. Then she stopped saying sorry and all she wrote about was home. *It's never so nice as home*, she wrote. *And always a wind. It's never clean. There's a lake*, she wrote, *bigger than all our acres put together, but I've only seen it once*. I left for the shop at half after six every morning, leaving Myrle to Mrs. Keyes, and dropped the letters in the garbage. Better to let her believe the letters were going out. Better to keep her busy, and me, I could read every single one and know more about my sister than I could ever guess.

"Just give me the money," she said once. Two months, and we'd never heard a word.

"Don't you trust me?" I asked.

Her face was pinched, her mouth tight. But those eyes of hers, they pulled on me like water did. "If you gave me some money, I could take them myself."

I stood at the door, Myrle sitting at her desk. She had that pencil in her hand, but she wasn't writing a thing. "You don't, do you?" I said. "You don't trust me."

She wouldn't look at me.

I opened the door, the voices of the other girls in the hall. Who could say it'd make one difference if I sent those letters? If anyone at home even cared? I grabbed my coat, swung the door wide, ready to slam it shut. I yelled at her, "It's not my fault no one writes you back."

The next morning, Myrle's desk was clean as a plate. Not a sheet of paper. Not a pencil in the well. I brushed my fingers across the surface and all I felt was grain. Inside the pocket of my coat, only lint. I walked to work with Charlotte and when we came to that garbage bin, I steered us away.

"Preston had a date last night, couldn't you tell?" Charlotte said. "He left at seven sharp, even changed his shirt. Who do you think she was?"

In the shop, Charlotte sat next to me at the machines with her mouth still running, her chair inches from mine. That girl with her elbows and knees, she was gone my second week, and I never got her name. But sitting next to Charlotte, that was something. Charlotte was an old hand. She talked a mile our first hour, never got caught. She had three years or more on most of us, from a boondock kind of town where everyone she'd ever known was buried or run off or too dumb for either one. She left when she was little older than Myrle, and she didn't care if no one married her or kept her in a kitchen, or so she said. She had a cigarette between her lips soon as she walked out the door, wore trousers more than not in winter. The smokes gave her the hips of a girl, and every other week her red hair seemed a different shade.

"What's up with you?" she asked.

"Nothing."

"Nothing," Charlotte parroted. "Liar."

My needle stuck. I stopped the machine and pulled the strip. Ten cents fine that would be. Another cent for every word if Charlotte kept on running, even if I tried not to listen.

"She didn't write a letter," I said.

Charlotte sighed. "So what? They never write back."

"Maybe they would."

"Maybe she's tired of it."

"Of what?"

"I don't know. All that . . . attention."

I bit my lip, my machine roaring.

"Come on, Esther, you know what I'm talking about. Everyone in that house of yours always following her around, watching, as if she was some kind of dolly they could dress up. Maybe she's figured she doesn't want it anymore."

"What do you know?"

"Myrle and me, we talk."

"I've never heard you talk about that."

"We talk a lot when you're not there."

I'm always there. But not when Charlotte got off first from shift, because of the old hand she was. Not when she woke up early and helped Myrle in the kitchen. All the time they spent together, without their thinking of me. An odd pair, with Charlotte tall and bright, hard as nails, and Myrle nothing next to her but a pale leaf. The two of them, whispering over plates on the other side of that swinging door. That time opened under me like a dark hole.

"Cheer up." Charlotte elbowed me and I almost lost a stitch. "There'll be a raise, did you hear? The union got them for us. Ten percent."

Another fine if I'd lost that stitch. Another if I couldn't keep my mind from letters. Myrle must have her reasons, but I couldn't think. A raise, that might give us enough for a pound of sugar every month, coffee even, the extra in a sock for safe-keeping under the bed. I wiped my forehead and started again.

"I'll tell you more at noon break," Charlotte said. "Just forty minutes."

I ducked my head. Break I might have to miss to catch up. Besides, I wasn't keen to climb those flights for a piece of bread. I was sweated right through. "The elevator," Preston said, "it's not for factory girls."

Factory girls. The way Preston said it, the name seemed a trick. Nothing a nice girl would try to be. And after that first day, I'd never seen the inside of that elevator. It made me dizzy, all its cables and strings. Preston as he loomed, his arm reaching over me to press the button. The man smelled strong as metal. Something that made a person want to take a bite. *Esther's got work in the garments,* Myrle had written once. *Save Sundays, I never see her in the daytimes.* Myrle's empty desk and now Preston in my head. That's where my daytimes went. Preston, in his office on the first floor, thinking about ten percent. I hated him at my back with his big hands watching us. But I hated it even more when he wasn't there.

Charlotte dropped back to her machine, half a sandwich in a napkin. Somehow break had come and went, my foot on the pedal still. She snuck the sandwich onto my table, covered it with scrap. *All that attention*, she'd said. Who didn't want that? And Myrle, she'd never seemed to mind it before. I gave Charlotte a smile thin enough it wouldn't bring foremen, but enough to tell her how empty my stomach was. I could eat that sandwich in the stall when they unlocked the doors for bathroom break, two hours off.

"After the last bell," Charlotte whispered. I could just hear her over the room's buzz. "Everyone's been asked to line up at the office. We have to get there in a hurry or we'll be waiting in that line for hours."

I frowned though my hands never stopped.

"Don't be so worried," she said. "It's the raise. They want to make a big show of it, give it out by hand."

"Number 57!" the foreman called. Charlotte snapped straight, her fingers fast. She seemed to work four pieces at once. The foreman circled our line and stood behind our chairs, watching our hands. Girls said he'd be good for a ring, but that ring would be small, his fingers no more than buttons and his ears wide as a chipmunks. I didn't want a man as hard as that. I eyed the sandwich hidden under that scrap, but didn't drop a stitch. "A pretty penny it'll be, right, girls?" the foreman said. Charlotte gave me a wink. A sandwich in the factory, that could cost us plenty. Still the man walked away, humming. I guessed even foremen got a raise after the seven o'clock bell.

*   *   *

At five after seven, we stood in our line. The air outside the windows was cold and black, as it had been that morning and the morning before. The line snaked over the gray tiles, workers pushing at each other's backs. A man as round he was tall pulled a chain from his jacket, giving his watch a glance.

"Ladies and gentlemen, please." He cleared his throat. "Workers, please, just a moment of your time." The line went quiet. The man slipped his watch in his pocket.

Charlotte leaned close. "That's Stanley Mills. He's the fat duck they brought from New York. Say he's reviewing the books."

"Ladies and gentlemen. I'm sure you've all heard about the concern over market numbers." A murmur from the crowd. At the far end, shouts. Mills wiped his face. "I'm here to insure you that Kuppenheimer and Company is as strong as ever, and that your company will remain in Chicago, where it was born. To prove this to you, we have decided to go forward with the raises the union negotiated and to which your owner, Henry Kuppenheimer, so generously agreed. We want to emphasize, however, that a company is only as good as the number of products it sells. Therefore, we are keeping the company store open late this week and next, newly stocked with a line of shirts, trousers, and smocks that we believe you'll find well within your means. These things were made by your own friends. You should be proud to wear them. We hope you understand how essential it is that our workers are not only satisfied with their wages, but that they put this money to good use. So remember, every dime Kuppenheimer's earns is money in your pocket too."

"My pocket's got a hole!"

"A hundred of those dimes ain't half a nickel to us."

Mills wiped his brow. "Well, yes. It all has to go around." He raised his hand again before stepping back. "Thank you for listening. And remember, this week and the next."

Voices echoed through the hall and the man hurried off. The squeak of rubber shoes, the stink of our uniforms. One by one we stepped into the office, and the guard at the door pushed a finger against his nose as if he'd never sweated once.

"Quarter an hour," Preston told us. It wasn't Kuppenheimer behind that door, but Preston, always Preston. The office was dark, save for those green underwater lamps, the curtains so thick they looked like blankets. Mills crouched by the wall, the arms of his chair pinching his stomach. Preston stood behind his desk with a metal box, two men in suits at his side. The men eyed his hands as he passed out the money, a clipboard and pen at their belts to cross off numbers, names. A quarter, that was more than ten percent. Of course they wanted to make a show of it. But when he counted out more for the man ahead of me, that quarter didn't seem like much. The man worked the looms, a dark knot of curls on his head and skinny as a rail. He pocketed his bills without a glance, as if the suits might take them back.

I did the math. "That man got forty cents. His raise was almost twice."

Charlotte hushed me. "Keep your voice down."

Preston looked away as he counted bills into my hand, his fingers on my wrist as if I might drop so much at once.

"That man got more," I said.

Preston closed the lid on his box. "You're going to rob that man of his wages?" He pressed his knuckles into the desk. I smelled that metal on his breath, the suits tapping their pens. "He supports a family on that, missy."

"Fifteen cents difference?"

"As your husband will make when you marry and no longer have to work."

"Phsst," I let out. The man from the looms, so thin you could see right through him, his fingers spindles, not enough for a woman to put a ring on if she tried.

"Girls can't work the looms," Preston went on. "A man could lose a finger every day when he does."

"I wouldn't lose a finger," I said.

"A girl like you," he said, "she'd look better outside this shop than in."

"Phsst."

Charlotte stamped my foot. For fifteen more cents I could buy myself a finger.

"That's right," Preston said. "You don't know what hurt is. That man does. He's a veteran. That's why he's forty cents."

Charlotte pinched my arm and hurried me out. Behind us, Preston went back to his box. Outside in the hall the workers were asleep on their feet. So much for the show, I thought. But a quarter, that was something at least. And Preston, he was even more. Every time he pushed at me he was, though I had to work him until he paid me any kind of attention. *A girl like you*, he'd said. Finally somebody paid a little.

It was almost curfew as we rushed through the streets. The line had made us late, and Keyes wasn't keen to open the door after she'd turned the lock. That'd be a lesson to us, she'd say. The woman was dropping the bolt when we hit the steps. "Good heavens," she let out. "Like the dark raised you up." She shook her head. "You missed your supper. I can't keep plates for you. If I ever started that, they might as well stop the clocks, but you'll find bread in the kitchen."

"Only bread?" Charlotte asked.

"It'll be a lesson to you, coming in late. So many of you girls late tonight. A half dozen I haven't laid eyes on yet. It's none of my business where a girl keeps herself, but if you want supper, you'll sit at the table tomorrow as you're intended."

Twenty-five cents, I almost said. That's what happened to the other girls, that and the line, while me and Charlotte stood up front and passed the others with our pockets full. Charlotte caught my arm. I guessed what she was thinking. If Keyes found out about the raise, she'd up the rent before we could turn our backs.

We hurried to the kitchen. A loaf of cracked wheat left from the morning, no butter. We broke off pieces with our hands. Charlotte stopped with her ear to the hall and went swift as a broom to the icebox. "I know just where she keeps the jam." The bread was dry as my fingers, but I didn't need iceboxes, not if Keyes might catch us. "Don't you worry," Charlotte went on. "I heard her tell Ellen she wanted to get rid of the whole lot. 'Can't fill the girls with sweets,' she said. 'It'll spoil them something terrible.'"

"That'd be a lesson," I said.

Charlotte grinned, pulling out a jar the color of blueberries. "Keyes is softer than she looks."

"Soft as cracked wheat."

"The nervous mother type. Anyone lays a hand on us, she'd give a limb to fix it. You and Myrle stay long, you'll find out."

The way she said my sister's name, it sounded sweet. Charlotte popped the lid, her ear to the hall again should Keyes get curious, and we dipped our fingers. On Charlotte's wrist, a scar. It looked like a cut from a knife, poorly healed. It took the light in that old kitchen to see it at all.

"What's that?" I pressed a finger to her wrist.

Charlotte jerked back. She rolled up her sleeve to show the scar. It traveled several inches up her arm. "This? It's something I did once, long time ago. I was paying too much attention."

"To what?"

She shook her head. "There are better ways to disappear from a place. You already know that."

She rolled down her sleeve. The jam had left our nails sticky and cold. No matter how we sucked, we couldn't get them clean.

"I know about you, Esther," she said. "You think people don't get you. But that's just you, giving them too much say."

We climbed the stairs stomach-sick. I opened our door and Myrle was hunched in bed under the dim lamp, her nightgown a tent from throat to shin, her head in a magazine. The cover of it was upside down. "I thought you'd never come."

I dropped my bag.

"Mrs. Keyes was at me again, complaining about the silver. I told her I'd never cleaned silver in my life. Ellen, she's the one who does it. But Mrs. Keyes made me try three times over. 'To learn it proper,' she said."

I shook my dress and apron off. Dust from my uniform filled the square of light. Slumped on the bed, I stretched my fingers, rough and red-crusted. I bunched them into fists and stretched them again until my knuckles went quiet.

"She's terrible," Myrle went on. "She never lets me stop, not for a minute."

"Not even a minute?" I asked. Myrle had a look on her face, the kind I'd seen every night for weeks, that worry of hers back for good. There was meat to her now. Keyes must have given her more than the rest of us because she cleaned the house, every scrap.

"It's not fair," she said. "I never get out of this place. You're off every day, working. Out with the other girls."

"You've got Ellen."

"Sometimes I don't even know if it's hot or cold outside."

"Cold." I pulled the magazine from her fingers. The pages had curled, but the smiles on those women were just as tight. What kind of Chicago they lived in, I couldn't guess.

"Esther." Myrle rested her head on my shoulder. Her smell in the room was larger than it'd ever been, that yeasty smell of bread. "I want to work the garments. I can run a sewer just fine."

"You never learned."

"I watched Mother dozens of times."

"You wouldn't make an hour." I stretched my fingers again. Sometimes unbuttoning was too much trouble, and if Myrle was asleep, I lay in bed uniform and all.

Myrle dropped back against her pillow.

"We got a raise," I said. "Twenty-five cents. So you don't need to work in a place like that. We'll have plenty."

"It's Mrs. Keyes."

"Stay put. Every girl here wants your job. And garments, you're too young unless you lied. Even if you tried it a week, Keyes would find another girl. Then how stuck would you be when you didn't like it. The both of us?"

"But Esther . . ."

"Just today, one of the girls went to the infirmary. Swung her hand and there was a needle. Sarah was her name. I don't know if she'll come back."

Myrle gripped her hands. It happened once, if not today, so surely it wasn't a lie. Preston liked to tell the story every chance he got. My sister had the best work in the house, the best this side of town, no matter how she whined. Girls could lose fingers too, I should have reminded Preston. And Myrle, she could lose plenty. The way a boy in the street stopped to lace her shoe. Men old as Ray, as Father even, turning to watch her. Always the same men, pretending to check their watches. I showed them what I thought with a thumb to my teeth.

Myrle groaned and I rested my hand on hers. A good inch longer my fingers had been, but not now with my hands so curled and Myrle's fat enough to make that ring on her finger squeeze.

"I'll send a letter for you anytime you want. Tomorrow even. That will give you something."

"They never write back."

"But they might."

"But they don't."

She closed her eyes. I turned her hand over in mine, laying it palm to palm. *Mrs. Keyes, Mrs. Keyes*, she complained. From her, the name sounded like hissing. In the mornings, that look on her face. Sleep was all I wanted, a few slow hours. But I couldn't stop thinking of letters. What she would have written. What I didn't know about her if I couldn't read what she sent. When finally her breathing went quiet, I stretched my arm to turn off the lamp, but with those fingers of mine, it took me three tries. *Don't go*, that look of hers said. *Don't live. Not without me.*

IV

At dinner the next night, Myrle wasn't in her chair. The girls sat over their plates with fists tucked between their knees, and Dolores didn't say a word. Across the table, Abigail stared at Myrle's place as if she'd gotten it wrong. Just an empty yellow plate between a crooked set of silverware, the striped padding on the chair's back pulling loose from its pins. The chair had nothing to say to us. Charlotte squeezed my knee, but I didn't look. Why was it my fault, where my sister was? Sick, I thought, and upstairs in the sheets. The way she'd always been.

Later in the front hall, Keyes stopped me. "Haven't seen your sister, have you?" She stood by the door, peeking out. The noises of the city grew in that alley three times over and the cold leaked through every window. The house could never keep the city out. The hall was narrow, and Keyes stood thick with the smell of baby powder. Daughters by the dozen, she must have thought us, lined up room after room like a carton of eggs.

"She must be upstairs," I said.

"When I knocked on your door, I didn't hear a peep." Keyes patted the pocket of her apron. She frowned and felt the pocket on the other side. Her hand swept over the table in the hall with its dish of lost things—barrettes, rubber bands, and pennies.

That's when I felt it, the itch in my chest. "What are you looking for?"

"Nothing, nothing." But it wasn't nothing. Myrle had stolen the same before, right from Father's ring. Keyes took hold of my chin between two knobby fingers, her eyes so gray I thought she could see right through me.

"Up the stairs with you," she said. "I'll be locking the door in ten minutes. Your sister better be in by then, or she'll have trouble. Can't imagine such a girl on those steps. But then I can't imagine any of you."

Upstairs, our bed was empty. I lay awake listening for the scrape of the door, the sound of my sister's footsteps. Outside, the alley had gone quiet. March, when the city smelled of old snow and the October leaves had thawed and turned to mush. That mush stuck to our shoes. Hung in bits on our coattails. At home, they'd be clearing the barn. Oiling the tractor, the fields still frozen. Father would walk the place as if chasing something. It was Father a girl didn't want to disappoint, though me, I always did. Myrle wasn't in our bed, she wasn't in our room. What would Father think?

I put out the lamp and turned my face to my pillow. The pipes banged. Like someone knocking at us from under the floorboards, she'd said. It used to be Myrle and me. Like twins, but different. One light, one dark. One pretty, one not. One shy as a bird and the one who made sure that bird never got hurt.

The doorknob rattled. In the dimness of the hall, Myrle stood in her coat, unwrapping her scarf.

"Where were you?"

She shuffled across the room and flipped off her boots. Under her coat, she wore one of my own dresses.

"I went out," she said.

"Where?"

She shrugged. "You go out."

232

"But you know where I am."

"Not always." She dropped her sleeping gown over her head, tugging my dress off from underneath.

"That's not the same," I said.

She crawled across me and turned to the wall. "I'm tired. Mrs. Keyes will have me up early again." I stared at her back, the curve of her hip. The sheet puckered when she breathed in. Quick to sleep like a cat, she was, and never a word more. She was here, but it wasn't any better. In the dark, I imagined her walking the streets in her boots and coat. She must have walked to the quietest part of the city, where the shore hit the lake. I didn't know what the lake looked like at night, if it looked like anything at all, or if it was only sound, a salty smell. It was something I'd never gotten used to, that fish stink. It clung to the vents of the buildings. To people's skin. If Myrle was lucky, the moon would come out, a tail of white on the water that went for miles. I imagined my sister following it, the way I would if I ever got the chance. But for Myrle, getting to that moon was easy. All she had to do was step onto the lake and walk.

The next week at the shop, I couldn't think. My threads snapped, the pedal growled under my feet, and the needle caught my thumb. I wrapped it bleeding with a strip of cloth. Charlotte didn't say a word unless it hinted at my sister's name. At lunch, I took my break away from all the talk, but the bell came fast. I hated those needles and scraps, the dark in the daytime, and that dragon that burned at a touch. Myrle had been out every night, and still not a letter. If I had kept the first, I could open it like something new under our lamp and read it like she was still talking to me, which she wasn't. I'd keep it under our mattress and listen to her voice in my sleep. *I'm sorry*, she'd say. *I didn't mean . . . I never wanted to leave like that.*

A cry from the corner. Charlotte shot out of her chair. "That's Abigail." The machines stopped and the lot of us went running after her, shoving to see. Abigail was on her feet, one hand out and the other clutching her face. She spun from one girl to the next. "Do you see it? Can you get it? Get it out!"

A girl gasped. "It's her eye."

Charlotte crouched in front of her, catching her arms. "Easy, Abigail. You just stay still."

"What's this here?" called the foreman.

Abigail's hand was full and bloody now, her voice keening. Charlotte held her waist, calming her. From between Abigail's fingers, something glinted hot and sharp.

"Out of the way. Here, here." Pushing Charlotte aside, the foreman caught Abigail under his arm and ran her from the room. Shut away in the elevator, the sound of Abigail's cries fell floor by floor to the street.

"What was that?"

"A needle break," Charlotte said. "Happens." She grimaced. "I got one in my cheek once."

I backed away. The floor was stained with Abigail's bleeding. This place, it cut every single thing. My sister and me, it cut all of us in half.

"What's wrong with Dolores?" another girl let out.

Dolores sat at her machine. The chairs around her were empty, Abigail's thrown to the floor, but Dolores gripped the seat of her chair like it might drop from under her.

"Don't tell anyone," she whined. "Don't you dare."

But already we could smell it. Her lap soaked and a puddle on the floor.

"We'll get you out of here," Charlotte said.

"But I can't."

Charlotte grabbed her coat and tied it around Dolores' waist. We got her to her feet. The other girls watched in a line like sheep.

"You girls best get to work by the time he's back," Charlotte snapped. She gave them a look, but I knew she didn't care a dime about work, foreman or not. She wanted them to worry about anything but us.

Outside it was already close to dark. We walked the mile or more to Mrs. Keyes, Dolores shivering. "What about Abby?"

"Poor thing." Charlotte bit her lip. "But I've seen worse. We've got to think she'll be all right."

We turned into the alley just as Myrle rounded the corner. My sister ducked her face into her collar, her eyes on her feet. If she saw us, she pretended she didn't.

"Gotta go," I said. Charlotte called after me, and Dolores, she was holding my arm. But it was Myrle, running off again to wherever she went. It was my only chance to find it.

Across the river, around the Loop, to the money part of town that we never came near. I finally caught up with her. Myrle was standing in front a theater that read C-H-I-C-A-G-O, the words bright underneath:

NORMA TALMADGE
ON SCREEN
THE SIGN ON THE DOOR

When a woman at the entrance raised a fuss by handing her coat to the ticker taker, fur hat and all, Myrle was already in.

"Hey!" the usher called when I tried it. "You got a ticket?"

I reached into my pocket.

"No ticket, no show," he said.

"But . . ."

He shooed me off with his glove.

"Fifty cents," the man at the counter said.

I reached into my pocket. Two quarters and a dime. All the extra I had for the month.

"If you don't got it . . ."

"I *got* it." I snatched the ticket out of his hand.

Inside, the ceiling was high enough to hurt necks. Red carpet and gold, a light of a hundred diamonds overhead. I felt dark as dark with all the fancy people there, the women in dresses down to their heels. White-gloved ticket takers of all things. A flight of stairs that swept to the upper floors like a tongue. Myrle, she was nowhere. BALCONY, my ticket said.

The lights flickered, the organ stamping. The place seemed to move underfoot, the balcony so high it felt like falling. I had to catch shoulders as I climbed the steps. When I found her, Myrle was sitting at the back in her coat, as high as she could get. That music, it was a reedy kind of roar. So full of light and air, I wondered how the place could hold so much at once. Myrle sat with her eyes closed as if that sound were just for her. And here it was, everything she'd been hiding in her head.

"Esther." Myrle leaned forward enough to nearly pitch herself out of her seat. She didn't seem surprised I was there. "Do you see it?"

"What?"

"Just wait."

But all I could see on the screen was a woman locked in a room. She had skin whiter than cream, a mess of curls on her head. She sure looked a star. She was trying to pick a lock, and behind her a man lay on a bed as if sleeping, but he wasn't. He had a gun in his hand, on his chest the bloom of something dark. On the other side of the door, the sign DO NOT DISTURB.

"The man was going to blackmail her," Myrle whispered. "But her husband shot him trying to protect her. Then he locked the room and left. He didn't know she was already hiding in there, a plan of her own."

The music was fast as running now, the sound jumping off the walls like bees. Norma was tearing at the door with all she had.

"Does she get out?"

"Sure. But not the way you think." She closed her eyes. The light from the screen was bright as suns. Already Myrle seemed to have left me behind.

"You don't want to go home, do you?"

"Home?"

"The farm."

She gave a quick shake of her head.

I reached for her hand. "What happened to your ring?"

"It hurt." Her fingers were puffy and fat. "Let's go." She took my arm and we scooted by people's knees. I didn't want to leave, not with the woman so close to breaking out of that room and my fifty cents, but Myrle was already down the stairs, her grip so tight I had to run to keep from falling. A mess of voices yelled at us from the seats. When I reached the bottom of the stairs, Myrle let go of my arm. She was out the doors, heading to the lobby. She didn't look back. In a flash, she was on the far side of that ruby floor, going along like something was chasing her. But the only thing behind her was me.

It took a few blocks to catch her. Myrle was breathing hard, walking in fits and starts. At the door of the boardinghouse, she pulled up short.

"Esther," she said, "don't tell Mrs. Keyes."

"Tell her what?"

"Anything."

When the door flew open, Keyes was in a fit. "Where have you two been?"

Charlotte stood at her back. "Is she sick?"

I didn't say a word, but Myrle was still breathing like that, leaning against the frame. Mrs. Keyes drew her up the stairs. In our room, Keyes snapped the door shut and laid her on the bed. She opened Myrle's coat, touched her forehead. She touched her stomach. Her hand jumped and she touched her stomach again.

"What is it?" Charlotte asked.

Keyes washed a hand over her cheeks. "Never thought a girl this old wouldn't know her birds and bees."

"She's pregnant?" Charlotte asked.

I dropped into the chair.

"You farm girls, you take the cake," Keyes said. "Don't your mothers teach you right?"

Mother, she had never told us anything. And Nan, she'd told us even less. All we knew we knew from cows and pigs.

But Charlotte, she didn't seem surprised. "Aren't you going to tell her?" she asked me.

"What do you know about it?"

"Tell me what?" Keyes said.

Myrle lay on her back, her face wet. Charlotte stared at me. Her or me, that stare said.

"There was a boy back home," I let out. "A neighbor."

"What boy?" Keyes asked.

I shrugged. "We're here, aren't we?"

"But doesn't he know?"

"He forced her, that's what he knows."

Myrle raised her head, as if telling was a choice. "He didn't."

"Yes, he did."

"He didn't force me. He didn't do anything."

"Are you forgetting how sick you were?"

Myrle's eyes went teary. "I don't want to remember it like that."

"Hush now, the two of you." Keyes blotted Myrle's face with a handkerchief and blotted her own. "Forced or not, I can't have a pregnant girl in this house."

"But she doesn't have anywhere to go," Charlotte said.

"She has a family, doesn't she?"

"They don't know," I said.

"But surely they would accept their own daughter."

"They won't even write her back," Charlotte said. "Tell her, Esther. All those letters she sent."

"Sure," I said. "She wrote some letters." All I could see was the tops of Father's knees. If he thought stealing was enough for that, what would he think of the Elliot boy stealing this?

"And you sent them for her."

"Sure I did."

Charlotte tilted her head. "Oh, my God." Her eyes narrowed. I shoved my hands inside the folds of my skirt. "You didn't, did you?" she said. "You never sent them. That's why they didn't write back."

"What's it to you? It was no good their knowing we're here. They'd make us come home. And Tom, he could do anything to her then."

The room went quiet, like the hush of those machines at the end of a shift.

Finally, Myrle spoke. "But Tom never did."

Charlotte huffed. "I can't believe it."

"Stop it," Keyes snapped. "I don't care about letters. We can't keep her here. There are rules. This isn't a charity. It's a decent house."

"Don't you dare send her away," Charlotte said.

"And who will pay for her? If she can't work. She hasn't been much help lately as it is."

Myrle called out, and I jumped from my chair, but she turned away. When she called out again, she said Charlotte's name.

"There are places these days that'll take a baby," Keyes said. "No one has to know."

"No," Myrle cried.

Charlotte took Myrle's hand. "Esther can pay," Charlotte said, "and me." She looked at me, then looked away. "I can pay."

I sat back. *Esther and me*, she'd said, but she didn't mean it. Charlotte didn't have sisters. But maybe now she had one. Maybe the kind who told her everything, the things my sister no longer told me. Charlotte and Keyes, they were watching me now as if expecting something.

"I'll help," I said. "Of course." Though I didn't know how.

But Myrle, she wasn't thinking of me anymore. It was all Charlotte. That red hair and her eyes like lights. Could be Charlotte was the reason Myrle's letters home didn't matter anymore. As if I had been the one in the loft with the Elliot boy. As if I'd known it could turn to bad. But I didn't. Still, I was the one who always got it wrong.

Five cents for every dropped stitch, five for backtracking, five for folding the collar so they couldn't iron it and sometimes even if they could. Five for needles and five if one broke because you weren't watching (an eye if you were watching too hard). Five for listening to Charlotte, but today she was quiet. All week at the house she'd kept her door closed, Myrle locked behind it. *She doesn't want to see you*, Charlotte had said. When I knocked, I could hear Myrle inside, padding about. One cent for being late, half a day for being late more than five minutes. Five if you had to get Mr. Preston to unlock the factory door, as I had every day since I lost my sister. Five more if Preston was in a mood. I hadn't got many dimes the week before or the one before that. The coming week I might have to owe.

If I stopped moving, I couldn't make mistakes. If I wasn't breathing, I would make even fewer.

Five past nine, still early in the morning. I sat back from my machine. Down the line, the girls in the same blouse, same dress, their hair caught back with the same cut of string. Even Abigail with that patch over her eye. If you looked too close at a thing, you got hurt. That's what Abigail knew. Best not to look at all. Electric, I once thought. But light like that only showed what a person couldn't have. I liked it dark. That needle, such a hot silver thing. I didn't dare touch it. If I wasn't working, there'd be no more needles. No more electric. I wouldn't go home. I wouldn't stay. I'd disappear even as I sat right here.

Five for disappearing. Five times five for every day you were gone and never telling anybody why. You owed ten dimes. You owed twenty. And all the time, Myrle had been growing bigger, those pipes in our room banging, Charlotte trying to get in. And now she had. The both of them, Charlotte and Keyes, saying everything would be all right. Just like home, no matter what my sister did. The way Mother held her and Father put his hand on her head like a cap. That heavy hand of his that was warm and never so sharp with Myrle the way it was with me. How many dimes was that?

A hand on my shoulder. I flinched. Preston stood behind me with the foreman. I threw that hand off.

"Number 57," Preston said. "Let's take a break, why don't we? Down in my office."

"A break?"

He nodded. Next to me, Charlotte worried her fingers.

"I don't need a break."

"Esther," Charlotte whispered.

Preston cocked his head. An old man. He was nothing more than that. Old men, you never could change their minds about you. I stood from my chair, looped one of Charlotte's curls around my finger, one last time. Charlotte touched the back of my hand.

"Watch yourself," she said. "I'm sorry. Really I am."

But I didn't know what she was sorry about. I wasn't sorry at all.

V

I took the train home. *I'll be back,* I'd told Myrle every day before I left. *Soon as I can.* And that quiet on the other side of the door said she believed me and didn't. With Charlotte around, she didn't seem to care. But I didn't have a dime anymore to keep the both of us there. Two charity cases, too much for Charlotte or even Mrs. Keyes. On the last night, Myrle asked me: "When?" I told her I didn't know. "But you can't come." With how far along she was, we could never knock on our door. We couldn't even cross the yard, for fear Father would see or Nan and then they all would know, and that would be the end of home. "That girl's close to bursting," Keyes said. "Don't you even think of tromping off with her to the middle of nowhere." Like a trick, now even Keyes took Myrle's side. As soon as I got money, I said, I'd be back. Soon as I could tell the story straight and bring her along, pregnant or not. Myrle opened the door. It was just enough to show a sliver of her eye and one raw cheek. She reached her fingers through the crack. I touched them with my own. "Wait for me," I said. "I'll come. I promise." She squeezed my hand and closed the door again.

I shared my seat with an old woman who wore a yellow flowered hat. She held it in her lap and stroked it with her thumb, stroking it until minutes after we left the station when she dropped her head to sleep. Out the window, the lake was gray and rough. The lights from the city faded, and all that was left was dark. Dark fields and dark roads, going no place I ever would know. My face peered back at me in the glass, dark as everything else. The train rocked, the wheels going full out. I could ride this train and never get off. Go west as far as the Dakotas, farther even, to a place where waking wasn't so hard and electric wasn't and knocking on a door was even less.

"Dear," I heard. I opened my eyes. "You were dreaming some sort of nightmare," the old woman said.

"What about?"

"Good heavens, I have no idea. I don't trust them myself."

"What?"

"Dreams. A person never knows whether they're up or down. Why, whenever I've slept through the night without one, it's a triumph. When you're older you'll feel the same."

Her face was puffy, her eyes red-rimmed like she hadn't slept in years. "I don't have a clue know how far along we are. Do you?"

I looked out the window. It was black as pitch, not a house, a tree. "We could be anywhere."

"Anywhere," she said. "That's a place."

"We could be nowhere too."

"Don't say that." She gripped her chest. "It's always better to have a place. Whether you like it or not. It makes a person somebody." She sighed like a great wind and peeled herself from her seat. "Now I'm off to the ladies. Would you mind watching my things?"

Down the aisle she waddled, balancing herself. The woman was as round as a peach. The door closed behind her with a bang. After a quarter of an hour, she didn't come back. I flattened my hand on the leather where she'd been and it was warm. As far as I could see, she'd left nothing behind. After a while longer, I wondered if she'd been there at all.

Home.

The fields weren't any different, a rough tide after planting, and the yard yellow with spits of grass. Those fields were low and hollow after Chicago. In the pasture, the cows dug their noses in puddles of rain. The house seemed squat, the sills wanting a coat of paint, and I couldn't do more than stand on the steps. It took me almost an hour to knock the first time. No one came. It was late afternoon. The porch was shadows, the crickets sawing. In no time, Lee would come in from the corrals or Ray, and I didn't want to be found at the door like an old cat. I knocked again.

The door opened. Nan stood with her hand on the knob, an apron at her waist. Taller than poles, she was, and sun-dark, but that hand of hers shone with a ring and she carried a bump under the front of her dress. A strand of hair clung to her cheek. She swept it back. I'd never thought of my oldest sister much, but now she seemed bigger than she ever was.

"Esther," she said, turning. Her mouth opened and she pressed her fingers to her throat. "It's Esther." In a rush, she folded me in her arms. The house behind her was warm and full. One voice and another, a scurry of them in the hall.

"Agnes!" Nan called over her shoulder. "Lee!" She held me tighter. "What a terrible child you are. What a terrible, terrible child."

*　*　*

"Your father will never believe it," Patricia said. She picked a lump of gristle from her teeth.

We sat around the table, every one of us in the same place, everyone but Father. He was off in his room, asleep, just like after Mother went. Next to Nan, in Myrle's chair, was Carl McNulty. His sleeve hung empty, he smelled a stranger, but the bunch of them acted like he'd been there all along.

Nan rested her fork. She hadn't touched her food. Since setting out the plates, she'd perched in her chair, her eyes on the hall. The others didn't do much better. Ray sat at the end, rubbing his hand. *Well now*, he'd said when the others rushed me on the porch. He'd given me a pat on the shoulder, worse than a dog. Outside and in, it was quiet. I wasn't used to that. In a place like this, a cry from an animal carried miles, right through the windows, as if it was in the room with us, and there was nothing to do but feed it scraps.

Nan folded her napkin in her lap. The sigh she gave. It could cut a girl to pieces.

"Oh, Nan, don't," Agnes said. Nan cupped her face. Carl reached for her while the rest of them dropped their heads.

"She doesn't know," Nan let out.

"Not now," Agnes said.

"Know what?"

Agnes was out of her chair. She gripped me by the arm. With a look, Nan tried to hold us in place. My oldest sister was younger than I'd ever seen her, her old bones with flesh on them, like what that man next to her did, he'd done in reverse, got her pregnant with herself. She'd never wanted to be our mother in the first place.

"Come on," Agnes said, tugging at me. "I'll show you."

*   *   *

We walked to the river that wasn't anything more than mud and weeds. The moon was out, the water black. Across the fields, the Clarks' kitchen was busy with shadows, but the Elliot farm was dark, not a spit of smoke. It looked like those houses that sat closer to town, where the farmers had given up the goose and moved off. Only squatters in those houses now, or emptied out, a sign from the bank staked in the yard. The Elliot house didn't have a sign. Even their fence was gone.

"About a mile off," Agnes started. "That's where they found her."

"Who?"

Her eyes narrowed. "Myrle, of course."

I turned my head. A mile off was more river, the place the water sank into a pool where we went swimming. Myrle always floated in her knickers, paler than any of us. But the way Agnes said Myrle's name, it sounded something worse.

"That's what I thought too," Agnes went on. "It can't be. The girl had been in the river for months, and she only came up with January thaw. By then, no one could recognize her. Just a girl, blond like Myrle, blue eyes. But no one else was missing. And we'd already found Myrle's dress in the washhouse." The corners of her mouth drew up sharp. "If it was just you who'd run off, we knew we wouldn't hear anything. Myrle was different. She'd at least try to write."

I crouched in the dirt and stuck my hand in the water, cold as nails. It wasn't so terrible what I did with Myrle's letters. Not so terrible as rivers.

"You can't tell," Agnes said.

"Tell what?"

"Where she really is."

"And where's that?"

"Chicago. Just like you."

I didn't answer her.

"They thought it was Tom Elliot who did it. He always did have a thing for Myrle. But they didn't have enough to arrest him. Still Tom was acting crazy. A week later, he put a gun to his head."

Tom and that loft in the barn. Sure enough, he must have felt guilty after that. Even if he hadn't taken Myrle to the river himself, maybe he drove her there with what he did. Maybe that's what he'd thought.

"But if Tom had killed her," Agnes went on, "he wouldn't have left her dress in our washhouse. And he wouldn't have torn it up like that. The way Mother taught us."

"If you know so much, why can't I tell them?"

"Because of Lee." She took a step closer. "I tried to tell them her drowning didn't make sense, but they wouldn't believe me. Wishful thinking, they said." She sighed. "Lee would die if he found out. Tom used Lee's gun."

"Lee'd never let that happen."

She looked away. "What I don't understand is why Tom didn't use his own. If he wanted to kill himself, I mean."

"What difference does it make?"

"Why don't you ask Lee? He tells you everything. Me, I can only guess." She took my hands. Hers were hot and small and nothing like I'd thought. "Just tell me," she said. Her eyes turned dark. "Is she all right?"

"She's fine."

Agnes let out a breath. Biting her lip, she started off.

"What about you?" I called out. "You ever think of leaving this place?"

"What for?" she shouted. "It's not like anyone gets anywhere." Before she was too far, she turned again. "By the way, Father's asking for you. 'She's come back.' That's what he's saying."

"He means Myrle."

"No, he means you."

Lee had his fire going in the smithy. He waited in the doorway across the yard. By the time I walked in, Lee was cross-legged on the floor, his head against the wall. I could have curled into his lap, fallen asleep right there and never talked about Myrle.

"Did I see you?" he asked. "In Chicago?"

I sat next to him, tucking in my skirts. "Don't you remember?"

He shrugged.

"You never should have been there, you know."

Lee stayed quiet.

"Agnes told me about the gun."

"Yeah?"

"What'd you do, Lee? You and Ray. It was the both of you, wasn't it?"

"It wasn't the both of us anything. The man was drinking."

"Who?"

"Tom Elliot."

"Tom is dead."

Lee's feet twitched. He closed his eyes. "We paid him a visit. A couple of days after they found her, after the deputy came. He and Old Elliot were sitting at the kitchen table, as if nothing had happened."

"Tom's wife?"

"Gone, I guess. Took the baby with her, what with Tom acting like he was. Heard she was scared." Lee wiped his mouth. "They weren't saying anything, just opened the door. Old Elliot laid out four cups. It was Ray who did the talking."

I could imagine them in that kitchen, though I knew I was remembering wrong. I hadn't been any taller than a table the last I'd seen it. Doilies on the chairs, knickknacks and flowers. That's when Mrs. Elliot was alive. But the way I saw it now, those doilies were dust. The knickknacks had cracked, the place running with dogs. And there were my brothers, kicking their legs like boys, the cups bigger than their fists by twice. As if everything in that place was too large.

"Crop rotations." Lee pinched the skin on his arm. "That's what Ray was talking about."

"Why?"

He shrugged again. "Using corn for a spell, then oats. 'Taking out one thing to save another.' Ray was always going on about that. After the bottle was empty, we took our hats to go. Even me, I'd had a few cups. Can't say I wasn't some dizzy with it."

"That all?"

"Ray insisted it was an accident. He was particular about that part."

"What was an accident?"

Lee frowned. I picked at a loose thread in my lap like it didn't make any difference what he said. Though it did. It made plenty.

"It wasn't any cold," he said at last. "Not after the thaw. But Ray walked home fast, and he rubbed his hands together like he was freezing. I couldn't figure that. 'Don't you worry about it now,' Ray said. Then he threw an arm over my shoulder." Lee shook his head, but I knew what he was thinking. It'd been years since Ray had done anything like that.

"It wasn't until the next day I figured the gun," Lee said. "I don't know why I left it. Ray said I'd brought it to show the Elliots, the gun being new and all. But I don't remember thinking it needed showing. The next day, that's when they told us about Tom."

"Ray," I swore. In the loft in the barn, that's what I saw. A gun out of nowhere. One good hand on the trigger, the other good for nothing much. Or maybe Ray didn't have to go that far. Maybe the Elliot boy just needed a little talking to. Crop rotations, sure. Taking one thing out to save another, though Ray likely said a lot more at the table with Lee forgetful and Old Elliot near to deaf. Tom was the only one he needed to hear it. Then a cocked and loaded gun left in the right spot. On the counter, by the door. Even on Tom's bed. A plain enough message to get Tom thinking he didn't have a choice, Old Elliot too deep in his cups to notice. And what did Tom have left? The wife gone. The farm a wreck. The loft, it was the perfect place. The kind to split a girl in half. That's why he'd pick it. A shot like that, it would've sent the animals bucking in their stalls. After he pulled the trigger, I imagined Tom breathing a skip or two. I could even hear it, the way it stuttered out of his mouth. A shot that might have sounded all the way to Chicago.

"Maybe Tom deserved it," I said. "Maybe he really did do something."

Lee sighed. "That doesn't forgive much." He rubbed at his eyes, as if they hurt him. "My head was some sore the next day, I know that. 'You don't remember,' Ray said. And it was true. Cups or no, these days I don't remember lots. An eye for an eye. That's what Ray said. And the deputy didn't seem to care much."

Lee's cheeks had gone pale as the wall. The fire, it was only coals. My brother was still the one who saved spiders. In the war, I don't think he even aimed his gun. Agnes was right. If Lee found out where Myrle was, found out his gun had taken a life for something less, even if he hadn't aimed the thing himself, it just might kill him on the spot.

"So you're back," he said.

"Maybe." I took off his hat, sat it on my head. "Ray and you, you buddies now?"

He smiled. "It's been a long time."

Without the fire, it was cold, but next to me Lee was a furnace. I pulled his arm around me and he drew me close. Outside, the cicadas thrummed, the fields nothing but leaves and crawlers and the river running. If we were quiet enough, we could hear that murmur against the rocks. If we were more than quiet, we could hear our own worries, his and mine.

Patricia peeked in Father's door. "He's asleep. We should wait." She was more than fat, her cheeks drooping like an old cake. The woman hadn't looked at me yet, not square in the face.

"Patricia," Nan scolded.

"All right. All right." Patricia opened the door.

Nan pushed at my shoulders to follow, but she stayed in the doorway herself. Patricia leaned over the bed. "He's such a sleeper these days. Ever since they found your sister." She clicked her tongue. "One day Lee caught him sitting on a wash bucket in the smokehouse with his eyes closed. You know what he had in his hands? A chick. Hadn't lived long enough to even grow fuzz. Your father almost froze out there." She busied herself straightening the sheets. "Oh, now, here he is."

A noise from the bed. Father blinked at me and blinked again. "*Wo ist die andere?*"

"It's Esther."

"Poor dear," Patricia said. "He must not know if he's here or there."

Father raised himself on his elbows. Patricia pinched my arm.

"*Ah, Esther,*" he said, wrapping his hand around my wrist. He held it to his chest and his eyes brimmed. "*Du bist zu mir zurückgekommen, sie aber nicht. Jetzt geh'nie weg von hier.*"

"What's he saying?" I asked.

"I haven't the faintest."

"You returned to him." This was Nan from the door. She looked in with her hand on her stomach, the way it always was now. "The other one didn't. Myrle, he means." She stopped, raised her eyes to mine. "But you, he's saying, you'll never go away from here again."

"I'll be," Patricia said. "He's sicker than I thought."

Never. The sound of it rung in my ears, no matter what Patricia said. Now *she* meant me when he said it, not *the other girl*, and that was something. Something grand. I thought of Myrle's fingers through the crack in the door, how with a touch they'd almost burned. We'd stayed like that until the whistles from the factories went, far off. *I'll be back*, I'd told her, *I promise*. And she'd only said, *When?* Myrle had never asked to come home. Those fingers of hers weren't anything like I knew anymore. That's what Chicago does to a girl, wringing you out until you become someone else. Maybe Myrle really was drowned, if that's what she wanted, to sink deep in the place where she had Charlotte and Keyes and I had only pinpricks. Maybe that's what the Elliot boy had done to her from the start.

And who was I to say any different?

Part V: The Birth of Norma Byrne

MYRLE

I

She was coming and I couldn't stop her. I wasn't about to try. I lay in the darkness of our room and didn't make a sound. The pinch was sharp at my back, my stomach a stone. The air felt restless and no end to it, save it was hushed like the inside of a box. Already I could imagine the curl of her hand in mine, her fingernails that would need trimming, and a thread of hair on her crown. A new little girl, just like that. As if I had done something to deserve her, and I wished I had.

"Charlotte," I called. She woke on the pillow next to me with those springs of hair in her eyes. When the light shone through the windows, I felt another one, sharper this time, with a twist in my insides. Charlotte took my hand.

We waited until the sun rose higher on the windows, the pains faster and the sheets hot to the touch. In the chair next to me, Charlotte worried herself into silence. By the door, Mrs. Keyes had abandoned the knitting in her lap. "At least it's a Sunday," she sighed. "We won't have those factories blaring at us." The alley outside was quiet as a church, the house too, the other girls still asleep. If it hadn't been for babies, I might have thought the three of us the last in the good wide world. If we spoke, something terrible would surely come of it. When the door finally opened, Mrs. Keyes dropped her head. "Thank heaven," she said and crossed herself. "The woman's here. We'll survive the day."

"Hold on, dearie," the midwife said as she bustled in. She was a small woman with a graying bun and round cheeks, but her hands were frighteningly quick. She dropped her bag and tapped Mrs. Keyes on the shoulder. "Get two bowls of hot water and a knife. Plenty of towels. And be sure that water's clean. The knife with it." Hurrying out, Mrs. Keyes opened her mouth as if she might cry. The woman winked at Charlotte and touched her hands to my stomach. "Nice and low," she crooned. "You shouldn't be much time at all." She washed at the sink and sat at the foot of the bed, pressing open my knees. "You'll feel my hand."

I winced.

The woman whistled. "She's upside down, that's the trouble. I'll have to turn her." She cocked her head. "You're a young one, aren't you? But that will be all right. Young ones have strength more than the old mothers. You might just have to bite your tongue a bit."

I knotted the sheet between my fingers. Charlotte sat with me on the bed, the bed far too narrow now and stiff at my back. When Mrs. Keyes returned, the other girls were awake in the hall, crowding together with their whispers. "You leave her alone, you hear me," Mrs. Keyes scolded them. "Myrle's got enough problems without you bumbling about." She fastened the lock and checked it twice.

"Here we go." The midwife reached under the sheet. "You try telling her to come out. Think on that." Charlotte's face shone. "Go on, Myrle," she said. "You yell all you want." But I couldn't catch my breath. The bed felt higher, the light from the windows streaming, and a pain tore through my insides to the back of my throat. "She's a mischief," the midwife swore, shaking her head. I wondered if telling her to come would do any good. What had Mother said? *It's a fine thing to be born, but it's none too comfortable. Fine things go like that.* But what did Mother know of comfort or finer things, when dirt clung to our house and even our gaslights left their smoky stains. I could see them flickering, high on the wall, and a flood of heat rushed between my legs. The midwife stood back. "My goodness," Mrs. Keyes said. There she was, my little girl. She was blood-thin and purple, a helpless bundle on a sheet. The midwife slapped her stomach and she cried out. "That's right." The midwife smiled. "Mrs. Keyes, you take her. We have some doing here." The woman drew out a needle and thread and a blackened bottle of whisky from her bag.

"Myrle, she's here," Charlotte said. "Look who she is."

"The lungs of an ox, I should say." Mrs. Keyes held the baby close so I could see her all at once. Her eyes were full, her hair pale as thistles.

"What should we call her?" Charlotte asked. "Helen?"

"Or Ruth," Mrs. Keyes said.

"What about Rose?" Charlotte asked.

"That's not a name," Mrs. Keyes said. "That's a flower. This one's a bona fide girl."

They waited for me, but I couldn't think. All the names I had imagined before, now they seemed less.

"You'll feel this one," the midwife said. A sharp prick and the light from the windows was high and white and flooded the place. I heard a wail, as clear as a bird and rising—the girl was a beauty with her noise. "Greta, that's a name for her," I said, letting my eyes close. "After Mother. Even Esther would like that." "Watch her now. She's going," the midwife called. "Myrle?" Charlotte asked. But it was the noise I wanted. It faded off now into the far corner of the room and the room with it—a noise I knew as well as my mother's voice, and I had always known it. *There's more to you than they think*, Mother had said. *Just looking at you, I can see it. Ten, twenty years to come. Just you wait.*

Twenty years, Mother said. But it took longer than she could have guessed. I remember sleeping on Agnes' porch with my sisters in the summertime, hours after the house had gone to bed. Through the screens, the cicadas hummed—*zikaden*, Mother called them. They sang the most when we were milking, at the end of the day and in the early mornings before we started our chores. Once we finished them, Mother would walk us to the river. "Look," she'd say, plucking a cicada off a leaf. She cupped it in her hand. They were ugly things—bright with circles of green, yellow, and black. Agnes stepped away and Esther made a face, but Mother curled her fingers around the insect as if something precious. "These nest only a few winters," she said. "But others burrow underground for more than seventeen years. When they come out, they are everywhere underfoot. And the way they sing, you can't hear your own voice. But after a few months, they are gone again. They leave only their shells." Mother waved her hand one way and another to show us. "Shells on every tree trunk and fence post." She blew on the cicada's back and it drew out its wings. Like glass, those wings—veined and thin, and the cicada didn't look so ugly then. I asked Mother if I could hold it, and she let it walk into my hand. When I tried the sound *zikaden* on my tongue, the creature thrummed against my skin. I blew on it the way Mother had done, its wings spreading. "Can you imagine?" Mother said. "After seventeen years, the world would be a very different place."

Those days, Mother brought us to the river whenever she wanted to tell us the names of things. "Spruce," she said. *Fichte.* "Nettles." *Nessel.* And *Elster.* "For the noisy magpie. That's what we named you for, Esther," Mother said. "And what a good name it was." Esther's cheeks grew dark. The next morning, Mother asked us to remember what she'd taught. Agnes always could, but Esther couldn't, and I for one didn't understand how something might have two names at once. Mother wouldn't give up on us, and soon the whole world and every leaf and twig had at least two names to call it by. Only in the year before the war did Mother stop her lessons. "Quiet," she'd say. "You keep those words in your mouth." Later when she took to her bed, we found her looking out her window as if she could see the shadows of every named thing now and forever in the paint peeling from the barn.

When Lee went to fight, Mother stayed in her room. She kept an oil lamp by her bedside so she could knit when she was awake. Father hung blue crinoline for her curtains, and through the end of October, the room filled with a watery kind of light. When Mother seemed bedridden for good, we sat with her with our schoolbooks. Agnes read aloud and Esther acted the stories out, but for me, I stayed close enough I could curl a length of her hair around my finger and feel the rise and fall of her chest. "Where I come from," Mother said, "words have juice to them. *Die Heimat. Die Sicherheit. Die Liebe.*" She repeated the sounds like a chant. When she caught us listening, she wiped a hand across her mouth. "Beautiful, yes?" she said. "Now be sure to forget them."

Agnes copied the words on a page of her book. I couldn't make sense of them. *Die, die,* I read over her shoulder. "That's not what it means," Agnes said.

"Don't you worry," Mother told us, clutching our hands. "You'll have Nan, as good as any mother. Girls should have their mother when they are young."

Before Agnes could stop her, Esther tore out the page and threw it into the fire. Agnes stopped copying Mother's words then.

It was late in November when Esther and I found Mother in her bed. She lay as she always did, her head turned to the window. Though her mouth was open, she wouldn't speak to us. We stood in the doorway pinching our fingers. "Mother," I whispered, as if I could wake her. Agnes broke through and dropped an ear to Mother's lips. "Hurry now," she said. "Get Father." The smell of Mother's room was close and sweet. She looked small as a pile of sticks under her blankets. "Go," Agnes shouted. Esther gripped my wrist and together we ran. We called for Father in the fields and the stables. We called for him in the barn. When at last he heard, he rushed straight to their bed and held Mother's hand. Nan hurried in, her face drawn. "Go on, you three," she said, her voice strange. "Get yourselves dressed." She gave us a kiss on the forehead and squeezed our shoulders, waving us off as if squeezing was enough. Father sat in their room and Ray came in from the fields, holding his hat. The three of us girls waited in the hall. We had dressed in our best, and Esther didn't tug at her collar or shuffle her feet. Nan shook her head. "I think we're to wear black," she said. Then she whispered to herself. "She never taught us this." Nan hurried into the room with a bowl of water and washcloths, but Father had already pulled the sheet and blown out the lamp. When he stepped into the hall, he drew the door closed behind him.

Later that night, we sat in the kitchen with the plate of cookies Mrs. Clark had brought. The plate had pretty white birds painted on the rim, but no one could eat from it. Mrs. Clark wept a bucket, or so Ray later said. But for himself, Ray hid his face for most of that day and the next. Mrs. Clark asked to sit with Mother in the parlor, but we brought her to Mother's bed and carried in a chair. "Where are the others?" she asked. "Who?" we said. Nan brought in another chair and sat with her herself. I watched them as quiet as I could from the door. While Mrs. Clark's shoulders shook, the sunlight fell through the window and crossed the room. I wondered if my shoulders should do the same, while my head felt swollen and my ribs were aching. Soon there wasn't much sun in the room at all. After the woman left, Nan took the plate full to the pantry and covered it with a cloth. Father stayed at the table, lifting his face from his hands. "*Mein Gott,*" he said. "I was in the barn." "What about Lee?" Esther asked, but Nan shushed her. "We'll be sending a message to the hospital," Nan said. "Then he'll come home."

In the early dark of the next morning, I went to Mother's door. Father snored in the kitchen. The others slept in their rooms. Mother lay in her bed, her eyes closed and her hands crossed over her stomach. Nan had washed and dressed her and tied her hair from her neck with a ribbon. Under her chin, another ribbon kept her mouth shut. I touched her cheek. It was stiff. Twins, they had called us, though I'd never let myself hope it. Still seeing her in that bed, I wondered if one day I might look the same. The thought should have worried me, with her skin so still and gray, but it didn't. Often I had pictured her face in a mirror when she was young—like mine but different. She had never told us why she left home back then. Was it a boy? A sister? Had she felt locked in a place, never alone enough for breathing? She had always seemed the staying kind. Same as me. But there was something now in the way she slept—as if she could go anywhere she wanted and by her own choosing. No one need ask her the reason why.

II

A knock on the door. These days, I open it no matter how late. A girl stands shivering on the steps in a jacket made for spring. She looks at me like the old woman I've become. The sign on the door says: WOMEN'S HOUSE OF BOARDING. Almost seventy years I've been in this place.

"I'm here for a room," she says.

I show her into the parlor where the couch has been re-covered more times than I can count, always white. The girl sits on the edge of the cushions with her fingers between her thighs. She's thin as a lily, her shoulders wings. With her dark coloring and eyes, my own hand looks bloodless in my lap. The girls these days wear their hair straight and long to their waists. They dress like men with their flat fronts, their legs as bare as faces, but they are good girls all the same.

"The board is two hundred a month," I start. "You get breakfast with that and your evening's supper. You'll have your own room and a bath down the hall . . . ." Something flits in the corner of my eye and I turn to see it. Nothing is there.

"You okay?" the girl asks.

"Oh yes, dear. I just lost track." I wash a hand over my eyes. "Do you have your papers?"

"Papers?" She looks around. *Code of the Boardinghouse Keeper*. The letters on the wall have faded in the frame, but still the girl covers her mouth. Her laugh is the first sign of pleasure in her I've seen.

"Maybe tomorrow?" I ask.

"Sure thing," she says.

I show her upstairs to her room. She takes a breath at the door before stepping in.

"You'll have time to rest before supper. When the others come off their shifts. That's about seven o'clock."

"Thank you, Mrs. . . ?"

"Byrne."

"Mrs. Byrne," she says. She stands as if chilled to the bone on the old rug. She doesn't seem to know what to do with herself. She's sixteen, seventeen, not a day more.

"Why don't you unpack your things. Take a little lie-down."

She nods but doesn't make a move. I close the door between us as softly as I can.

At suppertime, the girls crowd around the table and talk. They don't usually wear uniforms anymore, and they don't care about keeping their voices down. Charlotte and I think that's good enough. Factory work can still be had by the river, round the clock. But ours work as clerks in the shops, or maids and nannies. Some don't seem to work much. "Runaways," Charlotte whispers. We let them stay without their papers more often than not. Morning and night, we give them their meals, though the other houses have long ago stopped. The others aren't even houses anymore but tenements with hot plates, and no common rooms to speak of. "Full of criminals and addicts," Charlotte says. "Wards of the state." Charlotte is soft on our girls all the same. She leaves a chocolate on their pillows, keeps supper for anyone who's late. The house is ours to do with as we please. We needn't the money from renting. Still we answer the bell. A girl should have a good meal and a clean bed no matter what she's come from.

"The new one is nervous," I tell Charlotte in the kitchen.

"She'll be fine," Charlotte says. We are both older than God by now, or so Mrs. Keyes would tell us. We cling to the stair rails. Our stomachs are not so kind. Charlotte uses a cane, though she's the stronger between us, as she always was. The rest is a question of being content with the hour at hand. Charlotte and I sit together in the kitchen late at night. We sleep in the same bed to keep warm. But we sleep there even in the summer when it's hot enough for fans. On Sundays, we go to the market to fill our carts for the walk home. The rest of the day we stay at the stove, holding out our tongues for a taste from a spoon. This is how we fill ourselves.

Charlotte stirs a large pot of soup. A *Kuchen* bakes in the oven, after Mother's recipe, or what I could remember of it. *Die Heimat, Die Liebe*, I sing to myself. I never learned what the words meant. "Like a lullaby," Charlotte says. "Before I met you I thought all German sayings had something to do with pigs." At the table, the girls wait for their meal with tired eyes, but they never hurry us.

"Mrs. Byrne!" Charlotte and I turn our heads. It's our oldest girl, Gisel. Twenty-five with a scar on her cheek. I've never asked how she got it. *A boyfriend*, Charlotte thinks. The girl pushes the door open with her fingertips.

"Yes dear?"

"Arlene's sick. Can I take up a bowl for her?"

Charlotte's spoon bangs the pot.

"Of course," I say. "I'll bring it up myself." The door swings closed between us.

"That girl is sick every other week," Charlotte says.

"I was sick every other week."

"Well," Charlotte says. "Here's hoping this is different."

After supper, the girls carry in their dishes and line up at the sink to give them a good rinse. At the end of the day, their feet hurt and they lean against the wall. They aren't so terribly talkative now. I take up the soup for Arlene, leave it outside her room on a tray. The new girl's door is closed, but her music trails out loud enough. I'm not one for knocking to bother her. At the top of the stairs, I catch my breath. There's a flutter under my fingers when I touch my throat, the hard bone above my breast—it goes away as quickly as it came.

Down in the kitchen, I wash the table and hang the rag on its hook. Charlotte stays at the sink and sends me off with a wave. After so many years, she knows my habits as well as I know hers.

I step outside. In the alley, the light lists like a ship. It's the time of day I like best. In the summer, the sun lingers for a good hour after the dishes are done and the air is precious.

The lake is ten blocks. I make my way through the alley, past the iron works. On the other side of the river, some of the factories are closed. Some aren't even factories now but condominiums, though I'd never wish to live in one. "Not good enough for a dog," Charlotte says. But when I was young, the factories were everything. Work to keep a girl busy. Money of her own. Mother had once said the same of New York. *There are other places. So many people.* She took my hand and placed it to her heart. *The streets, the buildings, every week when I walked a mile to the market with my earnings, I could feel them beating.*

Later, I told Esther what Mother had told me. It was the first time Esther looked at me as something more than a sister. *We can go anywhere*, she said. *I'll take you myself.*

The years after Esther left did us some good. The beds were full. The factory gave Charlotte a raise, and Mrs. Keyes had meat enough for the table. Soon, Mrs. Keyes stayed in her chair in the kitchen and Charlotte and I ran the house. Late at night, the three of us sat to talk numbers and recipes. The work was something we chose. It was my word or Charlotte's that sent the girls to bed, the shopping lists written in my own hand, the three of us with keys no matter the hour. I thought of home only when the days grew quiet, one winter passing into the next. *Wait for me*, Esther had said, but I couldn't do much else. A train ticket, it was more than three months at Charlotte's wages. For the two of us, it was almost twice. I had no money for myself, save the few dollars Esther sent. Half a room and meals, that was more than Mrs. Keyes could afford no matter how many girls we had. After a while, Esther's letters went empty of dollars. *The bank wants Father's acres by the river*, she wrote. *Nan says we'll lose more if the weather doesn't turn. Ray and Lee will make themselves sick with the work, she says. But they do it together, I tell Nan.* Not a word about why she didn't come back. Worse yet, those letters never said if anyone at home asked about me.

I wrote dozens of letters myself. *Her name is Greta. She's fair like me, but sometimes she roars. I hope to be good at mothering, and you a good aunt. How much longer will you be gone?* I never sent the letter, not that one or the next. When I tried so much as write the address, my face grew hot. Though I believed my sister would keep the contents of my letters close, still I imagined Tom capable of any kind of knowing. And what if he learned of Greta? Would he try to take her for himself?

I shut the paper away in my desk. Still Esther wrote every few weeks. *Nan's got a daughter. She married Carl McNulty not long after we left. They've got that house of his, but they're always with us. And now Agnes is married too. He's tall as Lee and can carry her under his arm.* Over the years, Nan had another child, a boy named Lee, and Agnes had three girls of her own. *As quick as rabbits*, Esther wrote. *That's what Ray says. He eyes Patricia and her empty skirts when he does. But the way Patricia frets over them, you'd think they were hers.* Three, I thought. Now another girl wouldn't be so precious. Another wouldn't be welcome at all. I imagined Nan or Patricia discovering any letter I sent and cutting it open with a knife to read aloud at the dinner table. Then they all would know—that their sister had gotten herself in trouble. She'd only be a burden to them.

But if I didn't send word about myself, I could be anything they wanted. I could be better—the one who got away, living a grand life in such a grand place, no longer willing to play youngest. And Greta would be safe, no matter what. Before she left, that's what Esther had always said about us.

It was three years before Esther sent the letter about Father. She'd written it on a single sheet of paper, the print too small to read without a looking glass.

Ray was the one who found him in the dugout. We don't know when he snuck out. Nan says it doesn't matter a wink that no one went to the funeral except us, but Patricia was all done out about it. Lee didn't say a word to the preacher. Neither did I.

I shut myself away in our closet. When I closed my eyes, I heard only the blood in my ears and the river rushing above my head. I didn't breathe. I couldn't feel the cold or wet. When I opened my mouth, I could taste the snowmelt from the hills, and it tasted like home. Riding the current, I passed our yard as it had always been—the house, the dugout, the barn. The yard was there with its florid green, the patch of grass, always burning, and Father on the bank, striking at the water with his cane. When the sun came out, Greta floated at my side. *Are we fish now?* she asked, her eyes clear and bright. *Are we dead?* I said, *Yes.*

Father, if I told you what's become of me, would you understand? You locked us in that house, as if you worried we'd leave without a look back—the way you and Mother did. But locks don't stop a girl from thinking. And nails do even less. From the beginning, we believed that river would swallow us. *More and more, Julius,* I heard Mother say. *When is the land we have enough?* To lay your stake, you convinced Mother to follow you to the farthest place trains could run. Father, I have never had so much as a room of my own, in Chicago not even a bed—but Charlotte is the difference. Sometimes the person who never knew you or where you came from is the best kind.

We can go. It was Nan who said it first, months before Esther and I left. I woke to the sound of cracking, a draft. When I opened my eyes, Nan was sitting on the edge of my bed. She made sure I heard what she did. The thud of the nails as they fell and the window pried open, the sudden wind. She held a hammer in her lap as if a prized possession. *You can go if you want,* she whispered. *We all can.* When I sat up, she looked at me as if she hadn't expected me to have questions. *It isn't natural, living in a box.*

The letter about Father should have ended it, but I kept my promise to wait for several years more. Chicago was notorious then. That's what Esther would have known. But for the rest of us, it was only so much noise. We were dollar to mouth, the streets cold for walking in the winters, and the summers hot enough to drive us to the lakeshore. There were race riots near the stockyards and meatpacking plants, and Leopold and Loeb, the *Übermenschen,* were arrested like cowards for the murder of young Bobby Franks. Esther's letters slowed to one every three or four months. They were always the same. A half-page at most, scribbled with ink, running with names and events I didn't understand. *Agnes says little Martha might have broken her finger.* Or, *Nan told Patricia straight out she shouldn't say another word about the plates.* Or, *Old Tensley finally built his own shed, can you believe it?* No matter who Martha or Tensly were, or why Patricia worried about plates. Esther never did bother with explanations.

Greta was five years old when the last letter came. I opened it alone at my desk. The paper was flimsy, too small a piece to hold in a wind.

> *Dear Sister,*
>
> *I'm sitting for once, hardly time to breathe. I picture you in that house, all cozy. Say hi to Charlotte for me. And Keyes, is she always*

in your business? Agnes and those brats of hers are about to drive
me crazy, and I'm working from dawn to sleep and bored stiff.

Around here, Adam Haskett is the gossip. Remember him? He
finally married a girl. They have a baby, and that baby is older
than it should be by five months They only married last year.
There was a big to-do over it. Of course Patricia goes running her
mouth. People think a baby forgives everything, she says. But that's
Patricia, all angelic like. It only makes things worse, she says.
Think of the child!

My pencil's a stub. Got to run. Nan is calling.

You can't be mad forever, can you? Write me! Remember what
you promised?

E.

Greta stood in the doorway. "Mother?" With her quickness,
the girl could slip between shadows. She gripped my knees until
I lifted her into my lap.

"What's wrong?" she asked.

I wiped my face. "Reading letters."

"From who?"

"An old friend."

"Do I know her?"

"She should have known you, yes. But she lives very far
away. I'm afraid she's not much of a friend now."

Greta turned the paper over in my hands, trying to make
out letters, names. "Why do you read them?"

I folded the letter in half and slipped it back into its envelope. "I don't know."

"Auntie says it's time for dinner. You're late."

"Does she?"

"She says you must be feeding the birds up here for all she knows."

"Go on with you. I'll be right there. Just have to splash some water on my face."

The girl pouted, pulling my arm.

"Greta, go on."

At last she went, rushing down the stairs so fast I imagined her falling easy as a feather. Greta was as fierce as Esther, fiercer even. But Greta was kind, while Esther seemed to be growing less. *Remember what you promised*, she had written. And I remembered. I had waited for her even after Father went. *A baby. It only makes things worse*, Patricia had said. Esther was sure to pass the message on.

I shook the dust from her letters in my closet. There were dozens of them, some opened, some not. I tore them from their envelopes, skimming her awkward hand. *Wait for me.* She'd said it one way or another in each of those letters. Then what she meant but didn't say, nearly every time: *I'll never come.* With a pair of scissors, I started cutting. A corner from the first, another in half and half again. Soon I was cutting those letters into strips. *Sister, dear sister*, she had written. But none of those sisters were me. They were Nan and Agnes. Even Patricia. I had plenty of sisters here for myself. In only minutes, those letters lay in pieces at my feet, except one.

I sat at my desk and sealed the envelope again. It was dated only the week before. *Return to sender*, I wrote across the front. *No one here by that name.*

The next day at the courthouse, I asked for a form. *There's more to you than they think*, Mother had said. Twenty years and counting, I would have told her. When the form asked for the change of name, I wrote, "Norma Byrne."

Without even looking, the woman behind the desk struck the form with her bloody stamp.

I can't say I never imagined going back. After the country got on its feet again. After another war filled the factories with girls. Mrs. Keyes took to her bed and soon she was gone—I could have tried then. But no matter how often I wondered about home, Chicago was more. Before she went, Mrs. Keyes had left the house to us.

It would have taken a day on the train, a half for the drive. Every mile that passed, I knew I might still turn around. When I reached the house, I imagined myself too afraid to step out. Only the smell of dust and pigs when I rolled down the window, the whine of the weather vane on the barn.

A girl called to me from the porch. "They're all at the wedding."

I could picture her there, hiding behind one of the porch posts, almost as if I saw her myself. She wore her hair in a kerchief and pigtails, tall as a stalk. The buckets in her hands clattered at her thighs. The girl would never have known a stranger to visit the house.

"Whose wedding?"

"Why, Darlene's of course. Aunt Agnes made her dress."

I opened my door and stepped out, the heat of the sun in my eyes. "And your name?"

"Renie." She stood in the yard, awkward as a boy. Soon she was telling me her thoughts on weddings and dressing up in all sorts. "I'm not going," she said. "Any day, I'd rather do chores."

Of course. Her eyes had a sureness I knew. With her height and her cheekbones, the girl had to be Nan's.

"Weddings," I answered. "You know what they say. Never make too much of something. . . ."

"Mother says that too."

"Your mother, does she have many sisters?"

The girl stuck a knuckle in her ear. "She has two. But she used to have another one. As pretty as me, she said once."

"Did she now?"

"Very pretty, Mother said. But the sister drowned."

The yard rose up. I leaned against the hood of the car. I'd imagined the visit dozens of ways, but this one always repeated itself. "Are you sure?"

"Sure what?"

"That her sister . . ."

The girl tilted her head.

"Never mind." My hand burned on the hood and I shook it off. The wind struck, the barn door swinging. There wasn't anything but the dark hayloft and a bell ringing from an animal's collar, a curl of rope in the dust.

"What's your mother's name?" I said.

"Why, Nan of course. What's yours?"

"Something of the like," I said. "Some called her Nan. Some Margrit."

"That's a funny thing, to have two names."

The girl lifted her buckets again and made her way to the barn. The buckets banged as she walked, though she couldn't help but look back. I stood by the car under the sun. I had little energy left to explain myself. Before the girl disappeared again, I called out, "You tell your mother that her daughter loves her, you hear? Her youngest one. Tell her, her daughter loves her very much."

The girl stopped. "But I'm her daughter."

"That's right."

"What did you say your name was again?"

"Norma." My voice grew hoarse. "Norma Byrne."

"I've never heard Mother talk about you."

"No, you wouldn't have. She might not want to remember me now."

The girl shrugged. The buckets must have been heavy. Her fingers reddened where the handles cut. "You sound like her, you know," she called back. The cows lowed in the barn, and she hurried to answer them, the door behind her swinging shut. *Like Nan?* I thought. I imagined myself following the girl, asking her to explain—but I didn't dare step away from the car for fear it might disappear altogether. Besides, what more could I say?

I drove. Out along the river, where the water ran full and loud. On the banks were violets, sweet williams, bluebells, and bleeding hearts. The Elliot house was gone, nothing but planks in a dry bit of grass. When I passed the Clarks', three women stood on the porch in matching dresses. They had grown as large as their mother, the Clark sisters, and unmarried by the look of it, but maybe they were happier with that—they had their sisters, after all. When I raised a hand to them, they turned their heads to watch me as I drove on.

If I tried to imagine it again, I might take more time before I left. I might be sure to drop a stone at the door of Lee's shop.

That stone, it would be clean and white. Large enough he would pick it up before he stepped inside. With Lee, I always wanted to tell him no matter what he did, he did right.

But it all must be a dream. The kind I have in the dark when I can't sleep, and there's only Charlotte to tell me whether it's true or not. Because a river only runs in one direction, no matter what.

III

I walk to the lake. The boardinghouse is behind me, my arms snug to my ribs. There's a chill, worse than usual for this time of year, but I won't stop yet. The sun sits far in the west. I turn my back to it. Blocks away, the old Chicago Theatre is long closed, but there's talk of opening it again. Overhead, the sky has grown dark. When I raise my eyes to look, it blurs. I wonder if it's a summer cold I have coming on or something more.

"Hello, Mrs. Byrne. How's that girl of yours?" It's Josey. He owns the flower shop. Short and squat without a hair on his head, his smile turns his cheeks to baby fat. The shopkeepers like to talk to a person whether they've had a bad day or not and they always talk to me—I'm not in a rush.

"She's not so much a girl anymore, but she does all right."

He smiles. "I saw it in the paper, her show in London. A director now! I always took a liking to her singing voice, myself."

"Now she can do both."

"Sorry her own father can't see her. I know if she were my daughter, I'd be there in an instant. But you've done her straight."

"I'm afraid I haven't had much to do with it."

A widow. That's what they know me as, thanks to Mrs. Keyes. With her rosary, she prayed the lie would take—and for her, I never said otherwise.

"I'm sure her father misses her now," Josey says.

"I'm sure he would." In truth, I have no idea what has become of Tom Elliot, alive or not. Esther's letters never said, and I'm not sure I care anymore.

Josey hands me yesterday's newspaper and a single tulip, without its leaves. The newspaper has its coupons cut out, but I'm grateful for it.

"They've got a story about the Chicago in there."

"The river?"

"'A triumph of engineering,' they call it. Can you imagine, reversing the current like that?"

I shake my head, the light suddenly bright.

"You okay, Mrs. Byrne?"

"Yes, Josey. It's just the heat."

"Good day to you, then." He takes off his hat.

Mother, it's such a rush, Greta said last night into the phone. The line ticked, an ocean between us. I never imagined a girl could go so far. *I'll be home in three months,* she said. *Four tops.*

You'll be home when you're home, I said.

London is wild. I wish you could see it.

I stood in the hall with the cord bent around the doorframe. Outside, the windows showed little but a brick wall, even the bricks crumbling now. From the kitchen two floors down, Charlotte scolded one of the cats, "I bet you did, you nasty little thing."

Oh, no, I told my daughter. *I've seen quite enough.*

Today the lake seems more than ten blocks. The streets are nearly empty. At night, the young ones go downtown. Not here, where the workers' houses used to be. Here, which I'd always thought the heart of the city. When the shopkeepers pull the cages over their storefronts, there's a roaring in the street, but soon it's quiet. There's a man sleeping under his newspapers and I hurry by.

You have to be careful, Mother, Greta says.

But what can they do to an old lady, after everything that's already been done? Let the young be nervous for their own sake.

The lake swells with little but stones and grass between me and it. The water has flooded its banks. My bench needs a coat of paint, but then everything worth using does. I scratch at the flakes with a fingernail, feel them cut into my thumb. It's the time of year when the lake is warm as a bath. An old man passes, younger by at least twenty years. He keeps his hands in his pockets and nods at me as if nodding meant something. I shake my newspaper out.

RUDOLF HESS DEAD IN BERLIN

LAST OF HITLER INNER CIRCLE

My word. A suicide, no less. What was it Mrs. Keyes had said? *With a name like that, it's no wonder the man's a murderer.* But that was back in '47, when they hanged a man by the name of Hoess. A different Rudolph. *Hess, Hoess,* I could hear Mrs. Keyes saying. *What's the difference? Auschwitz,* Charlotte would have said to that. Greta was only twenty-six in '47 and already in New York. The girl never did bother much with names. In every school production she changed what she called herself, as if trying on a new coat. But in New York, they might have second-guessed if Greta had gone by *Hess* instead of *Byrne.*

The men are dead. I don't believe Greta ever knew we had such an ugly name. I had never thought it ugly myself.

Margrit Hess, Father had insisted for the top of Mother's stone. We children hoped to have the word *Mother* listed first. Still we were far too young to get a say in something like that.

We buried Mother in the northernmost field, close enough for her to hear the river—if hearing she wanted. It took Ray and Father a full day of digging, and not even Lee to help. Lee, who traveled two weeks on a boat and three days on a train once the telegram was sent. If he hadn't gone to war, it would have been Lee who built the box, Lee who did most of the digging. As it was, the grave wasn't very deep. Lee was sorry about that when he got back. We laid our flowers on the mound. At her head, a block of slate. *Mother*, it read, though second to her name. When Charlotte and I buried Mrs. Keyes, we inscribed *Mother* on it as well. I took it hard losing her, but Charlotte took it worse. The word *Friend* didn't seem enough for either of us.

A tap on my shoulder. "Norma?" The name isn't anything but a fly at my ear. "Norma?" again. And then the name I know better, the sound that fills me with something else altogether: "Myrle?" I turn my head. Charlotte stands behind me with a coat thrown over her nightdress and slippers on her feet. With her hair drained of color, she looks a ghost. The sun has set. The waves in the lake are quiet. There's a moon as yellow as a stone. It's the only way I can see her at all.

"You were gone so long," she says.

I shake my head to throw off the dust. "I'm fine."

She takes my arm and I ease myself up. Only when I press my fingers to the wood do I feel the cold of that bench. When we turn to the city, the lake stays dark at our backs. The gulls are gone. The shops are closed now. The walk feels longer than before, though I have Charlotte and her cane, tapping the cement. We are two old women leaning against each other for every step.

"Just a bit farther" she says. "We'll get you home. You must be coming down with that fever that's going around."

"I only lost a little time."

Charlotte squeezes my arm and doesn't let go. She studies me out of the corner of her eye. "We'll get you home."

I strain to look back. There's a young girl on my bench. Her name is Myrle. She was always murkier than anyone could have guessed. I watch as she walks into the lake, the water lapping her shins. She'll go deeper yet. Mother knew it when she filled our heads with the names of things. Because who says a person can't live more than one life?

"It was me," I told Charlotte after Greta was born. "I was the one who wanted to go." And Charlotte pretended that was the way it had always been. "Esther was too jittery here," she said. "But all you wanted was to get out of your room." She traced a finger across my palm. "Besides, you talk in your sleep."

That night before Esther and I left home, when everyone had gone to bed, I took Father's key while he slept and fit it in the lock. *We've got to know we've stolen the right one*, Esther had said. The bolt turned, the door opening. When I stepped out, there was nothing but a thin moon and my feet bare on the wooden planks. I felt my way down the porch steps, through the yard where the grass wet my shins. *Come right back*, Esther had said, but I wouldn't. Not yet. The river was quiet against the rocks as I picked my way out.

I had long hoped to try it. Since I'd found Mother so quiet in her bed. Since Tom had left me in the hayloft and Patricia made her announcement: *That boy's gotten himself engaged.* All those days spent in my room with my eyes closed, holding my breath—they were only practice for this.

At the river, the dirt turned to mud, the grass higher than my knees. I threw my nightgown on the bank and hugged three stones to my chest. As I waded in, the water was cold enough to burn. The moon barely showed itself. The river cut a trail between the fields. The cold changed to numbness the deeper I went, the current tugging at my feet. The water was soon at my hips. When it reached my throat, I dove in.

There is a place where a person is nothing. Where water is the same as breathing. This was it.

I sat on the muddy floor with the stones pressed to my chest and listened. My ears rang. My heart beating in them. I was more than frozen, the key sharp against the inside of my hand. For a while, it seemed the bottom of the river was what wanted me most. The weeds were knots, the mud pulling at my heels. But this was the agreement I had made with myself. I would pinch my nose. I would dive in. And if something in me wanted to stay with the river, I would.

But soon I felt it, that swelling in my stomach. My arms, that swelling said, they didn't want stones. I loosened my grip, let them sink. The key I held tight in my fist. I pushed at the mud with my feet, felt myself breaking through the surface. The air was clear and easy in a way I'd never known.

I made my way to the bank, heaving. On a rock, I sat out in the open and let the wind dry me as it could. There were the cicadas again. Farther out, the barn steamed with the animals sleeping. A noise in the meadow—a snake, a rabbit, a bird. I pulled my nightgown over my head, walked until the house showed itself. It seemed low and dull sitting there. I unlocked the door again and drew it fast.

A lantern blazed in the hall. "Why, Myrle," Nan said, "you'll catch your death."

The key I hid behind my back. The river ran down my leg. Nan's face showed sharp and pale, her arm trembling with the lantern's weight. Her eyes swept the mat under my feet. When she raised them to my face again, her look softened. She opened her mouth as if she might say something. Instead she smiled.

Oh, Nanny, you can come with us. I took her hand.

Nan's smile faltered. I wondered if I had spoken aloud. But Nan would never leave. She had let me go weeks before with the draft of that window. For her, she was as much a part of that house as the planks over our head.

"Go on," Nan said. She jerked her chin at the stairs. I squeezed her hand and ran. At the top, Esther closed the door and sat me on her bed. I was shivering enough for the two of us.

"Where were you?" she asked.

"By the river."

She frowned. "I don't think we should go. It's too far."

I held out the key to her and she gasped. My hand was bleeding. I'd gripped it so hard, it had made its mark.

"It's your turn," I said. "It's our only chance."

Esther stared at my hand.

I closed it and opened it again, bloodier now. "Take it."

She grabbed hold of the key. Closing her eyes, she slit her palm. It took her three tries.

"Promise," I said.

"Promise." She pressed her hand into mine.

"We're going," I said. "And we're never coming back."

285

* * *

Norma Byrne opens the door to the house. Norma Byrne climbs the stairs. If there is any part of me inside that old woman, it's the part that remembers Mrs. Keyes opening the door to our room all those years ago. Mrs. Keyes who was as wide as the rails. There seem a great deal more steps now than there were then.

I count them as I climb, though already we're halfway. "One, two," I start. "Eight," I say when I reach the landing. "Eight," Charlotte echoes without asking why.

In our room, Charlotte pulls back the sheets and I rest my head.

"Water?" Charlotte asks. She kisses me.

"They reversed the Chicago River, Charlotte. Did you know that?"

"Of course they did."

She turns off the lamp. Above my head, the ceiling shifts and the lights from the street, all those circles and lines, move as quickly as water in a glass.

The phone rings. Charlotte hurries into the hall.

"Who is it?" I ask.

"No," she says into the phone. "There's no one here by that name." The phone snaps in its cradle. "Norma?" she says, closer to me now.

The phone rings a second time. Charlotte turns her head and listens. "Must be her again." Then she's out in the hall and picking up the phone. "Well, yes. But Norma doesn't know anyone like that." The snap in the cradle again.

Charlotte grumbles as she returns to the room. Her neck is flushed with that old Irish blood, something I haven't seen in years.

"Some woman who says her name is Renie," Charlotte explains. "Do you know a Renie?"

"Renie?"

"She says she's someone's daughter." Charlotte shakes her head to think. "Bernadette's daughter, that's what she said."

"My sister Nan."

"I thought she said Bernadette."

"Is she all right?"

Charlotte drops her hand on my forehead. "What did you say?"

The phone rings again. Charlotte hurries into the hall. "Yes, yes, I might have been wrong. But she's feeling ill. Can I take your number?"

"Nan?" I call out.

"Yes, that's right," Charlotte says into the phone. "I have it. I'll be sure to give it to her when she's better."

Nan with a child. But of course that's what the letters said. I would have liked to see my sister's face again. I would have liked to know my niece, the one who'd rather do chores than dress for weddings. Maybe if I have energy enough, I could make the trip. The train isn't so many days now. When I try to imagine the place, it seems like a foreign country—if I ever knew it. But with those faces again, I might.

"Norma?" I hear.

A hand on my forehead. The hand is cold and smells of salt. "Is it Greta?"

"Are you all right?" Charlotte asks. "Can you hear me? I'm going to call the doctor."

"The doctor now?"

But Charlotte is on the phone again. "Yes, come at once. She seems very confused. Must you keep asking your questions?"

Greta is in England, I remember. The daughter doesn't feel the distance, but the mother always does.

"Look," Charlotte says. I open my eyes. Charlotte holds a yellow square of paper with numbers written in small sharp lines.

"Nan was like a mother to me," I say. "I never should have left."

"Norma?" But Charlotte's voice is distant now. I try to raise my head to hear her better.

"You stay still," Charlotte says. "They're coming. Can you wait?"

The bed lifts. A hand sweeps my face. Charlotte and her worries, but it'll be all right. They're coming. I'm not so far from home as I thought. So easy to have a number, to drop a line. So easy for them to be here at the door, less than a day's travel now, or so I've heard. Nan and her daughter, Renie. Father with his cane. Lee walking across the hill with his limp, but maybe he doesn't limp so badly now. Ray and Patricia, arm in arm. Agnes with her trio of children, taller than she ever was. And Esther, she's running ahead of them. She's already in the alley. She's knocking on the door. She knows just where to find me. *We're here for a room,* she says. *Of course. We just have to make the bed. Never mind your papers. How far have you come?*

Epilogue

August 18, 1987

Dear niece,

I have made a discovery. Do you remember the story I once told you about your two great-aunts who disappeared? I believe the youngest may be alive.

Your Uncle Lee has found a letter intended for him in our late Aunt Esther's belongings, though we don't know why she would have hidden it. The letter is undated but looks very old. It was written by one Mrs. Mary Keyes of Chicago. Lee would read me only part of the letter, but it was clear that Mrs. Keyes was trying to make amends: "Lord knows how heavily this has sat in my heart and for how long. Now that I'm ill, I'll never be able to forgive myself if I don't write. This is the truth: Your sisters were indeed living at this address when you came for your visit some years ago, and Myrle is living here still. She goes by the name Norma Byrne."

The letter troubled Lee, more than he seemed willing to explain. Still he thought it might prove that Aunt Myrle, your grandmother's last remaining sister, hadn't died, as was the family's belief. I wrote down the name "Norma Byrne" and called the residence. The woman who answered hung up on me twice only to listen the third time. She told me she was Norma's companion. I identified myself as Myrle's great-niece, her sister Nan's only

289

daughter, and said I was interested in how my aunt fared. The woman sounded elderly and quite distracted. She said Norma was very ill, but she would give her the information at a later time. If she found what I told her to be true, Norma would call back. Then the woman hung up.

Lee said he couldn't understand it. He was speaking of Esther's hiding the letter, of course. When it came to Myrle, Lee said, Esther was sensitive. He thought it nearly killed her when Myrle had drowned. She only mentioned it once, the way Tom Elliot had "done Myrle such a wrong." Lee said Esther never spoke of it again. I doubted I needed to tell him that the letter meant Esther had lied. Your uncle nursed Esther to the end in the old family house, though she'd grown irritable. When I last visited, she gripped my hand in the parlor where we sat near the fire and whispered something I never will forget. "I let her do what she wanted." That's what she said. When she repeated it, Lee hushed her. Back then, I thought it was Myrle and Tom she meant. Now I'm not so sure. I worry for Lee alone out there without his sister. Since the letter was found, his health has turned, and he won't speak Esther's name, even when asked. I don't know what bothers him more, that Myrle might be living or that Esther hid the truth from him. Strangely enough, I think for him the latter might be worse. Aunt Pat said she'd send over one of Agnes' girls to look in on him and see to it he has food in his stomach. I'll check on him myself.

As for me, when I was young, I remember a woman stopping by the farm. I never thought much of it. But after she left, your uncle took to carrying around a white stone. Mother said she'd never seen him so pleased, not since the day his sister Esther had come home. He didn't give his reasons, Mother said, almost as if he didn't understand it himself. Still Mother seemed pleased when hearing of the woman's visit as well, though she never said why.

It has been two weeks now and I'm still waiting for Myrle to call. If she doesn't soon, I will call her again. I'll keep you updated.

Much Love,
Aunt Renie

Acknowledgments

Thanks for the support and encouragement of my readers Steven Beeber, Karen Halil, Laura Harrison, Daphne Kalotay, Linda Schlossberg, Dawn Tripp, and Lara Wilson. Thanks also to my longtime writing friends Patti Horvath, Jane Rosenberg Laforge, Kate Southwood, Elisabeth Fairfield Stokes, and Michelle Valois, as well as my writing cohorts Sari Boren, Steven Brykman, Alexandria Marzano-Lesnevich, and Ilan Mochari.

Thanks to the GrubStreet staff and friends for doing what you do and being who you are, especially Lisa Borders, Eve Bridburg, and Chris Castellani, for helping build the Novel Incubator Program, which made me a better teacher and writer. Thanks to all our Incubees for your energy and talent. You inspire me every day.

Thanks to Brandeis University for allowing me to teach and write "in residence." Thanks especially to Steve McCauley for shepherding me through the process.

Thanks to my editor, Corinna Barsan, for her continued zeal this second time around and her exceedingly smart pencil, as well as to the entire Grove Atlantic staff. Thanks to my agent Esmond Harmsworth and the Zachary, Shuster, Harmsworth agency team, notably Janet Silver and Lane Zachary.

Thanks especially to my family: my mother, Lorene Hoover, for inspiration and editing; my sister, Lisa Carstens, and Mike, Hannah, and Cayla; and my brother, David Hoover.

Thanks always to Randy Bailey for his love, patience, and support, for putting up with this strange kind of life, and for giving me a second family.

Finally, thanks to my late cousin, Hazel Hoover, for her offhand remark that "you look just like one of your great-aunts," and to my late Aunt Irene (Renie) Israel, who despite being ill, opened a family album in her lap and told me about the two sisters who "disappeared," showing me the photograph that began the whole thing.